Praise for

THE UNMAPPED CHRONICLES BOOK ONE:
CASPER TOCK AND THE EVERDARK WINGS

"A humorous adventure that resonates on multiple levels." —*Publishers Weekly*

Praise for

THE UNMAPPED CHRONICLES BOOK TWO:
THE BICKERY TWINS AND THE PHOENIX TEAR

"This title stands out, not only for lovable secondary characters, but for the exquisitely horrible sibling rivalry. . . . Children will fall in love with the twins soon after meeting them." —*SLJ*

Praise for

THE UNMAPPED CHRONICLES BOOK THREE:
ZEB BOLT AND THE EMBER SCROLL

"A fantastic ending to an endearing series."
—*Kirkus Reviews*

Also by Abi Elphinstone

The Unmapped Chronicles
#1: *Casper Tock and the Everdark Wings*
#2: *The Bickery Twins and the Phoenix Tear*

Sky Song

THE UNMAPPED CHRONICLES

- BOOK THREE -

Zeb Bolt and the Ember Scroll

ABI ELPHINSTONE

Aladdin

New York London Toronto Sydney New Delhi

ALADDIN
An imprint of Simon & Schuster Children's Publishing Division
1230 Avenue of the Americas, New York, New York 10020
First Aladdin paperback edition August 2022

Originally published in Great Britain in 2021 by Simon & Schuster UK Ltd.

Also available in an Aladdin hardcover edition.

Cover designed by Heather Palisi
Interior designed by Mike Rosamilia
The text of this book was set in Truesdell.
Manufactured in the United States of America 0722 OFF
2 4 6 8 10 9 7 5 3 1
The Library of Congress has cataloged the hardcover edition as follows:
Names: Elphinstone, Abi, author.
Title: Zeb Bolt and the Ember Scroll / by Abi Elphinstone.
Description: First Aladdin hardcover edition. | New York : Aladdin, 2021. | Series: The Unmapped chronicles ; book three | Summary: "In this final adventure in the Unmapped Kingdoms, a young orphan rises up to stop the evil harpy Morg once and for all"—Provided by publisher.
Identifiers: LCCN 2021009389 (print) | LCCN 2021009390 (ebook) | ISBN 9781534443136 (hardcover) | ISBN 9781534443143 (pbk) | ISBN 9781534443150 (ebook)
Subjects: CYAC: Foster children—Fiction. | Blind—Fiction. | Dragons—Fiction. | Trust—Fiction. | Magic—Fiction. | Adventure and adventurers—Fiction. | Fantasy.
Classification: LCC PZ7.1.E465 Ze 2021 (print) | LCC PZ7.1.E465 (ebook) | DDC [Fic]—dc23
LC record available at https://lccn.loc.gov/2021009389
LC ebook record available at https://lccn.loc.gov/2021009390

For Hana Lily Suzuki

Welcome to the Unmapped Kingdoms . . .

Most grown-ups are far too busy to believe in magic. They have newspapers to read, bills to pay, phone calls to answer, and—most time-consuming of all—children to nag. But if grown-ups were a little less busy and a little more curious, they might notice some of the things that children see. Unlikely, impossible, extraordinary things. Like portals to secret kingdoms that reveal the truth about how our world actually began . . .

In case you're wondering, it all started with an egg. An exceptionally large one. And when this egg hatched, a phoenix emerged. It wept seven tears upon realizing it was alone, and when these tears fell, the Earth's continents were born, forming the world as you and I know it. The phoenix called these lands the Faraway, but they were dark and empty places, so, to brighten things up, the phoenix shed four of its golden feathers. And from these feathers grew secret, unmapped kingdoms, invisible to the people who would go on to live in the Faraway. These kingdoms held all the magic needed to conjure sunlight, rain, and snow, and every untold wonder behind the weather, from the music of a sunrise to the stories of a snowstorm.

Now, you may have encountered wisdom before: grandparents are wise, librarians are wise, and some (though not all) elephants are wise. A phoenix is wiser still, and this particular phoenix knew that if used selfishly, magic will grow strange and dark. But if it is used for the greater good, it can nourish an entire world and keep it turning. So the phoenix decreed that those who lived in the four Unmapped Kingdoms could enjoy all the wonders that its magic brought, but only if they worked to send some of that magic out into the Faraway so that the continents there might be filled with light and life. If the Unmappers ever stopped sharing their magic, the phoenix warned, both the Faraway and the Unmapped Kingdoms would crumble to nothing.

Next, the phoenix set about choosing rulers for these kingdoms. And being such a wise creature, the phoenix gave squabbling kings, queens, and politicians a wide berth when deciding who to appoint. Instead, the phoenix chose the Lofty Husks—magical beings all born under an eclipse and marked out from the other Unmappers on account of their wisdom, unusually long life expectancy, and terrible jokes. In each kingdom the Lofty Husks took a different form, from wizards and golden panthers to ancient elves and snow eagles, but they all ruled fairly, ensuring that every day the magic of the phoenix was passed on to the Faraway through the weather.

The four kingdoms all played different roles. Unmappers in Rumblestar collected marvels—droplets of sunlight, rain, and snow in their purest form—which dragons transported to the other three Unmapped Kingdoms. There, they were mixed with magical ink to create weather scrolls for the Faraway: sun symphonies in Crackledawn, rain paintings in Jungledrop, and snow stories in Silvercrag. Little by little, the Faraway lands came alive: plants, flowers, and trees sprang up, and so strong was the magic that eventually animals appeared and, finally, people.

The phoenix looked on from Everdark, a place so far away and out of reach that not even the Unmappers knew where it lay. But a phoenix cannot live forever. And so, after five hundred years, the first phoenix died and, as is the way with such birds, a new phoenix rose from its ashes to renew the magic in the Unmapped Kingdoms and ensure it continued to be shared with those in the Faraway.

Time passed and every five hundred years, the Unmappers learned to watch for a new phoenix rising up into the sky to refresh the Unmapped magic and herald the arrival of another era. Everyone believed things would continue this way forever. . . . But when you're dealing with magic, forever is rarely straightforward. There is always someone, somewhere, who becomes greedy. And when a heart is set on stealing magic for personal gain, ancient decrees and warnings can slip quite out of mind. Such was the case with a harpy called Morg who grew jealous of the phoenix and its power.

Almost four thousand five hundred years ago, Morg cursed the nest of the phoenix on the night of the renewal of magic. No new phoenix appeared, so Morg seized the nest as her own and set about seeking to claim all the magic of the Unmapped Kingdoms for herself.

But, when things go wrong and magic goes awry, it makes room for stories with unexpected heroes and unlikely heroines. Perhaps you have heard about the girl from Crackledawn who sailed to Everdark to steal Morg's wings, the very things that held the harpy's power? Maybe you know about the boy named Casper who journeyed from the Faraway to Rumblestar to destroy those same wings so that the Unmapped Kingdoms and the Faraway might be saved from ruin? Possibly you have come across the Petty-Squabble twins who traveled from the Faraway to Jungledrop to find a mythical fern that banished Morg from the Unmapped Kingdoms and restored rain to our world? Or you might just be one of those wise children who sense the ways of dragons and know that they are now roaming the Unmapped Kingdoms, scattering moondust from their wings to keep what is left of the Unmapped magic turning until Morg dies and a new phoenix rises. And rise it must, because the magic is fading every day, despite the dragons' efforts to keep it alive, and it will not be long before it vanishes altogether. For only the arrival of a phoenix can restore what Morg has destroyed and renew the kingdoms to their former glory.

There is still one story to be told, one final adventure waiting to take us to the Unmapped Kingdoms. The Petty-Squabble twins might have adventured through Jungledrop, trapped Morg in a never-ending well, and saved the world from her dark magic . . . but all things eventually come to an end—even never-ending wells. And from an underground world, Morg has been patiently scratching her way, ever closer, to the Faraway. She knows that if she can get ahold of the immortalized tears of the very first phoenix that fell there when our world was born, she can use their power to break back into Crackledawn, an Unmapped Kingdom she still has followers in after a visit she made there many years ago. Then she can seize control of the Unmapped Kingdoms once and for all.

Day after day, Morg has been following the pull of the phoenix-tear magic, and tonight she has reached an entrance to the Faraway. But the harpy is too weak to break the boundary into our world, so she waits in the darkness beneath an abandoned theater on Crook's End, a dimly-lit and mostly-forgotten side street in Brooklyn, New York. Once, this street boasted a string of restaurants and lines of excited theatergoers, but as the neighborhood grew rougher and more dangerous, people moved away and the restaurants and theater closed.

No one lives on Crook's End anymore. But all that is going to change, because an eleven-year-old boy is on the run and his feet are pounding nearer and nearer. He does not know that it is magic leading him toward this deserted street. But there cannot be phoenix tears, a harpy, *and* a portal to an Unmapped Kingdom close by without there being consequences.

And though Zebedee Bolt might not be the kind of child who has time for magic, it very much has time for him. Morg needs somebody to let her into the Faraway, and the Unmapped Kingdoms need somebody to kick her out once and for all. Zeb needs no one and trusts no one and that is all well and good, but trying to escape magic when you're hurtling toward it is like trying to stop eating a doughnut when you've already taken the first bite. Quite impossible. You may as well just get on with it and accept that while magic throws its weight around, you're in for a bumpy ride. Especially if that ride involves dragons rather than doughnuts, because dragons, as Zeb is about to find out, are even wilder than magic. . . .

Chapter 1

Zebedee Bolt was good at running away from home. He'd done it enough times, after all. And not the half-hearted wandering off that involves shouting at your parents, storming to the bottom of the garden, then slinking back in time for tea. When Zeb ran, he crossed bridges and raced through unfamiliar parks, safe in the knowledge that he had memorized all the latest tricks from the Tank (a survival expert who did deeply uncomfortable things, like drink his own sweat and make rescue ropes out of his beard hair, on his television show).

But Zeb was always discovered in the end. And this was because he found it almost impossible to rein in the Outbursts. These episodes came upon him without warning and consisted of an embarrassing amount of sobbing on street corners. By the time he'd got a grip on himself, various grown-ups were usually stepping in to bring his getaway to a close.

You see, Zeb wanted to be tough. He longed to be like the Tank, who could escape any situation, like surviving weeks in the wild on a diet of grasshoppers, or emerging from a tussle with a bear with nothing but a bit of light bruising. But when you've got no money, a limited supply of food, and no friends to fall back on if things go wrong, it is a bit harder to remain upbeat.

So, while Zeb's getaways always started well, it wasn't long before the fear and panic kicked in. Where, really, was he running to? What hope was there for an eleven-year-old boy alone in New York? Who actually cared about what happened to him? Not that he ever talked about his feelings to the grown-ups who found him, the social worker in charge of him, or the foster families he'd lived with. Because talking meant trusting. And trusting other people had gone out the window years ago for Zeb.

Tonight would be different, though. Tonight he had remembered cookies. And he had made a solemn vow in front of the mirror that he wouldn't burst into tears and get found, not even when it got dark, or a little bit scary. Because Zeb had had enough of being passed around people's homes like an unwanted package, enough of hearing the same things whispered about him by the foster families he'd known: *He's so quiet. Why does he never smile? Is he always this moody?* And, overheard this morning, from foster parents Joyce and Gerald Orderly-Queue of 56 Rightangle Row, Manhattan, while on the phone to his social worker: *We've had him for six months now, and it's simply not working. He doesn't smile; he doesn't laugh; he barely even talks! And he spends so much time shut away in his bedroom, he is almost certainly plotting something dreadful. So before he poisons us in our sleep, or worse, sprays graffiti all over the sitting room, we'd very much like to hand him back.*

Their words jostled in Zeb's ears as he ran over the Brooklyn Bridge. It was always the same thing; he was never what foster families wanted. And while the welfare agency in charge of him had placed dozens of other children in loving homes, those—like Zeb—under the care of social worker Derek Dunce hadn't had the same luck. Derek Dunce was a buffoon of a grown-up who was capable of messing up even the simplest of things, like walking down a corridor. Finding loving families to nurture and understand vulnerable children was completely beyond him. So, like a disappointing meal in a restaurant or a faulty coat from a department store, Zeb was always sent back to the welfare agency in the end.

Zeb had crept out of Number 56 Rightangle Row for good over an hour ago, as soon as he'd gobbled down his dinner and finished talking to himself in the mirror. Now he was on the run, and though he wasn't sure where he was running to, he kept going, even as the dark settled in and the city lights began to glitter. He pulled the hood of his jacket up, partly because he'd once seen the Tank do the same, moments before facing down a lion, and partly as a precaution. If the Orderly-Queues had sounded the alarm and the police were out looking for an eleven-year-old boy with blond hair, green eyes, and a fondness for hysterical crying, Zeb wanted to be disguised.

He turned off the bridge and hurried into the heart of Brooklyn. The place was buzzing. People poured in and out of restaurants, music sailed through open windows, and taxis honked. For a second, Zeb allowed himself to wonder what belonging to a neighborhood like this, with family and friends around him, would be like. Bike rides with a mom and a dad in the park? Weekend cinema trips with kids from school? Sleepovers at the neighbor's house?

A longing grew inside Zeb and with it, a lump in his

throat—the first sign of an Outburst. He swallowed it down, then did what the Tank did when the going got tough: some jaw clenching, followed by a grunt. Instantly, he felt better, and as he made his way on through the crowds, he reminded himself that dreaming up family and friends was pointless, because you could never count on other people. Not when they'd let you down time and time again. Humans, Zeb had come to learn, were a bit like vegetables. They claimed to be full of all sorts of good things, but ultimately, they were pretty disappointing.

According to Derek Dunce, Zeb had been born in the Bronx, his mother had died when he was only a few months old, and his father had wanted nothing to do with either of them. At first, those responsible for Zeb had hoped that the foster homes would be temporary, that he might soon be adopted into a loving family. But because Derek Dunce was entirely unqualified for his job, the foster parents Zeb had encountered were the sort of grown-ups who only really wanted uncomplicated children, the types who may throw the odd tantrum around mealtimes and get in a flap about having their toenails cut, but who generally just got on with growing up.

Zeb was not one of these children because it is hard to

get on with growing up when being loved hasn't happened first. His Outbursts led to him being labeled a "difficult child," and at the string of schools Zeb had been to, he'd never made friends. He kept to himself, too wary to let his guard down even for a moment. It was a lonely business, but it was better than trying to make friends only to move again.

Zeb slowed to a walk as he made his way on into the city alone. He left the bustle of restaurants and bars behind him and turned onto sleepy side roads lining closed parks, until the neighborhood began to fray and become a less-visited sort of place. Zeb gripped the straps of his rucksack. This was the farthest he'd ever come by himself. He contemplated a brief sob before thinking better of it and walking on through the trail of autumn leaves.

It was quieter here—and darker. Many of the street lamps had fizzled out, and the moon was tucked behind the clouds. Zeb went on into the shadows, unknowingly drawn by the pull of magic. The streets had emptied, and now the night belonged to strays: a prowling cat, a dog hunting for scraps, and a rat scampering into the gutter.

Zeb stopped again, and the panic swelled inside him. He had pinched a sheet of tarp from the Orderly-Queues' garage because the Tank was always talking about thinking ahead when building a shelter. But how did you know where to set up camp? Should you just curl up beneath the tarp with your cookies and hope for the best?

As if the city could sense Zeb's unease, a breeze came out of nowhere, stirring a handful of leaves at his feet before nudging them on down the road. Zeb found himself following the leaves as they tumbled one after the other down the street and across another road.

He passed a discarded newspaper and only half registered the headlines:

GLOBAL TEMPERATURES SOAR

POLAR REGIONS MELT AT RECORD SPEED

ARCTIC ANIMALS FACE EXTINCTION

SEA SWALLOWS COASTAL TOWNS

In the last hundred years, there had been two major climate disasters. A series of hurricanes that had nearly torn the world apart, then a drought that had starved the planet of rain for months on end. And now huge chunks of polar ice were melting each day; the polar bears and beluga whales were almost extinct; the rising sea was flooding entire cities; and the hottest summer on record had seen raging wildfires across the world. Millions had lost their homes, thousands had lost their lives, and the Arctic and the Antarctic were disappearing at terrifying speeds. Everyone living in a city by the sea was nervous—everybody except Zeb. Because stopping global warming wasn't top of his agenda tonight, or any night really. Preventing an Outburst and finding a place to hide was.

Zeb followed the leaves until they settled at the foot of a signpost that marked the start of a street so dark, it looked like the mouth of a cave. Zeb felt his knees wobble and a familiar lump slide into his throat. To prevent an episode of uncontrollable howling, he puffed out his chest, raised his chin, and focused on the fact that there was nothing and nobody waiting for him if he let an Outburst loose now. Joyce and Gerald Orderly-Queue had shown more affection for the Saturday crossword than for him. He *had* to go on. He had to start a new life on his own.

He looked up at the street sign. It was rusted at the hinges and the lettering was chipped, but he could just make out the words.

"Crook's End," he murmured.

He took a small step closer. There were more signs nailed to the buildings: PABLO'S PIZZAS, PASTA HEAVEN, BROOKLYN BURGERS. But these restaurants looked like they'd been boarded up for a while now, and at the end of the street, closing the road off into a dead end, was another building. It was taller and wider than the others, and the stonework above the old wooden door was a little fancier.

Zeb glanced at the faded sign hanging above the door: THE CHANDELIER, it read, and beneath it was a list of what appeared to be outdated showtimes.

"A theater," Zeb whispered. "All the way out here." He eyed the door, which had been padlocked shut. "Grown-ups, they always focus on the doors. . . ."

But Zeb knew, from personal experience, that if you could escape a building in a number of ways: out of a window, via a skylight, down a fire escape—then there were multiple points of entry, too.

He settled for a ground floor window now, one covered with planks that had rotted through. He pulled them away to find a grubby pane of glass, and he hadn't expected to see much when he pressed his face up against it. But at that precise moment, the moon edged out from behind a cloud. And because the roof of the theater was in need of repair, the moonlight slipped in through the cracks and shimmered on the most enormous chandelier Zeb had ever seen. Hundreds of glass droplets hung from the domed ceiling, glinting silver like a giant's crown.

The moonlight was so bright that Zeb could see quite clearly inside now. Beyond a tiny foyer, the theater opened to reveal a balcony of seats up high, and down on the floor, more seats arranged in rows and draped in cobwebs. These led up to a stage fringed by tattered curtains and covered in dust. The stage was empty but for one thing. And when Zeb saw what it was, a small smile escaped his lips.

"A piano," he breathed.

You see, Zeb had not been brewing poison or shaking up cans of graffiti paint inside his bedroom on Rightangle Row. He had been teaching himself to play the keyboard he'd found under the bed there. Music, it turned out, was the one thing that could blot out everything else for Zeb. As soon as the first few notes of a song sounded, the rest of the world fell away. And while music didn't seem to be a priority for the Tank, Zeb *had* watched an episode where the survival expert fashioned a rescue horn out of an ox's thighbone, so he decided it must be all right to play a few sonatas from time to time.

Zeb gazed at the grand piano, sleek and black, as if it had been cut from midnight. And suddenly he forgot all about Outbursts and disappointing foster homes. He heaved the window up until there was space enough to climb through. Then, throwing one last look down Crook's End to check that he hadn't been followed, he squeezed himself into the theater and closed the window behind him.

It was absolutely silent inside, and Zeb winced as his footsteps bit into the quiet. But he made his way past the stalls, beneath the chandelier, and toward the stage. In the wings and scattered in moonlight, Zeb could see old set designs piled up on top of each other—mountains, palaces, and jungle trees—as well as heaps of abandoned props. Birdcages stacked up beside lamps, parasols left on sagging armchairs, and typewriters plonked on old trunks. Zeb was relieved that he would be spending the night curled up in an armchair rather than huddled under the tarp outside. Now, though, he wanted to play the piano—while the moonlight was at its brightest and everyone else was asleep, so that whatever he played would go unheard and he wouldn't be caught.

He sat on the stool before the piano. The keys were coated in dust, and Zeb wondered how long the instrument had stood there unused. He blew the dust away, and the chandelier glittered mischievously above, as if inviting him to play. Perhaps if Zeb had known that the real danger that night didn't lie out on the street but *under* it, he would have gotten up there and then and left Crook's End. But Zeb did not know that a harpy was waiting for him beneath the theater. And so he played the tune he loved most, the tune he chose whenever he felt afraid and alone, because it carried him back to a memory of long, long ago. He played it softly, slowly, but even as the first few notes tiptoed out into the empty theater, Zeb felt a sense of calm settle inside him.

He forgot about the Orderly-Queues. He forgot about eating lunch alone in the school cafeteria. He forgot about nights spent crying under his duvet. Instead he thought about the mountains, palaces, and trees in the wings of the theater, and as he played, he imagined they were real and that he was walking among them in a land far away. On and on Zeb played, unaware that deep underground, below this very piano, Morg's dark magic was stirring.

Chapter 2

The cookies didn't last long. In fact, by the next morning, Zeb had eaten all twenty-four of them and polished off his bottle of water. But a quick snoop around the theater showed him there was a dressing room with a sink, running water, and a working toilet, and several packets of jelly beans in a box in the foyer. Not enough to throw a dinner party, but enough to keep an eleven-year-old going for a day or two.

Zeb still wasn't entirely sure what his plan was. He just knew that inside this theater he had a bed, a piano, and lots of places to hide if someone came looking or a bout of explosive crying took hold. So, until the jelly beans ran out, there was really no need to leave.

He rooted through the props and placed all the slightly

scary ones in a bathtub he'd spotted at the back of the theater. Waking in the middle of the night to find himself face-to-face with a witch mask wedged down the side of his armchair was not an experience he wanted to repeat. He spent a large chunk of the day in front of a dressing room mirror, flexing his undersized biceps in preparation for intruders. Mostly, though, Zeb found himself counting down until moonrise and the silvery hours that followed when the rest of the world had gone to sleep. Then it would just be him and the grand piano, safe in the knowledge that nobody would hear.

Only somebody *did* hear.

Several streets away, there lived a young woman with fire-red hair called Fox Petty-Squabble. As an eleven-year-old, she had spent her days bickering with her twin brother, Fibber, but all that had changed after an adventure in the Unmapped Kingdom of Jungledrop, where they had banished Morg down a well and restored rain to our world. That was some time ago, and Fox was almost thirty now, but she could remember the glow-in-the-dark rainforest as if it were yesterday. And now that the world's climate was spiraling out of control again, faster than any of the scientists had predicted, Fox lay awake wondering whether there might be trouble in the Unmapped Kingdoms once again.

Fox was a social worker now. She had dedicated her life to helping others. But she knew that if Morg was behind this latest climate emergency, she'd need to go back to the Unmapped Kingdoms to sort things out. The only snag was that like last time, she'd need a phoenix tear to get there. There were only five of these tears left, and who knew where they were? She and Fibber had only stumbled across one the first time because an old antiques collector called Casper Tock had thrust it into her palm.

That night, Fox listened to the sound of the piano, so faint that at first she thought she was imagining it. But it was there, just at the edge of her hearing—music so beautiful it was like listening to waves rolling. It had been the same the night before, too, as she lay in her bed struggling to sleep. So, who was sitting down to play the piano in the middle of the night?

She sat up, padded across the bedroom of her top floor flat, and pulled back the curtains. Was the music coming from Crook's End? That would be impossible—no one lived there anymore. When she had visited the theater a few years ago, the week before it closed, she had most definitely seen a grand piano up onstage as part of the last production. Surely there was no one inside the Chandelier after all this time?

Now, most people would think twice about venturing into a boarded-up theater at night. But when you have faced cursed trees and demon monkeys, you find yourself blessed with more courage than most. So Fox bundled on some clothes and made her way out into the dark.

Zeb, meanwhile, was halfway through a piece of music he had composed the week before. It was low and brooding, inspired by an episode of *The Tank*, where he'd watched his hero hypnotize an elephant while simultaneously building a campfire. Zeb couldn't read music. He'd never had lessons, and he'd always played the Orderly-Queues' keyboard with headphones plugged in so that no one would poke their head round his door and tell him to be quiet. But he couldn't help feeling that music was, rather curiously, in his bones. Melodies seemed to come to him far more easily than family and friends. Zeb had put his musical talent down to a strange stroke of luck, but there was more to it than that. Magic was at work here. And this magic knew that one day Zeb would need his secret talent to work a miracle and save the world.

Zeb closed his eyes as he played, lost in the rise and fall of the notes, but when he opened them, he shrieked. There was a woman with bright red hair standing in the foyer! Zeb hurtled offstage into the wings, grabbed a vicar's robe from a pile of costumes, and threw it over his hoodie and jeans. Then he waited, crouched on the ground with his heart thudding, as the footsteps came nearer.

"I won't hurt you," the woman said. "I just want to talk."

Zeb burrowed deeper into the vicar's robe, instantly regretting it as a form of cover and cursing himself for playing the piano in the first place. The Tank would never have let a midnight concerto give him away.

"You're good at the piano," the woman said. "Really good."

Zeb could tell she was close. He risked a peep out of the vicar's robe and squeaked. The woman was on the stage now, and she was looking right at him. Zeb held her gaze and tried his best to look fierce. Being hard-core was exhausting, especially when all you wanted to do was burst into tears, but right now it was absolutely necessary. Zeb continued to glare at the woman. Would his biceps be up to the challenge if she got tricky?

"Why are you in here all alone in the middle of the night?" the woman asked.

Zeb pursed his lips and said nothing. Well-meaning members of the public often stepped in at critical points during his getaways, but they didn't care what happened to him in the end—not really. Once they'd phoned the police and an officer had come round to collect him, he wasn't their problem. But this woman didn't reach for her phone. She knelt down on the stage in front of Zeb instead. And smiled.

"Do you enjoy playing the piano?" she asked.

To his horror, Zeb found himself nodding inside his robes. What was he *doing*? If you were on the run, you didn't engage in chitchat about music! He did some jaw clenching and a small grunt to make up for it.

The woman kept talking, and Zeb noticed her voice was gentle, quite unlike the clipped tones of Joyce and Gerald Orderly-Queue and the dull drone of Derek Dunce.

"I'm hopeless with musical instruments," she said. "But I did go to an orchestral concert in Germany a few years ago, in a little village called Mizzlegurg with a dear old friend called Casper Tock, and the pianist there was quite something." She paused. "Almost as good as you, in fact. She was from Nigeria—and they say when she plays, the clouds part."

Zeb was unsure how to respond. An Outburst didn't seem to be brewing anymore, but he didn't exactly want to get himself caught up in a conversation either. Which is why he was surprised to hear himself say, "You heard Alaba Abadaki?"

The woman's face lit up. "Yes! That was her name!"

Zeb had heard the famous pianist a number of times on the radio in his bedroom, and he could only imagine how brilliant she must have been to see. But he tried not to dwell on this thought—he had a conversation to shut down and a visitor to dispose of before his getaway got completely out of control.

"I'm Fox," the woman said.

Zeb stiffened inside his robe. This did not sound like the end of a conversation. Why wasn't this woman dragging him off to the police station?

And then Fox said: "I'm a social worker, and I live nearby."

Zeb narrowed his eyes. The last thing he needed was a social worker foiling his escape, though she did seem very different from Derek Dunce. Her voice was softer, her eyes were brighter, and she didn't fill the silences with pointless suggestions.

"I want to help you," Fox said.

Zeb glowered at her. "I don't need help. From anybody."

Fox held up a half-empty packet of jelly beans and smiled. "Looks like you're almost out of these."

Zeb snatched the packet from her and shoved it under his robe.

"Listen," Fox said. "Why don't I take you out for some proper food? There are always a couple of diners open through the night. You can order anything you want: a burger, a plate of fries, a milkshake—whatever. And we can have a little chat."

Zeb's stomach growled at the mention of burgers. But the "little chat" did not sound good.

"I'm staying here." Zeb flapped his robe dramatically to make his point. "I'm not going out for food *or* back to a foster home ever again."

Fox looked at the boy sadly. She and her brother had been miserable and lonely as children. She knew what it was to feel unloved by grown-ups and she recognized it before her now.

"I can't force you to come with me, Zebedee."

Zeb flinched. "How do you know my name?"

Fox nodded toward the foyer. "It's inked onto your rucksack."

Zeb picked at his robe. The Tank could have warned him that taking named belongings out into the wild might be problematic.

"Go away," he muttered after a while, even though the thought of how he was going to find food once the jelly beans ran out was starting to make him feel uneasy.

He expected Fox to stand up, whip out her phone, and call in reinforcements. But she understood that children were complicated creatures, and though she knew she ought to walk Zeb to the police station, she sensed he wasn't the sort of child who was ready to give in just yet.

"Life won't always be this hard," Fox said softly.

Zeb blinked. He wasn't used to tenderness, and Fox had caught him off guard. Zeb tried to steel himself, but it was too late. Her kindness had triggered an Outburst, and though he swallowed and swallowed to force down the lump in his throat, Zeb had to face facts: The tears were coming whether he liked it or not.

"One day, things will be better," Fox went on. "Brighter." Zeb rubbed the first tear away, and Fox leaned in a little closer. "One day you will realize that you matter."

A second tear dribbled down Zeb's face and soon his cheeks were streaked. He brushed the tears away, but more fell, so he buried himself under his robe, where it was safe, and sobbed. And the more he sobbed, the angrier he felt. He had been doing just fine until Fox showed up. Now he was having an Outburst, and the whole getaway was lurching to a close. Zeb waited, again, for Fox to haul him up and insist he come along to the police station with her. But she didn't, and for a wild moment Zeb found himself wondering whether perhaps she really might be different from all the other grown-ups. He stamped the thought out as quickly as it had come—Outbursts always played havoc with his emotions.

"I'm going to hurry back to my flat and get my purse," Fox said. "Then when I come back, maybe we can have another think about that milkshake?"

Zeb sniffed. As far as he could tell, he had three options: wait here under the vicar's robe in the unlikely event that Fox kept her promise and came back for him; run off once again into the night; or sail out of New York on a raft built from theater props like the Tank would do. Zeb wiped his nose, forced the Outburst away, and tried to make a decision. It was pointless, really, because the harpy underground had been listening to everything. She had her own agenda—and it had nothing whatsoever to do with what Zeb wanted.

Fox stood up. "I'm coming back for *you*. I promise. Just stay here until then."

She turned and hurried out of the theater. And as soon as she was gone, the whispers started.

Chapter 3

Tucked under the vicar's robe, Zeb didn't hear the whispers at first. He was too busy trying to work out what he thought about Fox. But as he shrugged off his costume, he heard faint scratches of words coming from the direction of the piano.

"F-Fox?" Zeb called nervously. "Is that you?"

There was a brief silence. The chandelier sparkled in the moonlight. Then the whispers resumed, a little louder and more urgent than before. Zeb frowned—they seemed to be coming from *inside* the piano.

He eyed the instrument from the wings of the stage. This was not good. His survival training hadn't factored in the possibility of whispering pianos. The whispers grew louder, and Zeb realized they were saying one word over and over again, which slid down his spine like ice.

"Zebedee. Zebedee. Zebedee."

Zeb let out a terrified moan. Why was there a voice inside the piano calling his name? He'd looked inside earlier when blowing dust off the strings and there hadn't been a person hiding there. But more than that, this voice didn't sound as if it belonged to Zeb's world—it was the kind of voice rust might have if it could speak, and yet there was an edge to it that sounded somehow female. Zeb gulped. Was the theater haunted? Was this a ghost lurking inside the piano?

He tried to move. Perhaps running off again *was* the safest bet, because now that the Outburst had passed, he felt fairly sure it was madness to think he could rely on Fox. What would make her any different from the other grown-ups he'd met? All that talk of burgers and milkshakes was probably just a trick to get him out of the theater. For all he knew, Fox could be at the police station right this moment turning him in. But when Zeb made to move, his legs wouldn't budge. Fear held him just where he was. Right where Morg, the whispering harpy, wanted him to be.

"I can summon anything you want," the voice was saying now. "A getaway plane, riches galore. A place of your own miles away from anybody else so you never need to bother with other people again. With my magic, *anything* is possible."

Zeb was still too frightened to move. This ghost, or whatever it was, seemed to know things about him. Had it been listening in on his conversation with Fox? But alongside Zeb's fear, curiosity emerged. Nobody had ever promised him getaway planes, riches, and remote hideaways before. Zeb shook himself. He had watched close to a hundred episodes of *The Tank* and not once had his hero mentioned magic. But despite knowing it didn't exist, Zeb found himself imagining the possibilities of a future built with magic: a palace in the Himalayas; a castle in some remote forest in Finland; a fortress in Outer Mongolia . . . Zeb blinked to stop himself getting completely carried away.

But the voice went on, laying its promises at Zeb's lonely feet. "You could have a castle with a hundred floors and a grand piano in every room. You could have rooftop swimming pools and a private cinema. You could be so filthy rich you would never want for anything."

Zeb steeled himself again. Getting sidetracked by something as ridiculous as magic was bound to end in disaster. He tried to focus on the voice itself instead. Was it actually coming from the piano, or was it all in his head? He stood up on shaking legs and made his way toward the instrument. Holding his breath, he peered inside. No ghost looked up at him, no hideous specter leapt out. There was nothing inside the piano, just the strings and hammers—and the voice.

"I am not of your world, Zebedee. I am a creature trapped just beyond it because the journey here has taken nearly all of my strength. With your help, I will be able to do extraordinary things. Magical things that could change your life."

Zeb stared at the piano in disbelief. The voice was real, and it was definitely coming from inside the piano. So, what if it really *did* belong to a creature somewhere beyond his world—did that mean magic was real? The thought was so completely absurd that Zeb almost lost his balance. He tried to think rationally, as the Tank would do. Perhaps this piano was some elaborate mechanical prop from a past performance that had been programmed to speak nonsense after someone played it. But the voice had called Zeb by name. . . .

"There's got to be an explanation for all this," Zeb said in a trembling whisper.

"Magic," the voice replied. "And once you accept that it exists, we can get down to business. And getaway planes . . ."

Zeb chewed his nails. It was muscles, not magic, that got you out of scrapes. Wasn't it?

"I could slink off, I suppose," the voice said. "Find someone else to shower with riches and—"

"Don't go," Zeb blurted. And then he found himself saying: "If, by some miracle, magic exists, how can you change my life when you're in one world and I'm in another?" He paused. "What if you're just like everyone else I've ever met: full of promises you can't keep?"

"Oh, I'm not like anyone else," the voice replied. "I will keep my promise to you—if you keep a promise for me in return."

Zeb frowned. "But how can a voice keep a promise? It doesn't make sense."

A silence followed and Zeb inched closer to the piano. Had he blown it by asking too many questions? Had the creature sloped off to pester someone else? Then Zeb's skin tightened. The air inside the theater was changing. It had felt stale before, but now it felt alive, charged. The moonlight throbbed, and then, into the silence, there was a rush of wind that seemed to come from the piano itself.

It tore through the stalls, whipping up clouds of dust from the seats before spiraling round the chandelier. Zeb gasped as the light rocked back and forth, gathering momentum as it swung. And then a gust wrenched it from the ceiling and sent it hurtling down toward Zeb. He dived sideways and covered his eyes as the chandelier smashed onto the stage with a deafening crash.

Zeb opened one eye to see thousands of glass droplets strewn like shattered ice across the stage. Then the voice spoke again.

"I will keep my promise, Zebedee. I will conjure you a new life if you bring me the droplets still hanging from the chandelier. The ones that are glowing."

His ears still ringing from the crash, Zeb glanced at the chandelier. It was turned on its side and most of the glass had shattered, but Zeb could see a cluster of droplets dangling down that were perfectly intact. They were small—no bigger than marbles—and they were shining with the blinding blue that belongs to kingfishers and jungle frogs. Zeb's eyes widened. Whatever this creature was, it was powerful. It wasn't even *in* Zeb's world yet, and somehow it had torn down a chandelier.

"Time is running out," the voice crooned. "You cannot make a noise that loud without somebody coming to investigate. That meddling woman might come back. And she'll come with more than her purse." The creature hissed. "She'll come with the full force of the law on her side, and when the police see the mess you've made of that chandelier, they might even lock you up. After all, nobody wants a vandal in their neighborhood."

"But Fox said she was coming back to take me out for food. She—" Zeb stopped, realizing he'd been quietly believing in the social worker all along. What was wrong with him tonight? Why was he suddenly believing in unlikely things left, right, and center?

The voice cut into his thoughts. "You know as well as I do, Zebedee, that the social worker has gone to the police. And if you turn away from me now, you'll be back where you were: alone and unhappy and utterly without hope." There was a pause. "Bring me the droplets, boy."

Zeb looked from the chandelier to the piano. It was one thing admitting that the voice was probably right about Fox, but it was quite another to go believing in magic. "If—if you still have enough magic to summon a wind and pull down a chandelier, why can't *you* summon the droplets?"

"Because those droplets are filled with a different magic

from mine," the creature snapped. "They are immortalized phoenix tears, shed a long time ago, and phoenix magic has a will of its own, which, right now, is sitting stubbornly out of my grasp. I can sense this magic, though, even without seeing it, and when it is brought to me, I will use it to help you. I will build you an almighty home filled with pianos." The voice paused. "But perhaps you don't want my help. Perhaps you've got your life all figured out and it's time I left you alone."

Zeb knew he was running out of time and options. With no money or connections, he could only run for so long, and who knew what punishment might lie in store for him if he was accused of vandalizing the theater when he was eventually caught? He thought again of the creature's offer: a getaway plane, riches, *and* a home. For the first time in his life, there was a chance for him to escape—*properly* escape—and now that it had been dangled in front of him, he couldn't pass it by, no matter how unlikely it all seemed.

"Well?" came the voice again.

Zeb imagined his palace in the Himalayas. He'd never thought about living in a grand home before, but now one was forming in his mind. He could see his bedroom: a glorious four-poster bed and a piano pushed up to a window overlooking snow-capped mountains. There was a heated rooftop swimming pool, too. And a landing pad for his getaway plane. He wasn't sure *how* he'd go about flying this getaway plane, but perhaps when you had magic on your side, *how* wasn't so much of an issue. Maybe the voice inside the piano could demand pilots as well as planes and no one would bat an eyelid. The palace grew and grew in Zeb's mind until the possibilities of it all outweighed the doubt and he found himself daring to believe in magic.

He tiptoed over the glass until he came to four glowing droplets. Up close, they shone so brightly that he blinked. Reaching out a hand, he yanked them from the chandelier. He was so keen to claim his reward, he didn't notice a fifth droplet that had broken away from the others and was tucked beyond the stage curtain—beyond the creature's radar, too.

"Yes," the voice breathed as Zeb made his way back toward the piano. "I can feel the phoenix magic stirring now."

The droplets tingled in Zeb's palm, and a thrill rushed through him as he thought of what lay ahead. Would the getaway plane appear in Crook's End the moment he handed the droplets over? Perhaps he'd arrive at his rooftop swimming pool for a quick dip before bed.

The creature's voice, rich with desire, gave one last order as Zeb drew close: "Drop the phoenix tears into the piano, Zebedee."

Zeb held the droplets above the strings and, for a moment, he wavered. Why, just as he was about to secure himself a brilliant future, had the image of Fox drifted into his mind? He cast her away and hardened his heart to any shred of possibility that she might have kept her promise and come back to help him. That just wasn't the way people worked. He let the first three droplets clatter down into the piano, but he held on tight to the last one, just in case he needed some bargaining power during the exchange of riches.

For a few seconds nothing happened, and Zeb wondered whether perhaps he'd gone mad and simply imagined the voice altogether. Then an arm burst out from under the strings and hammers. A thin arm, covered in black feathers. Zeb recoiled as five clawed fingers reached out toward him and gripped him by the shoulder. He tried to yank himself free, but the fingers were strong and only held tighter.

Then, in one swift pull, they dragged him down into the piano.

Chapter 4

Zeb kicked and screamed. He was tumbling down and down into darkness. Where were the strings and hammers inside the piano? Where was the bottom of the instrument? He shrieked as clawed fingers scrabbled at his hand, then the last droplet was gone and Zeb's body brushed past something cool and hard, like stone. He landed with a thump on a heap of soil, and as his eyes adjusted to the gloom, his whole body filled with dread.

Somehow, he had fallen through a crevice of rock into a very large cave. A mass of tangled roots covered the roof, and tucked into their folds were hundreds of skulls that shone with an eerie green light. Jagged rocks lined the cave, several shadowy tunnels led off from it, and at the far end, there was a throne carved from stone and wrapped in spiderwebs.

In front of Zeb, dusting herself free of soil, was the creature. She had a black-feathered body, talons instead of feet, and a mangy pair of wings sprouting from her back. Over her face she wore the pointed skull of a long-dead bird and Zeb could see two yellow eyes shining with menace behind this skull. They blinked, and Zeb scrambled backward. Then the creature laughed darkly, and as she raised the glass droplets in her hand, Zeb noticed her wings begin to change. They grew bigger and stronger as more and more feathers appeared, until they were no longer the tattered, limp things they had been. They rose up either side of the creature, huge and black, like a cape of oil.

"Almost five hundred years I have waited for this moment!" the creature cried. "I have crawled through darkness day after day, night after night to find enough phoenix magic to restore my strength and begin my reign. And tonight, I have succeeded!" The creature cackled and her laugh echoed down the tunnels. "I, Morg, am a harpy filled with magic once more!"

Zeb was now so frightened he thought he might be sick. Magic was real; that much was clear. But what he hadn't expected was for it to be so utterly terrifying. Even the shadows seemed to shrink with fear every time the harpy moved, and Zeb noticed the crevice he had fallen through had now closed up completely.

Morg slipped the droplets into a pouch around her neck, then turned her attention to Zeb. "Welcome to Hollowbone, my underground lair, a land so full of darkness it barely belongs to any world at all."

The cave was so quiet, Zeb felt sure the harpy would hear his heart thumping into the silence, but he willed his words on, despite his fear. "You—you said you'd summon anything I wanted. So I'd like to climb inside my getaway plane, collect my riches, and get out of here. Please." He looked around him. "Maybe you could park the plane in that tunnel over there—*with* a pilot inside it, because I can feel an Outburst coming and I'm not sure I can sob and steer at the same time."

Morg flexed her wings. "There is just one small thing I still need you to do, Zebedee. One last item I need you to bring me for my powers to be *fully* restored."

A shower of black sparks fell from the harpy's wings, singeing holes in the stone floor as if it had been made of paper. Zeb flinched. If this was the harpy before she came into her full strength, he didn't dare imagine what she might be like at the height of her powers. Zeb forced himself to his feet nevertheless. He needed to show Morg he meant business, even though he was so scared he could barely breathe. "You—you look like you've got plenty of magic to be getting on with things yourself, and I—I kept my side of the bargain. So, I'd like to get going in my plane now."

Morg picked up a stone and Zeb watched in horror as she crushed it into a handful of dust. "Your time will come, Zebedee. But until it does, I need you to listen and obey."

Zeb tried his best to steer the harpy back to their bargain. "But you said—"

Morg growled and Zeb watched, wide-eyed, as the rocks lining the mouths of the tunnels sharpened into spikes. She took a step closer to Zeb and the air chilled.

"Have you ever wanted something, Zebedee? Wanted it so badly you would do almost anything to get it? And I'm not talking about getaway planes or rooftop swimming pools. . . ."

Zeb was too petrified to speak or look up, but he could feel the harpy's eyes boring into him.

"What about power?" Morg continued. She stalked over to her throne, then sat upon it with her wings tucked up behind her. "You could build a home in the most remote part of your world, but there would still be a chance—however slim—that someone would find you and drag you back to your old life. And then all this would've been for nothing."

Zeb was silent for a moment. He was aware that he was treading a fine line between having a conversation and being crushed into a handful of dust. And yet when he raised his head, he found the harpy glaring at him so intently he felt compelled to reply. "What—what are you suggesting?"

The harpy cocked her skull mask to one side. "That we build a new world. A world where *we* are in charge."

Half an hour ago, Zeb would have scoffed at the idea, but now that he had been yanked from Brooklyn, dragged down into an underground lair, and was face-to-face with a magical creature, it didn't seem so far-fetched. More than this, though, Zeb was in the grip of Morg's magic now, and the possibility of a safe new world had grown legs of its own, filling Zeb's mind until he could barely remember the city or the house he'd been running from.

He shifted under the harpy's gaze. "You're *sure* this is possible?"

"*Anything* is possible," Morg spat, "if you have enough magic. The only reason I didn't mention it to you earlier was because building a new world comes with"—she paused—"a catch. And you seemed to be taking such a long time to decide on what to do with yourself; I thought it best not to fluster you further."

"Would the catch still mean I get a plane and riches and a palace in this new world?"

Morg nodded.

"And we wouldn't have to live next to each other or anything?" Zeb grimaced at the thought. "You could be in charge of one half of the world and I could rule the other?"

"Correct. There will be more than enough magic for both of us to live the lives we want."

Zeb weighed all this up, then he took a deep breath. "What exactly do you want me to do? And what's the catch?

The harpy leaned forward on her throne, and in a singsong voice she began to tell Zeb a story. "Before I came along, a phoenix ruled the world from Everdark, a hidden land just like Hollowbone here. It's halfway between the Faraway—where you're from—and the Unmapped Kingdoms, magical lands where sunlight, rain, and snow are conjured."

Zeb pulled himself onto a rock and tried his best to follow.

"It was the phoenix's job to watch over these four kindgoms and ensure the Unmappers who lived there shared their magic with the Faraway, so that your continents might be filled with light and life. Phoenixes are weak, though. Every five hundred years the reigning one would die and a new phoenix would rise from its ashes to watch over the Unmapped Kingdoms. But then I came along . . ." The harpy smirked. "I rose from the ashes of the last phoenix nearly five thousand years ago. And do you think watching over other people and sharing magic with humans is something I do?"

"Er, no," Zeb replied hastily. "Smashing chandeliers and hauling people into pianos is more your style."

"You're catching on." Morg steepled her clawed fingers. "Without a new phoenix rising every five hundred years, the Unmapped magic is beginning to run out. The kingdoms' dragons may be scattering moondust to keep what is left of it going, but every day a little more fades. Only the birth of a new phoenix can restore the magic I have destroyed so far. So, now is my time to act."

Zeb inched a little further inside his hoodie. He was still coming to terms with the harpy and now there was talk of dragons, too. . . .

"Three times over the last five thousand years I have tried to steal the Unmapped magic. And three times I have failed.

But this time, I will seize it all and then I will have the power of the elements on my side." Morg's wings shimmered. "I will command the sun to scorch, the rain to unleash mighty storms, and the snow to cast the fiercest blizzards, until every Unmapper is destroyed. Until the Kingdoms of Rumblestar, Jungledrop, Crackledawn, and Silvercrag are no more. Then I will use this Unmapped magic—the most powerful magic of all—to build us both a new world."

Zeb was starting to feel alarmed. "But if you get rid of these Unmapped Kingdoms, doesn't that mean the Faraway, where I'm from, goes too?"

"And there you have the catch," Morg replied. "The Faraway will vanish, and all the people with it." She paused. "But your world hasn't exactly been kind to you, has it, Zebedee?"

Zeb looked down. There were eight billion people on planet Earth and not one had shown him they cared. That social worker called Fox might have claimed to, but who was to say she would actually have come back? And as for the Unmapped Kingdoms: He'd only heard about them for the first time just now. So, it should have been easy for Zeb to wash his hands of the lot of them.

"You're quite sure the only way to build a new world is to

wipe out the Unmapped Kingdoms *and* the Faraway?" he said.

"Of course I'm sure," the harpy snapped. "I wouldn't be wasting my time with you if there was another way."

Zeb was trying extremely hard to focus on power and riches instead of world annihilation, but it was proving harder than expected. "Does wiping everyone out seem a little bit"—he searched for the right word—"*drastic* to you?"

"I knew you'd be too weak for this," Morg hissed.

The harpy stood up, and as she raised her wings, a flurry of black sparks danced around her. Zeb didn't know much about magic, but he could clearly sense that a whole lot of trouble was about to come his way.

"Wait!" he cried. "I wasn't saying I wouldn't help you. I was just—just—thinking things through."

Sparks poured from Morg's wings, hissing as they hit the ground. "You're either in or you're out, Zebedee." She took a stride closer and her dark magic crackled. "Which is it?"

Zeb knew deep down that even though he was unsure about erasing humankind, he was trapped in Hollowbone with the harpy, and unless he went along with her plan, he was as good as dead. He tried to focus on the end result: Once the new world had been conjured and he and Morg had gone their separate ways, no one, least of all Derek Dunce, would meddle in his life ever again. Zeb would finally be in charge of his own destiny, like the Tank himself, only smaller and with less facial hair.

Morg was cradling a ball of black sparks in her hands now and as she raised it high, Zeb knew he had to make his decision now.

"I'll—I'll do it," he stammered. "I'll help you find whatever it is you need to build another world."

Morg let the ball of dark magic fizzle to the ground, then she folded in her wings and sat back down on her throne. Zeb blew out through his lips.

"I plan to use the last of the magic inside the phoenix tears you brought me to break open a portal into the kingdom of Crackledawn," Morg explained, "where sunlight is made. I went there after leaving Everdark years ago, and I still have followers there. Midnights, I call them. They know that without a phoenix, the kingdom's magic is hanging by a thread, so they have seized upon Crackledawn's vulnerability, and for the past decade they have been making things even trickier for the Unmappers and their precious sun scrolls. *This* is why your climate has been spiraling out of control again. Just as it was when I meddled in Jungledrop and you had no rain for months on end, and when I broke into Rumblestar and you were plagued by hurricanes."

Zeb thought of the soaring temperatures, melting ice, and rising sea levels, the families who had lost homes and loved ones, and the TV footage showing polar bears stranded on melting ice. All that had happened because of this harpy?

"Smudge and Bartholomew might have locked me back in Everdark," Morg muttered. "Casper Tock might have flung me out of Rumblestar, and Fox Petty-Squabble might have trapped me in a never-ending well after banishing me from Jungledrop five hundred years ago. But this time will be different. This time all the phoenix tears are here." She patted her pouch, unaware that in her greed at becoming a harpy again she had been careless and overlooked the fact that there was still one phoenix tear unaccounted for. She crooned on, blind to her mistake. "This time no pesky eleven-year-olds from the Faraway can use the tears to enter the Unmapped Kingdoms and thwart my plans."

Zeb's pulse quickened. The social worker back in the theater had been called Fox. And hadn't she mentioned going to a concert with somebody called Casper Tock? But the harpy had talked of meeting Fox five hundred years ago and that couldn't possibly make sense . . .

"Does time pass in the same way in the Unmapped Kingdoms as it does in the Faraway?" he asked, trying to keep his voice calm.

The harpy shook her head. "One year in the Faraway is almost thirty years in the Unmapped Kingdoms or in Hollowbone."

If time back home passed that slowly, then it was possible that five hundred years could have gone by in the Unmapped Kingdoms since Fox had beaten Morg as an eleven-year-old, because that would make her about thirty now. Could the social worker called Fox, who he had only spent a matter of minutes with, have been mixed up in this so-called Unmapped magic too? Had she battled the very harpy Zeb had just made a deal with?

For a wild second, Zeb wanted to rush back to the theater and find Fox. He'd been reluctant to talk earlier, but now there were dozens of questions he needed to ask. What if she really had saved the world from Morg and here he was about to destroy it? Was a world worth saving just for one person?

"This Fox Petty-Squabble," Zeb said slowly. "What color was her hair?"

The harpy looked at Zeb intently, as if reading his mind. Then she said: "Red."

Zeb's eyes widened. But before his thoughts could gather any more momentum, Morg spoke again.

"Fox Petty-Squabble, who you did indeed meet in the theater tonight, is one of the nastiest humans I have ever encountered. There she was promising to help you and acting like she cared. But what would you think if I told you that in her quest to save the Faraway, Fox betrayed her own brother? She lies, you see, and she only ever thinks about herself. She'll stop at nothing to ensure things go her way." Morg cackled. "And there you were hoping that there might have been just one person in the Faraway who actually cared about you."

Zeb felt a familiar hurt sweep through him. He didn't know this Fox person at all, and though he was still wildly unsure of the harpy, she did at least seem like the kind of creature who got stuff done. Zeb thought of the crevice of rock he'd fallen through and how it had closed up, sealing his way home. He knew, deep down, that he didn't really have a choice in what he was about to do. The harpy had him trapped.

He pulled his shoulders back and raised his head. "What needs to happen next?"

Morg rose from her throne. One flap from her wings and she was at the roof of the cave, her talons latched on to the tangled roots. She tugged one of the skulls free, and as she swooped back down, Zeb noticed it wasn't shining green like the rest. The light inside this one was gold.

"Being trapped in a never-ending well has its advantages," Morg said. "You're forced to dig yourself out, and five hundred years of digging is bound to throw up secrets. . . . I found Hollowbone eventually and tucked into a crack in the rock here, I found one half of the long-lost Ember Scroll. It tells the story of how the world began. And the very first phoenix hid it here to keep it safe from harm because it knew how secret in-between worlds like Everdark and Hollowbone are."

Morg stroked the skull, and Zeb noticed the light inside it was moving. He edged forward. And as he peered through the eyes of the skull, he saw two gold wings, no bigger than a swallow's, hinged together at the center.

"The Ember Scroll is made up of two parts, which have been separated over the years: the scroll itself, which is a piece of sacred parchment, and these wings, which are made from phoenix feathers soaked in Stargold. Once the wings are fixed to the parchment, the Ember Scroll can fly out over the Unmapped Kingdoms."

Zeb watched the little wings open and close, and he felt suddenly glad of their light in the deep, dark cave.

"Legends claim that the story written on the Ember Scroll is waiting for an ending, for someone to write a new phoenix into life to ensure peace and prosperity forevermore for the Unmapped Kingdoms and the Faraway, no matter what happens to the magic there now." The harpy snorted. "If I can find the scroll and write my *own* ending onto it—where I steal the Unmapped magic and build a new empire—I will break the cycle of the phoenix magic once and for all, and my words will ring true for eternity."

Zeb looked up at Morg. "But how do I fit into all of this?"

"The phoenix was a creature of fire and flame, and many believe it placed the Ember Scroll somewhere hot, somewhere far out of reach."

Zeb swallowed. He didn't like the sound of where this was heading.

Morg's eyes glittered behind her mask. "You, Zebedee, are going to steal the scroll from the sun."

Chapter 5

WHAT?!" Zeb spluttered. "How on earth am I going to get to the sun? And how am I going to survive that scorching furnace of gas if I do get there?" Even the Tank would have drawn the line at this.

But Morg raised the skull containing the Stargold Wings and simply said: "Stargold. Whoever carries it is protected against fire."

Zeb's palms were beginning to sweat. He was all for siding with the harpy if it meant conjuring up a new life, but what she was suggesting was impossible! "Can't you carry the Stargold Wings and I'll just cheer *you* on from down here?"

Morg shook her head. "I am a creature of darkness and shadows, like my Midnights. Not even Stargold can protect us from the sun. But you will be safe. Phoenixes have a sentimental fondness for humans, so anything imbued with their magic will help you."

"But the sun is huge!" Zeb cried. "A hundred times bigger than Earth, according to my science teacher. So if, miraculously, you find a way to get me there, how am I going to locate a tiny piece of parchment? It'll take me forever!"

"Magic is drawn to magic, Zebedee. When the Ember Scroll senses its wings are nearby, it'll come to you."

Zeb slumped onto a rock and ran a hand through his hair—it was a lot to take in. "How do I know you're telling the truth about all this? How do I *know* the phoenix magic will protect me?"

Morg set the skull with the Stargold Wings inside down by Zeb. "Because I'm trusting you with this—the very thing I need to build a new world." The harpy stalked off toward one of the tunnels. Then she stopped at the opening and looked back over her shoulder. "And because, much as I hate to admit it, phoenix magic is strong; it's what saved Fox Petty-Squabble from me in Jungledrop."

Morg swept off down a tunnel, her wings trailing behind her. And though Zeb scooped up the skull and made to follow, the spiked rocks lining the tunnels crunched closer, barring his way. Zeb gulped. He might have been interested in Morg's offer, but one thing was crystal clear: Until he found the Ember Scroll, he was little more than the harpy's prisoner. So, no matter how impossible or terrifying the journey to the sun sounded, he knew he had no choice but to do it.

Zeb looked about him—he wasn't sure if it was night or day beyond the cave. Hollowbone had swallowed all sense of time. And having grown used to the clatter of New York City and the comfort of hearing and playing music, he found the cave's silence smothering. But he was tired, and he figured that sleep was probably a good idea considering the scale of the task ahead.

Zeb glanced at the Stargold Wings fluttering like a trapped moth inside the skull. He didn't know what to make of phoenixes. But the fact that one had befriended Fox, even though she'd apparently betrayed her own brother, didn't fill Zeb with much enthusiasm. Although there was something comforting about the Stargold's glow, as if someone had remembered to save a little piece of light for Zeb should his world come crashing down.

Zeb woke with a start, a few hours later. Morg was towering over him, her wings bathed in the cave's green glow.

"Ready?" she muttered.

Zeb felt for the skull containing the Stargold Wings and hauled himself up. He couldn't help thinking a bit more problem-solving and even a spot of breakfast might have been sensible before journeying to the sun. But he was too scared to suggest it in case the harpy started juggling balls of dark magic again. Besides, Morg seemed to have other plans anyway.

"Follow me," she said, whipping her wings round toward a tunnel.

The stone spikes barring the way slid back, the harpy hurried through, and Zeb followed nervously. Now and again there was a candle perched on a rock, casting a flickering glow on the wet stone, but more often than not, Zeb had to feel his way on through the darkness.

Eventually, the tunnel widened and a green glow slipped inside from somewhere up ahead. Then the rocks pulled back and Zeb found himself in another cave. It was as big as a stadium, with stalactites dripping down from the roof and thousands more skull-lamps lining the walls. But what made Zeb shiver was the lake that filled it. The water was black, lit green in parts by the lamps. It was eerily still, and all around the edge lay heaps of broken bones.

Zeb's toes curled inside his sneakers. The cave was completely silent—even quieter than the cavern he'd slept in, if that was possible. And this was the kind of silence that comes before something terrible happens. Glancing down at the skull in his hand, Zeb noticed that the Stargold Wings were shivering.

He turned to the harpy. "Could we just have one little chat about how exactly I'm going to reach the sun and what I—"

The harpy, Zeb realized, wasn't listening to him at all. She had taken the phoenix tears out of the pouch around her neck and was staring at them intently.

"There are only four." She seized Zeb by the scruff of his neck. "Where's the fifth?"

"There—there wasn't a fifth," Zeb stammered.

The harpy hissed. "Turn out your pockets."

Zeb did so. "See—nothing. There were only four phoenix tears in the theater."

Morg shoved him aside and curled her fingers over the tears she had. "There is one last phoenix tear unaccounted for, but even if it is found somewhere in the Faraway, I am on the cusp of entering Crackledawn. No one can stand in my way now."

She held the tears high and they pulsed blue. Then the lake

rippled, even though there was no wind, and the harpy shouted: "Arise, broken bones! I built you from the dregs of my magic, but I am growing in power. With this phoenix magic here, you will become my followers! My Midnights!"

The silence seemed to swell. Then came the sound of bones clanking. And Zeb watched in horror as, one by one, skeletons rose up from the heaps of bones lining the lake. Necks cricked and limbs twisted, until an army of gaping mouths and empty eye sockets turned to face Morg.

She crowed with delight. "The day is drawing near when I will steal *all* of the Unmapped magic and use it to conjure you Midnights a whole new world!"

Zeb made a mental note to build a very high wall separating his side of this new world from Morg's.

"Now, though," the harpy said, "you will follow me as we break into Crackledawn to steal the Ember Scroll."

The skeletons let out a ghostly cry, but Zeb's eyes slid to the lake. It was moving again. Ripple after ripple broke the surface, then the water began to fizz and boil. Zeb's heart thumped. Something was coming, something big.

Morg raised the phoenix tears once again, and as they glowed, the lake erupted. Water spewed over the skeletons and up rose a towering ship. The deck was black, the rigging was black, the sails were black. And the sea serpent carved into the prow was blacker still.

"All aboard *Darktongue*," Morg shrieked, "my ship built from shadows!"

The skeletons reached for their boned spears and began banging them on the cave floor as they marched into the lake toward the ship. Zeb wanted to shut his eyes and disappear. His getaway, which had begun just with running over the Brooklyn Bridge, was now reaching unforeseen levels of terror. He knew he had to hang in there if he wanted the new world and all its possibilities, but that didn't stop him feeling the need for a quick whimper in the shadows. He shuffled back inside the tunnel with the Stargold Wings.

The harpy's clawed hand dug into his shoulder. "Leaving so soon, Zebedee?"

"I—I wasn't leaving," Zeb spluttered. "I was just—just getting a better view."

"Good," Morg replied. "Because you will be lost for eternity if you slink back inside those tunnels. There's no way back to the Faraway from there. But climb aboard *Darktongue*, and a new world awaits."

She stalked off toward the ship. Zeb bit his lip to stop it trembling, then he steadied his legs and forced them into a swagger, the kind of walking the Tank did when he was about to face extreme danger. Zeb's swagger was more of a hesitant limp, but it nudged him forward and, moments later, he found himself aboard *Darktongue*, which Morg's Midnights had steered to the shore.

The Midnights poured over the ship, letting down sails, sorting the rigging, manning the wheel at the helm, and unfurling a shining black flag from the crow's nest. As *Darktongue* pulled back from the shore, Zeb threw one last look around the cave and was surprised to see a large heap of bones in one corner that didn't seem to have become a terrifying Midnight. But he quickly forgot them as the ship began to gather momentum, speeding toward a vast wall of rock at the far end of the cave.

"We'll be killed if we charge into that rock face!" Zeb yelled.

Morg was up on the deck at the prow now, her wings outstretched and rippling, her hands clasping the phoenix tears. She had been waiting for this moment for a long, long time. And as the last of the phoenix magic burned blue, there was a loud crunch and the rock face before them slid back, like a giant stone door opening.

Light poured in, the blinding white light of a sun just risen, and Zeb raised a hand to cover his eyes. There were new sounds now too: seagulls crying and waves roaring, and Zeb almost wept with relief at hearing these noises because it meant the eerie silence and never-ending darkness of Hollowbone was coming to an end. He could taste salt on his lips and feel wind ruffling his hair. He lowered his hand from his eyes. An ocean spread out as far as he could see, diamond-bright under a wide blue sky. Zeb felt almost dizzy thinking of how far he'd come from Brooklyn. Dragged down into an underground lair and then forced out in a totally new world through a portal Morg had opened.

The harpy screeched with delight as *Darktongue* forged its way into Crackledawn. Then the Midnights banged their spears on the decks and cheered, and even Zeb managed a shaky smile. Morg had done what she said she was going to do: She had broken into the Unmapped Kingdoms. And now Zeb was moving closer to a brand-new life.

The harpy laughed as she tossed the phoenix tears, now drained of magic, overboard. Then she leaned over the sea serpent prow and smiled. Because there were creatures waiting for her as the ship sailed out of Hollowbone. Followers who were rising from the depths of the ocean to swim alongside *Darktongue*.

Zeb leapt back from the edge of the ship as an enormous eel with purple skin, flickering gills, two forked tongues, and a single roaming eye surfaced for a moment, then sunk out of sight. Then came a red kraken with enormous suckers and slime-drenched skin.

"Ogre eels and fire krakens!" Morg cried. "So my army of Midnights grows! I thank you for your work here. Your dark magic kept me alive as I clawed out of the never-ending well, found Hollowbone, and made my way on to the Faraway! I am looking forward to helping you drain this kingdom of magic and put an end to all those who live here!"

Zeb began doing some wild jaw-clenches. Anything to distract himself from the reality of Morg's plans and the sea monsters racing along either side of the ship. He looked out over the ocean again. Had there not been ogre eels and fire krakens splashing about, Zeb figured this world would look a lot like his own, though something about the air here felt different, as if the wind might be carrying secrets. He shrugged off his hoodie. It was warm in this kingdom, tropically warm. He tried to imagine what kind of creatures might live in a land like this and found himself looking for the seagulls he'd heard earlier. But they were nowhere to be seen now, and despite the heat, Zeb shivered suddenly. The birds might have flown off, but surely there should have been others, or at least some fish beneath the surface of the sea. But there was nothing. No sign of any boats either. And Zeb wondered then whether the wind might be carrying fear as well as secrets.

He glanced behind him. Only the mouth of a cave remained of Hollowbone, a yawning darkness behind them in a sea of infinite blue. But from it, there came a cry. And it was much, much louder than the shrieks of the seagulls earlier. Wilder, too. Then a clanking rang from the cave, and Zeb thought of the heap of bones he'd seen left behind.

The clanking gave way to a steady, beating *whrum*. Zeb swallowed. Whatever it was that was coming had wings.

And then one last Midnight bound to Morg's will burst out of Hollowbone: a dragon built of bones.

Zeb ducked as it raced past the ship, breathing blasts of red-hot fire, before climbing up into the sky. Its tail slithered like a snake's, but the bones lent every movement a hollow clatter. The dragon's wings were more like giant fingers, its skull was horned, and its cry sent shudders through *Darktongue*'s sails.

But when Zeb saw Morg look from the dragon to him, then back again to the dragon, he knew that this Midnight had been called for a purpose.

This was his ride to the sun.

Chapter 6

D*arktongue* moved through the sea like a knife. Quick, smooth, quiet. Morg leaned over the prow of the ship, whispering instructions to the ogre eels and fire krakens under her command.

Zeb maneuvered himself and the Stargold Wings to the opposite end of *Darktongue*, a safe distance from the sea monsters, and looked out over the stern. The kingdom of Crackledawn on the far shore seemed to be buzzing with life and magic—a magic wholly different from Morg's. This was playful and full of color and so crammed with wonder, it made Zeb's jaw drop. He glimpsed a pod of multicolored dolphins leaping through the waves and, a little distance away, a diamond-shelled turtle turning somersaults beneath the surface. Pockets of land were dotted here and there—one little island with thousands of gold shells glittering on the sand, and another with feather-tailed monkeys leaping between palm trees.

Zeb shifted uncomfortably as he remembered that he was part of a plan to wipe all this out. Morg's Midnights, it seemed, had already started. A patch of sea went suddenly black for no reason, and on the surface a shoal of fluorescent fish floated, lifeless. An island they passed that might once have been covered in palm trees was home to burned timber. And a cluster of caverns signposted THE SIGHING CAVES were making the situation *very* clear as their cave mouths sighed their way through all sorts of depressing puns: "Might as well cave in and die with so little Unmapped magic left in Crackledawn!" and "We're on rocky ground these days!"

Zeb was beginning to think it strange that he hadn't seen any of the people from the kingdom yet—Morg had called them "Unmappers." But then *Darktongue* rounded the Sighing Caves, and a little farther out to sea, rocking on the waves, was a magnificent dhow boat. Its polished deck shone in the sunlight, its golden sail billowed in the wind, and from the stern a cluster of people were hauling in nets. Zeb hadn't been sure what to expect from the Unmappers, but they looked more or less like ordinary people. Barefoot men and women dressed in knee-length tunics gathered at the waist with a sash of leaves. Within seconds of seeing *Darktongue*, they all started shouting.

"Leave the nets!"

"Dark magic ahoy!"

Zeb watched as the Unmappers raced across their deck, yanking at the rigging and readying the sail. But Morg's eyes were set on this boat now, and *Darktongue* was charging toward it at lightning speed.

The Unmappers' shouting grew more frenzied, and Zeb could almost taste their fear; he knew the horror of being ambushed by dark magic. "It's—it's *Morg*!" they screamed. "She's returned! With a dragon! SOUND THE ALARM!"

An Unmapper scrambled to the bow and yanked the large silver bell there. A clang rang out, louder than any bell toll Zeb had ever heard, and all of a sudden, he found himself desperately wanting the Unmappers to escape. But it was too late for alarm bells and escape plans now. *Darktongue* was closing in on the dhow, and as it swung close, Morg raised her terrible wings and her Midnights leapt aboard.

Zeb watched, horrified, as the skeletons screeched and hurled their spears. The Unmappers didn't stand a chance, Zeb could see that. He buried his face behind the skull he held as the Midnights swarmed the boat, turning each terrified Unmapper into a pile of dust with every jab of their spears. Then, minutes later, all was silent. Zeb peeped out from behind the Stargold Wings to see the Midnights clattering back aboard *Darktongue* and Morg raising her gaze to the bone dragon. It hurtled down from the sky and, with one blast of fire, set the Unmappers' boat alight.

All trace of the dhow and its crew sunk from sight. Zeb knew the harpy was powerful—in just one day he'd seen her crush stone, raise skeletons to life, and break into a magical kingdom. None of that could hold a candle to what he'd just seen. Morg's magic had destroyed a ship full of Unmappers in front of his very eyes. And if this was how sick he felt now, then what would he feel like after wiping out four kingdoms worth of Unmappers and an entire civilization back home?

He sneaked a look at the harpy. She was laughing wildly and her Midnights were cheering. All Zeb wanted to do was run away. But he was trapped aboard *Darktongue* now, and if he backed out of the bargain he'd made with Morg, he knew he'd be killed in seconds. Perhaps there was a chance he could get Morg to create a new world but somehow avoid exterminating quite so many people? Surely there were loopholes with magic?

Darktongue pushed on through the ocean, then Morg stalked across the ship toward Zeb. She ruffled her wings and a hunk of bread, a piece of shriveled fruit, and a flask of water appeared at Zeb's feet.

"Breakfast," she muttered. "You'll need it before your journey."

Zeb watched the sea where the Unmappers and their dhow had been just moments before. "You—you destroyed them," he said quietly. "Every last one."

Morg nodded.

"But—but they didn't seem to be doing any harm."

The harpy took a step closer. "I did tell you, boy. To build a new world, I will destroy *everything*." Her wings twitched. "Eat. Now. You'll be leaving shortly."

Zeb squinted at the sun and gulped. He was feeling too sick to eat or drink, but he did anyway, even though the bread was stale and the fruit was partly rotten, because he knew if he backed out now, he'd be going the same way as the Unmappers he'd just seen.

"My dragon will carry you to the sun," Morg said. "And the Stargold Wings will form a shield of safety around you both. Then, when you are close enough, the Ember Scroll will sense its missing magic and come to you."

Zeb slid a glance up at the dragon. It was gliding above *Darktongue*'s sails, its boned wings cutting the sun into slithers.

Trying his best to be brave, Zeb cleared his throat. "Then I bring *you* the Ember Scroll, *you* write *your* ending"—he figured this wasn't the time to discuss possible loopholes in magic—"and we get to build a new world before going our separate ways?"

"That is the deal," Morg replied.

She bent down and took the skull containing the Stargold Wings from beside Zeb. Then she squeezed and the bone fell away, like powder, until all that was left in her hands were the little gold wings. She held them tight as they flapped inside her palms, then pushed them down into the empty pouch around her neck before passing that to Zeb.

"Keep ahold of these wings, Zebedee. Our future depends on them."

Zeb slipped the cord around his neck, and as the pouch lay flat against his T-shirt, he felt the Stargold Wings move—little flutters like a frightened heartbeat.

Morg unfurled her own wings and the dragon, sensing her wishes, swooped down toward the ship.

"This time things will go my way," Morg sneered. "This time the Faraway child is on *my* side."

The dragon landed with a crunch on the prow of the ship, and it bent its head to listen as Morg hurried toward it. At first all that Zeb could hear from the other end of the ship were a few growls and whispers. But then their conversation became clearer, louder, as if someone had turned the volume right up. There wasn't much phoenix magic left in Crackledawn, but what remained knew that children from the Faraway could, when push came to shove, save the world, if they had the right information. And so, unbeknown to Zeb, the phoenix magic stirred now so that he could hear the harpy's *real* plan.

"He's a nobody," Morg was saying. "All I need you to do is carry him to the sun and ensure he brings me back the Ember Scroll. Don't even stop to sink the ships you pass. I'll take care of them—and all the Unmappers living on Wildhorn. Go straight to the sun with the boy."

The dragon grunted.

"Then once he's handed me the Ember Scroll, get rid of him," Morg snapped. "Burn him to a crisp. Because there won't be any room for Faraway boys in my world of dark magic."

Zeb felt his stomach churn. He had only trusted the harpy

to help him because he had seen her power, which, compared to the lukewarm promises of the grown-ups he'd known, made him think she could be worth siding with. All along, the harpy had never been planning to keep her side of their bargain. And having seen how she dealt with those standing in her way, Zeb realized that despite his desperation, he had been wrong to trust her.

But the truth stung all the same. He had been let down—*again*. And for a moment he thought he could feel an Outburst brewing, but it was something else: the faint flutter of the Stargold Wings against his chest. He had an object the harpy needed, so there was still a chance in all of this to come away with something. Because if Zeb found the Ember Scroll and kept it for himself, then who was to say he couldn't write an ending of his own onto the parchment, one that didn't involve quite so much extermination? Who was to say he couldn't use the Unmapped magic to destroy Morg and build his own world, exactly as he wanted it. A fabulous continent all to himself, then another (significantly less interesting) one to house all the people he couldn't face wiping out but couldn't face living alongside either.

The dragon thumped down onto the deck, then made its

way through the skeletons toward Zeb. He was frightened still—after all, he'd seen this dragon drown a ship—but now his fists were curled into angry balls. Because he had a new plan and it did *not* involve trusting anyone else ever again. He wasn't sure *how* he'd get away from the dragon after grabbing the Ember Scroll, but his new continent would be a place without others or their broken promises.

The dragon snarled as it approached Zeb, and it took every single scrap of courage Zeb had left to climb up its rib cage and onto its back. He sat astride it, trembling as he held on to the spiked bones that forked down the length of its neck. Then he forced himself to imagine he was the Tank, facing down a lion, before turning his gaze toward the sun.

The dragon lowered itself into a crouch, nodded to Morg, then launched off the ship into the dazzling sky. Zeb clung on, his eyes watering in the wind, his heart pounding. The dragon beat its mighty wings as it soared out over the sea toward the newly-risen sun, leaving Morg's sea monsters and skeletons to hunt down the Unmappers. And Zeb tried his best not to think about the fact that he was riding a beast that planned to burn him to a crisp.

Chapter 7

Back in the Faraway, Fox Petty-Squabble stood on the stage in the empty theater, cursing herself for having left. The boy was gone. And she might have believed he had run away, were it not for the smashed chandelier and ruptured piano. These were signs of a struggle, and from the look of the hooked scratches etched into the wood inside the piano and the black feathers scattered about the strings, she had a horrible feeling she knew who was responsible.

Fox clutched the side of the piano. If Morg had somehow escaped the never-ending well she and her brother, Fibber, had trapped her in so long ago, then her suspicions about the climate had been right. It *was* spiraling out of control because the harpy was on the loose once more. She must have gathered enough power to come to the Faraway with the aim of stealing the one thing here that could open a portal for her back into the Unmapped Kingdoms: a phoenix tear.

Fox wondered then about two things: Was it a coincidence she had been living so close to a legendary phoenix tear and she had been the one, out of everyone else, who had come across Zeb tonight? Or did magic have a plan in all of this? For her *and* for Zeb . . .

Fox looked around. There were no feathers or talon marks anywhere but the piano. She must have come for the phoenix tear—and somehow poor, vulnerable Zeb had got tangled up in her quest—then left.

Fox sat down on the stool. She should never have walked away from the theater. In trying to do the right thing, she'd messed up completely. Now it was *her* fault the boy was caught in the harpy's plans. And if she knew Morg, these plans would be nothing short of world domination. She hung her head as she imagined Zeb a prisoner of Morg's, remembering all too well how terrifying the harpy could be. Fox had encountered her for the first time in a forest called the Bonelands, and if a golden panther called Deepglint hadn't stepped in to rescue her, she wouldn't be here today.

Fox thought again of the phoenix tear Morg had come for and of the stories she had been told about these tears out in Jungledrop. And then something occurred to her. The very first phoenix had wept *seven* tears to conjure the Faraway's continents. Casper Tock had found one, then he'd given another to her and Fibber, which they'd shared to get to Jungledrop. Which meant there were still five phoenix tears unaccounted for. So, could there be a sliver of a chance that there had been *multiple* phoenix tears in this theater Morg had been drawn to and one or more might still be here now? Fox stood up. She couldn't help feeling that she and Zeb had been drawn together tonight by magic for a purpose. Perhaps both of them had a role to play in saving the Unmapped Kingdoms and the Faraway from Morg.

Fox thought of the phoenix tear she had been given by Casper Tock. It had been small, no bigger than a plum stone, and it had glowed a mysterious blue. Fox scoured the stage for anything that might resemble it, raking through shattered glass, overturning trunks and armchairs in the wings, and shaking out every dusty robe. There was no sign of a phoenix tear, but Fox didn't stop looking. She would keep on searching, even if it took her all night, because she had made a promise to Zeb.

The night ticked on, and still Fox searched. But when she nudged the stage curtain while rooting through a box of props, her heart quickened. There was a glow coming from beneath the curtain. She yanked the folds of tattered velvet aside, and there, on the ground, was a phoenix tear glowing in all its glory—the one that Morg had left behind.

Fox picked it up, breathless with hope. "This," she said, clasping the tear tight, "this changes everything."

She didn't know which Unmapped Kingdom Zeb and the harpy had gone to, but with phoenix magic on her side, she knew she'd find them. She thought of how the phoenix tear had worked for her last time. She had opened a train door and been catapulted off to the kingdom of Jungledrop. And with Casper Tock, it had been the door of a grandfather clock that had led him to Rumblestar. Fox glanced across the stage to the nearest door to her. A trapdoor in the stage itself, used by actors for surprise entrances.

Fox bent down over the trapdoor and wished her brother, Fibber, was with her. They had loathed each other before their quest in Jungledrop, but their adventure in the Unmapped Kingdoms had made them the best of friends. They often spoke on the phone long into the night about their travels through Jungledrop's glow-in-the-dark rainforest. But there was no time for phone calls now.

Holding the phoenix tear to her heart, where her hopes were mounting, Fox laid an ear to the trapdoor and smiled. Because she could hear something impossible: waves crashing. So, with the promise of magic ringing in her ears, she pulled open the trapdoor and climbed inside.

Zeb, meanwhile, was clinging on to the bone dragon for dear life. *Darktongue* was miles behind them now, a mere speck on the sprawling ocean. They raced on toward a cluster of boats full of terrified Unmappers sailing away as fast as they could. Zeb supposed they'd heard the alarm bell tolling and were doing their best to hurry out of harm's way. But what hope did they have with Morg and her Midnights in pursuit? They'd be found, in the end, and then the harpy's magic would finish them off.

The dragon kept going. It didn't even slow when they raced over a large, jungled island signposted WILDHORN that looked, to Zeb, like a pocket of magic still flickering in an otherwise dark and brooding ocean. There were tangled trees filled with exotic fruits, feather-tailed monkeys, and large silver bells that rang out as if the kingdom itself was now sounding the alarm too. From the dragon's back, Zeb glimpsed waterfalls flowing in figure-of-eights while down by the shore there were caves lined with gold and a beach hut called the Cheeky Urchin. Wooden walkways linked this island to a cluster of smaller islands surrounding it, and Zeb could just make out hammocks strung between trees there and armchairs laid out on the sand. But there were no Unmappers to be seen. Not even aboard the huge ship called the *Jolly Codger* that was moored in the bay. Its sails had been converted into trampolines and its rigging into swings, making it look more like an abandoned playground than a boat. But there were no children playing on it. If Unmappers lived here on Wildhorn, they must have heeded the alarm bells and hidden. Zeb chewed his lip as he remembered Morg's words to the dragon. She was heading for this very island. And how long would it take for her army of Midnights to storm ashore and find all the Unmappers?

The dragon raced away from Wildhorn, on and on over the blackened sea. Then gradually the water began to turn blue again, and the dragon surged upward into the sky as it began its journey to the sun. Zeb glanced down and let out a moan. They were far, far above the sea now, and the sun's warmth prickled his skin. He tried to fix his eyes on the sun itself, but its blinding light made him turn away. He still had no idea how he was going to get away from the dragon after finding the Ember Scroll. But the Tank was always reacting to things as they happened—it was just part of being hard-core—so Zeb very much hoped a plan would come to him at the right moment.

Little did he know that the phoenix magic locked inside the Stargold Wings had a plan too, a plan that was already whirring into life all the way back in the Faraway as Fox Petty-Squabble made her way into Crackledawn. Morg had been right about *some* things. Whoever gave the Ember Scroll an ending really would have the power to restore hope to the world or destroy it forever. And the parchment for this scroll really *was* lost. But it wasn't anywhere near the sun. It was somewhere else entirely. And though the Stargold Wings were small, they knew that Zeb, and Fox Petty-Squabble, needed help.

And so it came as a nasty shock to Zeb when the Stargold Wings inside the pouch around his neck began to move. It was more than the tiny flutters he'd felt before. Now the wings were pushing down so hard Zeb had to struggle to keep his head up. The dragon flew on, unaware of the Stargold Wings' mischief, and it was only when Zeb cried out that the dragon took notice.

"I—I can't keep my balance!" Zeb yelled.

But by the time the dragon had swung its head round, it was too late. The Stargold Wings yanked Zeb's neck—hard—and the force wrenched him from the dragon's back and sent him tumbling through the sky.

Chapter 8

Zeb would have screamed if he could. But he was falling too fast to make a sound. Down, down, down he plunged, sure that this was the end. He was going to die—alone and unloved—as soon as he hit the sea. And the dragon knew this too. The Faraway boy was Morg's only hope for the journey to the sun, and he had the Stargold Wings, so they *couldn't* let him die. The dragon was diving as fast as it could, but it didn't have phoenix magic on its side, and Zeb was falling faster.

He hit the sea like a bullet, and though the impact should have killed him, it didn't, and while the dragon circled the sea for a trace of the boy or the precious pouch he had worn, the Stargold Wings hid Zeb underwater in a cocoon of magic.

The dragon circled and circled, but neither the boy nor the

pouch came to the surface. It shook its horned head, let out a furious blast of fire, and then, because it knew it now needed the help of others to sort things out, it sped back toward *Darktongue*, growling uneasily at the thought of facing Morg's rage. But it knew that fire krakens were used to sniffing out magic, so they might be able to find the Stargold Wings, and Morg would just have to come up with another plan to seize the Ember Scroll.

Zeb wasn't entirely sure what had happened in the minutes after he hit the sea. He'd been gearing up for Certain Doom, but he was, surprisingly, very much alive. He wasn't in pain, his limbs were still moving—in fact they were thrashing about in a tightly-woven net, bound some way above him in a knot—and, miraculously, his lungs had a little air left inside them. He had the feeling that he had been carried quite some way underwater—in a strange sort of bubble—before he had ended up in this net.

The net wasn't filled with fish but with gold jewels the size of pebbles that seemed to be making all sorts of faint but unmistakably peculiar noises: hiccups, sneezes, giggles, and hums. No matter how much Zeb wriggled, he couldn't seem to escape, and now, someone, or something, was dragging the net up to the surface.

Zeb's thoughts whirred. The Stargold Wings had most definitely thrown him off the dragon. But why? Had they sensed they were about to be used for evil? Whatever the reason, they had somehow kept him safe underwater, and Zeb found himself thinking of something Morg had said: *Phoenixes have a sentimental fondness for humans, so anything imbued with their magic will help you.* If the phoenix magic was, ultimately, pitted *against* Morg, perhaps this net that he was in wouldn't be manned by some dreadful ogre eel.

There was a short, sharp tug and Zeb burst out of the water to find himself face-to-face with a girl. She had brown skin and dark hair, bound into a long braid, and there was a purple chameleon perched on her shoulder.

The chameleon yelped and then, to Zeb's amazement, it spoke. "I thought you said you were hauling in one last net of sunchatter, Oonie?! But you've gone and caught a *boy*!"

The girl blinked as she heaved the net over the edge of the boat and Zeb—together with a handful of whispering gold jewels—spilled out onto the deck. The vessel was much smaller than *Darktongue*, and thankfully, it didn't look as if it had been carved from shadows. A wooden sunshade had been erected over the stern, the sail seemed to have been made of gold leather littered with black ink that spelled out various words—GOLDSHELL COVE, THE SIGHING CAVES, WILDHORN, THE GAPING GULF—and the girl and the talking chameleon on board looked confused rather than up to their necks in evil.

Zeb waited for the Stargold Wings to do something miraculous, like untangle him from the net, chuck the girl and the chameleon overboard, and help him sail on toward the Ember Scroll uninterrupted while looking fabulously important. But that didn't happen. The wings were no longer tugging or glowing, and it is hard to look important when you have seaweed wrapped round your ear and gold jewels burping at your feet.

Oonie wiped her hands on her tunic, then cocked her head toward the chameleon on her shoulder. "Do I untie the No-Go Knot? What do you think, Mrs. Fickletint?"

The chameleon's scales flashed red, then blue, then yellow, before settling purple again. "Oh, I'm all flustered, Oonie. First thing this morning we hear an alarm bell from the north ring out over the ocean, then there's a message from the Lofty Husks saying the worst has happened: Morg is here in Crackledawn, and we should sail back to Wildhorn immediately. *Then*, we hear that an army of skeletons and ogre eels are holding everyone on Wildhorn captive, the Lofty Husks are being stripped of their magic, and as the only ones still out at sea, we should gather in as much sunchatter as possible before fleeing for our lives. And then *he* turns up all covered in seaweed!" She drew a big breath. "It has been *quite* the morning!"

Oonie looked Zeb up and down. Her eyes were the shining brown of conkers, and yet they never fixed on Zeb's own eyes. They roamed over him, as if the girl was looking *into* him and rummaging through his secrets.

"He's not one of us, is he?" Oonie said after a while.

"No," the chameleon—who must have been called Mrs. Fickletint—replied, her large eyes fixed on Zeb. "I—I think he's the Faraway boy spotted riding Morg's dragon over Wildhorn. How on earth he found his way into the Unmapped Kingdoms, I've no idea. . . . But if he's on the harpy's side, he's probably terribly dangerous, so we should hurl him overboard immediately."

Zeb's eyes widened.

"Boys are usually pretty straightforward," Oonie mused. "Pin them down, refuse to feed them, and in the end, they tend to do what you want them to."

Zeb gulped. He'd come across girls his age back home but none as forthright as this one. She looked like the sort of child who could run a country, steer a boat, and wrestle a giant squid all at the same time. He would have to be on his guard.

"How dreadful are you, boy?" The spikes lining Mrs. Fickletint's chin quivered. "Full to the brim with evil or just gently simmering with wicked thoughts? Because if you lay one finger on Oonie, or me for that matter, I will—I will"—the chameleon flashed pink, then orange—"I will send you to bed with no lunch!"

Zeb was inwardly relieved by the chameleon's threat. Missing a meal was small fry compared to being set on fire by a dragon. Perhaps he could handle these two after all. He glared at the pouch around his neck in case the phoenix magic needed a little nudge to get going, but still the Stargold Wings ignored him. So, he unhooked the seaweed from his ear and tried to push his way out of the No-Go Knot instead. That, also, got him nowhere. He scowled up at the girl and the chameleon. "I'm not working for Morg, if that's what you mean."

Oonie put her hands on her hips. "Then why did we get a message from the Lofty Husks—rulers of this kingdom and the wisest magical beings in Crackledawn—reporting a Faraway boy had been seen on Morg's ship *and* on the back of her dragon?"

"I *was* riding her dragon, but I"—Zeb paused—"hopped off. Turns out making a pact with a harpy isn't a good idea."

"YOU MADE A PACT WITH MORG?!" Mrs. Fickletint spluttered. "The most dangerous creature in the Unmapped Kingdoms?! The one who has been sending ogre eels and fire krakens to sink our ships and curse our sunchatter for the past decade?! Do you have any idea how many of Crackledawn's Unmappers have died at the hands of that harpy? HUNDREDS!"

Zeb thought of the ship he'd seen the dragon sink, then looked at his feet. "If you had nothing and nobody back home, then you found yourself dragged into a harpy's underground lair, you might have done the same. I gave her a phoenix tear or two, and she promised me a new start. But it was all lies." He glanced up. "Do you think I *want* to be mixed up in what she's doing here? I didn't even *know* about Unmapped Kingdoms until yesterday!"

For a moment, Mrs. Fickletint's face softened a touch and Oonie grew quiet, as if weighing Zeb up.

"Not that it matters now," Zeb mumbled, ringing water from his T-shirt. "Because I'm finding the Ember Scroll for myself, not the harpy."

Oonie stiffened. "If Morg is here and she's after the Ember Scroll, then the end really is closing in, Mrs. Fickletint. The Unmapped Kingdoms have been fending her off for thousands of years, but if she gets hold of that scroll, she only needs to write her own reign into life to finish us all off." She narrowed her eyes in Zeb's direction. "And you think *you're* going to find this scroll when not even the Lofty Husks or the legendary explorers like Nefarious Flood could find it?"

Zeb squared his shoulders. "Yes. Because when I'm not chitchatting inside fishing nets, I'm very hard-core. It'll only be a matter of time before I'm finding the Ember Scroll, writing my *own* ending onto it, and conjuring up a brand-new world."

"And do away with the Unmapped Kingdoms and the Faraway?" Mrs. Fickletint clutched her tail in horror. "Oh, you are a wicked, wicked boy after all. I should wash your mouth out with soap!"

"There won't be time for that," Zeb replied. "Once the magic in the Stargold Wings gets going again in a few minutes, I'll be gone." Zeb didn't dare admit that he had no idea *how* the wings worked or whether they *would* actually help him again, but the Tank often stressed the importance of buying time when planning an escape, so he blustered on regardless. "The wings and I usually travel by underwater bubble, you see"—he patted the pouch around his neck—"and considering Morg's bone dragon couldn't find us, I very much doubt you'll stand a chance of catching me."

The chameleon was now staring at him with her mouth wide open. And when Oonie spoke, her voice was altogether different.

"*You* have the Stargold Wings?" she breathed. "I thought they were lost forever."

Zeb shifted. In trying to be hard-core, he'd gone and blown the fact that he was in possession of something extremely valuable.

Mrs. Fickletint leaned forward on Oonie's shoulder. "If the wings have been found, then maybe there's hope left after all. . . ."

Oonie nodded excitedly. "Crackledawn was on its last legs even before Morg showed up. The Lofty Husks said we only had a matter of weeks before the Unmapped magic disappeared completely. It'll be *days* now the harpy's here, but if the Stargold Wings can lead you and me to the Ember Scroll, then maybe we could write a future for the world." She was pacing up and down now. "We could bring back a phoenix and save the Unmapped Kingdoms and the Faraway before Morg wipes it all out!"

"Hang on a minute!" Zeb cried.

Mrs. Fickletint ignored him. "Oonie, dear, just because you learned about the Ember Scroll waiting for an ending in *A Brief History of Phoenix Magic* by Percival Yesteryear, doesn't mean *we're* the ones to finish it off. We should take the Stargold Wings to the Lofty Husks immediately. They'll know how to find the scroll and sort things out, especially if it really is, as rumors claim, as far away as the sun."

Oonie threw her hands in the air. "The Lofty Husks are prisoners back at Wildhorn, remember, and they're being stripped of their magic as we speak! You heard what Greyhobble said: We're the *only* Unmappers still out at sea! All the other Sunraiders made it back to Wildhorn . . . so we must be Crackledawn's last hope!"

Zeb tried to butt in, but Mrs. Fickletint jumped down off Oonie's shoulder onto a bench and raised her voice over his. "This is about you proving yourself again, isn't it, Oonie?"

Oonie said nothing, but her jaw was tense.

Mrs. Fickletint sighed. "When will you learn that being a captain isn't about sailing the farthest or the fastest or signing up to the biggest adventure? There's more to it than that. You don't need to spend your whole life trying to be tough just because of the way you were born."

Zeb looked Oonie up and down. He was missing something, clearly, but he couldn't work out what.

"You don't think I can manage an adventure this big, do you?" Oonie snapped.

"That's not what I meant," Mrs. Fickletint replied. "And you know it."

Oonie looked out over the sea. "This is different from everything that's happened before. If we don't grab the Stargold Wings off the Faraway boy and use them to find the Ember Scroll, there will be no more Crackledawn. No more Faraway. The world as we know it will vanish!"

Zeb gave a defensive huff from inside the net. "You can't just grab the Stargold Wings off me."

Mrs. Fickletint spun round to face Zeb. "How do we even know you've actually *got* the Stargold Wings? You could be a spy . . . on Morg's side all along!"

Zeb shuddered at the thought. "I don't want anything to do with Morg ever again. She let me down, same as everyone in my old life let me down. I'm not on her side. I've never had *anyone* on my side, and that's the way it's going to stay."

Oonie sized Zeb up once more. "He's scared, Mrs. Fickletint. You can tell that as well as I can. So, we've *got* to trust he has the wings, because finding the Ember Scroll and bringing back a phoenix is our only hope against Morg."

Oonie cracked her knuckles, and Zeb cursed himself for not doing more work on his biceps back in the theater. But before Oonie could do anything too disastrous, a sharp cry loaded with fury rang out across the ocean, making them all jump.

"M-Morg's dragon . . . ," Zeb stammered.

Oonie's and Mrs. Fickletint's eyes widened.

"It must have told the harpy that it lost the Stargold Wings!" Zeb cried. "Now it's probably roaming the ocean with her in search of them!" He shook the net frantically. "Quick! Get me out of this!"

Mrs. Fickletint's scales lost all color. "This is what happens when you take on saving the world, Oonie! You wind up with a dragon on your heels!" She glanced at Zeb. "If he wasn't sitting there looking so feeble and frightened, I'd say we chuck him overboard and sail away. . . ."

"And lose the Stargold Wings?" Oonie cried. "Not likely."

Mrs. Fickletint threw up her paws in despair, then leapt

from the bench and wrenched open a little trunk beneath it. "Ignore the boy for now, then, and all the sunchatter we pulled up in the net with him, until we've told the ship where to go, at least! The dragon's cry came from the north, so we must go south—as fast as we can!"

The chameleon took out a quill from a pot labeled SQUID INK and wedged it in Oonie's hand. And had Zeb not been quite so scared, he might have wondered why Oonie hadn't reached for the quill herself.

The girl bent over the sail and wrote two words in the messiest handwriting Zeb had ever seen: The BLACKFANGS.

Mrs. Fickletint's eyes widened. "We can't go there, Oonie! It's out-of-bounds and terribly dangerous and—and—you haven't had nearly a big enough breakfast to take on the razor-sharp rocks that line the southern boundary!"

"I know that only the legendary Nefarious Flood has sailed beyond the Blackfangs and survived to tell the tale," Oonie said, "but we can't go back to Wildhorn, and out here in the open we'll be seen. We *have* to go that far south because, past the Blackfangs, Nefarious's maps mention hidden islands. We can lie low on one of them while we come up with a plan to find the Ember Scroll!"

"I promised the Lofty Husks I'd look after you!" Mrs. Fickletint shrieked. "Not put you center stage in a battle against Morg!"

The dragon called out again, and Zeb clutched his knees up to his chin. The screech was a little closer this time, and the lantern fixed at the prow of the boat began flashing.

"Now the Bother-Ahead Beacon is *red*!" Mrs. Fickletint wailed. "That means the fire krakens are on their way too! Oh, to be aboard the *Kerfuffle* on a day like today!"

Zeb's heart pounded. He'd glimpsed a fire kraken while on *Darktongue* and he did *not* want to see one again. He began tearing at the net with his hands and teeth, but the No-Go Knot held fast. Oonie, on the other hand, moved with unflappable calm. She placed two hands on either side of the gold sail, and before Mrs. Fickletint could argue again about the destination, the *Kerfuffle* was off.

It charged through the waves as it made its way south, away from the cries of the bone dragon and the fire krakens racing through the sea beneath it. Zeb let out a yelp inside the net, because Oonie was now advancing toward him, and she was wielding a knife.

"You said you'd be grabbing the Stargold Wings off me!" Zeb cried. "You never said anything about a knife!"

Oonie sliced through the net as if it had been made of thread, and the sunchatter clattered to the ground, a cluster of muffled whistles, chuckles, and snorts. Ignoring them, Oonie jabbed her weapon in the direction of the stern behind her.

"You're our prisoner now, so get below deck; whatever Mrs. Fickletint might say, we need those Stargold Wings. The *Kerfuffle* is powered by phoenix magic, so it can outpace fire krakens and ogre eels when it reaches full throttle, but with Morg on the loose, we'll need to keep out of sight until we're sure it's safe."

The dragon screeched again, and Zeb threw himself over the benches toward Mrs. Fickletint, who was trying, in vain, to yank a trapdoor open. Zeb's heart skittered. He had been adamant he wanted nothing to do with the girl and the chameleon, but it very much seemed like he was on the brink of a voyage with them.

Chapter 9

The *Kerfuffle* sped on, its golden sail juddering in the wind. Zeb couldn't see the dragon—only miles and miles of mirror-bright sea—but he could hear it screeching, and the Bother-Ahead Beacon on the prow of the boat was still bright red.

Mrs. Fickletint hopped up and down. "Gah! The enchanted trapdoor has gone and changed its security lock again! It was LIFT earlier—Laugh Intensely Five Times—but now it's saying YANK and I can't for the life of me remember what it stands for!"

Zeb threw a panicked glance at the trapdoor under the chameleon and the four golden letters spelling YANK on top of it. Then Oonie began frantically nodding her head and blurting out a strange kind of song that started high, then dipped low.

"Yodel and Nod Knowledgeably!" she cried between outbursts.

The trapdoor sprang open, and Zeb glimpsed steps leading down into the hull. Mrs. Fickletint scampered to safety, then Oonie disappeared through the trapdoor. With the dragon's cries ringing in his ears, Zeb hurried down after her.

It was not dark and cramped inside the hull as Zeb had imagined, and this was because the *Kerfuffle* was simmering with magic. There couldn't possibly have been room for a sweeping staircase leading down into a large cabin lit by lanterns, and yet there was. Because magic deals in impossibilities all the time.

Zeb pulled the trapdoor shut, drowning out the cries of the dragon, then inched down the stairs in disbelief. There was a long wooden table, raised on crab legs in the middle of the room, spread with maps and leather-bound books, and two cubbyholes either side. One contained a stove and numerous pots and pans, the other a little bed in front of a circular window looking out to sea. There were barrels crammed with gold jewels labeled SUNCHATTER and shelves cluttered with glass bottles, spinning globes, ink pots, and silver quills. And, at the far end of the cabin, there was a fire of blue flames blazing in a hearth before two threadbare armchairs.

Zeb could no longer hear the dragon calling. The boat really did seem to be racing away from danger, as Oonie had said it would. The girl and the chameleon breathed a sigh of relief. As did Zeb. And so incredible was the *Kerfuffle*'s cabin that Zeb almost forgot about being cross and hard-core.

"There's no way all this can fit under the boat . . . ," he murmured. "It makes no sense."

"Magic never makes sense," Oonie replied curtly as she stepped down into the cabin. "It just settles in and gets on with stuff."

From inside a jug on the table, Mrs. Fickletint raised a scaly brow at Zeb. "Oonie and I have been on board the *Kerfuffle* for six months now, and we're only just getting to grips with all its quirks—but don't you go thinking we've lost control of things around here. You're our prisoner—one false move from you, we'll feed you to the fire krakens."

Oonie spun the knife in her hand, and Zeb froze on the stairs. But then a miniature toad popped out from beneath a rug and began burping the alphabet backward. This was followed by a very large turtle—which Zeb had assumed was ornamental—that started scurrying around the cabin, straightening rugs and closing trunk lids.

Mrs. Fickletint tried to keep her eyes on Zeb, but the turtle was proving a noisy distraction. "I'm all for employing a hurtle to keep the cabin shipshape, Oonie, but this one has no idea how to follow instructions. I distinctly told it that cabin cleaning was *tomorrow* and ironing was today." The chameleon narrowed her eyes at the alphabet-burping toad. "And as for you . . . I swept the place for sea-hoppers after the commotion your lot caused when we stepped on board for the first time, and yet you just won't leave, will you?"

"Stop fussing, Mrs. Fickletint." Oonie hadn't shifted her gaze from Zeb. She raised her knife in one hand, then thrust out an open palm in Zeb's direction with the other. "Hand over the Stargold Wings. Or else."

Zeb leapt back a step. "The Stargold Wings are going to help me build a new world, but—but I was thinking that when I find the Ember Scroll, I could write a very small continent for Unmappers and"—he motioned toward Mrs. Fickletint—"talking chameleons, if you'd like?"

Oonie snorted. "That is the most stupid—and selfish—thing I've ever heard. Everyone here knows that if you steal the Unmapped magic to build a new world, you lose the Unmapped Kingdoms and the Faraway. You wipe out *everyone*."

Zeb looked at the floor. Surely Oonie didn't know *everything*. There must be a way around mass extermination when you had the most powerful magic of all in your hands?

Oonie was having none of it. "I'm the captain of the *Kerfuffle*, so as long as you're on board, you'll be following *my* rules. And I'm telling you that once we've shaken off Morg, we'll be using the Stargold Wings to find the Ember Scroll. Because this ship is now on a mission to save the Unmapped Kingdoms and the Faraway."

Mrs. Fickletint flounced dramatically over the edge of her jug. "Does nothing I say sink in, Oonie? Must you leap toward risk quite so enthusiastically?"

Oonie groaned. "This is a voyage we *have* to make, Mrs. Fickletint. Every day, another boat is drowned by the fire krakens and another Unmapper dies. Every day, a little more of Crackledawn's magic fades. The water in the Gaping Gulf used to be so turquoise it glowed in the dark, but you've said yourself the sea there is black and all the sunchatter on the seabed is cursed. Then there was that Sunraider who said he saw a whole pod of silver whales washed up, dead, on the shore. And maybe Wildhorn has managed to cling on to its waterfalls and golden caves, but Morg and her Midnights are there now too. What do you think that means for our home—my hammock hanging from the snoozeaway tree and all my sea trinkets lining the branches? For your hollow inside the wibblebough sapling beside it and the little armchair Mr. Fickletint carved from enchanted driftwood? For the waterfall we love to swim beneath with your twenty-seven children? There'll be nothing left. No Unmappers, Lofty Husks, or magical creatures either."

Tears stood in Mrs. Fickletint's eyes now. "No more sipping wibblejuice at the Cheeky Urchin with the family after a day out Sunraiding with you. No more nights watching shooting stars and wishing on them for a phoenix to return."

Oonie took a deep breath. "If we don't write a phoenix into life on the Ember Scroll, there will be nothing to go back to. It'll be over for the Unmapped Kingdoms and the Faraway forever."

Zeb tried to think of the Faraway, and all its disappointments, rather than imagine Oonie's home and Mrs. Fickletint's enormous family. "I don't care what happens to the Faraway. It's not as if I have friends or a family to go back to," he muttered.

But as he said those words, the little pouch around his neck began to glow again.

Mrs. Fickletint sat bolt upright in her jug and gasped. "The Stargold Wings—they really are inside that pouch, aren't they? They're shining!"

Zeb's heart quickened and Oonie took a step closer. "If they're shining, that means there's still phoenix magic left inside them. They might be able to show us the way to the Ember Scroll. . . ." Oonie turned to the chameleon. "The Stargold Wings led the Faraway boy to *our* ship and now they're glowing. It feels like they *know* we've got a part to play in saving the world. So, what do you say, Mrs. Fickletint? Are you in?"

The chameleon looked from the pouch to the girl, then with a weary sigh, she said: "Of course I'm in, Oonie. Wherever you go, I go too, especially when it comes to saving Crackledawn. I just—I just wish you'd see that you don't have anything to prove in all this. That the way you are is absolutely enough." She paused. "And that if we fail, which we might well do, it won't be your fault."

Zeb sensed there were things about Oonie he didn't understand, but he realized something about the chameleon then—she was loyal. And quite without warning, Zeb felt a yearning deep inside him for friendship, for someone to say they'd be rooting for him on this voyage. He told himself to get a grip.

Mrs. Fickletint took a deep breath and jabbed a paw in the direction of the lanterns dangling from the roof. "The Bother-Ahead Beacons down here are no longer red. They're yellow, which means we've outsailed the fire krakens—for now. . . . But those beasts can sniff out phoenix magic better than most creatures. They're the ones cursing our sunchatter, after all, and turning the ocean black. So, if they gain ground and catch even a whiff of the Stargold Wings, they'll be onto us in a flash. Somehow, we need to ask the Stargold Wings where to go for the Ember Scroll. And we need to do it fast."

Oonie smiled at the chameleon, then she turned and set a very determined foot on the first stair. "If you hand over the Stargold Wings right this instant, we'll keep you hidden from Morg and her Midnights for the duration of this voyage. Try anything funny, and we'll shove you up on deck to be eaten by that fire kraken Mrs. Fickletint mentioned."

Zeb wasn't about to give up on his plan of building a new world for himself, but he didn't fancy being gobbled up by Morg's Midnights either. He was starting to realize he needed to work with the girl and the chameleon, for the time being, anyway. So, he lifted the pouch from his neck and thrust it into Oonie's palm.

"I have no idea what's going on with the magic in this place, but I do know one thing: None of us are going to get what we want if Morg is alive. I'm in for this voyage because we both need the Stargold Wings to find the Ember Scroll. You can write the harpy out of existence, and *I* can use all the Unmapped magic to sort out who's living where."

Mrs. Fickletint winced. "Not *quite* in the spirit of things, but I suppose it's a start. What do you think, Oonie?"

The girl shrugged, and then her face, lit by the glow of the Stargold Wings, broke into a smile. "This," she whispered, holding up the pouch as she felt her way over the wings inside, "this feels like hope."

Oonie made her way carefully down the stairs and placed the pouch on the table.

"Watch out!" Zeb called, rushing after her. "The wings might fly off?!"

"You can't hope in something without trusting it first," Oonie replied. "It would be like wishing on a star without believing in the night."

She opened the pouch, and the Stargold Wings fluttered out. They hovered above the maps on the table, and the cabin fizzed with magic. The multicolored sand in the glass bottles on the shelves swirled, the sunchatter in the barrels whispered, and the pages of the books on the table rustled.

Then the wings flew over to the blue flames at the end of the cabin. There was no wood paneling boxing the boat in here, just large oval windows looking out into the deep blue sea. The wings hovered before the fire, and even Zeb couldn't hide his wonder as they scattered gold sparks, which settled in the air as recognizable shapes against the flames.

"Words," he breathed. "There are words in the fire!"

Zeb, Oonie, and Mrs. Fickletint walked closer, spellbound by the magic of the Stargold Wings, until they were all standing before the flames. And so enthralled was Zeb that he didn't notice Oonie nudge the chameleon and whisper, ever so quietly: "What does it say?"

Mrs. Fickletint began reading aloud:

"Sail on south to the Final Curtain.

Step beyond all you know is certain.

Seek the cave that has never been found.

Claim the scroll before the moon is round."

The sparks faded, and Zeb shook himself. "Seek a cave that has never been found?"

"Before the next full moon?" Mrs. Fickletint cried. "It's

a well-known fact that Unmapped magic is at its strongest when the moon is round, but the next full moon is in just four nights' time!"

"And what kind of place is the Final Curtain?" Oonie said. "It doesn't sound like the Ember Scroll is up at the sun. . . ."

Zeb stared into the flames, hoping more words might appear. The Stargold Wings slipped soundlessly away from the fire and flew into the pocket of his jeans. He wasn't used to things sticking around, but something about the wings choosing to settle in his pocket made him feel just a little bit less alone.

Mrs. Fickletint tilted her head toward Zeb. "You may have given up on the Faraway and all the magic keeping it alive, but I'd say magic clearly hasn't given up on *you*."

From the tone of the chameleon's voice, Zeb wondered whether Mrs. Fickletint's opinion of him might be changing a little. He was a prisoner aboard the *Kerfuffle* still, but he got the impression that being held captive by Oonie and Mrs. Fickletint might be somewhat different from being trapped by Morg.

Oonie was back at the table now, rummaging through the maps there. "We've no idea what kind of landmark the Final

Curtain is, but the message from the Stargold Wings told us to 'sail on south,' which means the Blackfangs is the right destination, for now. The only confusing thing is that there's no mention of anything of note *beyond* the southern boundary. Nefarious Flood just sketched out a few islands with the words: 'Not Much Here, but Worth a Visit If You're Really Bored (and you've got the stomach for the Blackfangs).'" She sighed. "It's too risky going up on deck now to write a new destination onto the dragonhide sail, but once we reach the Blackfangs, we'll need to tell the *Kerfuffle* to sail on to the Final Curtain, whatever that might be. Then we'll just have to hope she knows where to go. . . ."

Zeb was watching Oonie carefully now. Because the maps spread over the table, he realized, were blank. At a glance, Oonie looked like she was scouring them, but close up Zeb could see she wasn't using her eyes at all. She was using her hands, *feeling* her way over the parchment, and in the light cast by the Bother-Ahead Beacons, Zeb could just make out the little bumps that seemed to be guiding her thoughts.

Then suddenly Mrs. Fickletint's words earlier made sense. There *was* something different about the way Oonie had been born.

"Braille," Zeb said quietly as he remembered the boy in his class back home who read stories by running his hands over bumps on the page because he couldn't see. He looked up at Oonie. "You're blind."

Chapter 10

Mrs. Fickletint flashed green, shot out of her jug, then began a charge across the table toward Zeb. But Oonie knew the ways of the chameleon better than anyone else, so she felt about over the table until she reached the reptile, then she scooped her up into her hands.

"It's okay, Mrs. Fickletint," she whispered. "It's okay."

Oonie looked at Zeb. The same way she had when Zeb stepped aboard the *Kerfuffle*. Her eyes didn't meet his exactly, but they fixed on a part of him all the same, as if she had found something in him that even he didn't know was there. She raised her chin, daring Zeb to make a wrong move.

Zeb was quiet for a moment. This was, after all, a girl who had a knife in her pocket and most probably wrestled giant squid in her spare time. She looked stronger than all of his class back home, stronger than many of the grown-ups he'd met too. And she seemed so completely in charge on the *Kerfuffle*, it felt impossible that she couldn't see.

Zeb tried to imagine how he would feel without his sight, how frightened he'd be of the dark magic racing after them. But Oonie had an instinct for where things were, and she moved with a calm sort of confidence that made her seem much older than she really was.

"There was a boy in my class back home who was blind," Zeb found himself saying nervously. "He scored top grades in every test he took, and he made a speech in Debating Club last term about how he wanted to run for president one day."

Oonie held her head high as if considering this. Then she shrugged. "I would never work in politics. Not nearly enough voyages."

She turned back to her maps, but Mrs. Fickletint wasn't through with Zeb. She wanted to make sure he knew who he was messing with.

She puffed herself up on Oonie's shoulder. "Six months ago, Oonie was chosen by the Lofty Husks themselves to become Crackledawn's youngest Sunraider."

"That's enough, Mrs. Fickletint," Oonie warned. "We've got work to do."

The chameleon, who was entering her stride now, dropped down onto the table and wagged a paw at the boy. "Normally, you have to wait until you're eighteen and you've reached the end of your formal lessons to roam the seas for sunchatter, the gold jewels found on the ocean floor that whisper the magical sounds of the sun—"

Zeb started. "Sunlight makes a *noise*?"

"Every sunrise and every sunset you see in your world is, in fact, a symphony," Mrs. Fickletint explained. "A unique piece of music made up of a thousand sounds hauled up from the bottom of the sea by Sunraiders here in Crackledawn."

Zeb wasn't sure how many more surprises he could handle in one day. There should be some sort of limit, he felt, because all these revelations were making him feel very unsettled. But the idea that sunrises and sunsets might be symphonies was, to him, the most magical thing he'd heard so far.

Mrs. Fickletint went on. "Sunsmiths on Wildhorn tip the sunchatter into cauldrons and mix it with marvels to form ink. Then they use this ink to write symphonies onto the sun scrolls, which they play once on the organ in

Cathedral Cave before sending on to the Faraway."

Zeb was struggling to keep up, but as he eyed the barrel of sunchatter beyond the table, he was filled with a sudden desire to hear all those sounds strung together in a melody. He tried to focus on the logistics of this to make sure he wasn't being taken for a fool. "Marvels," he said. "What are they?"

Oonie was still feeling her way over the maps for anything that might resemble the Final Curtain, but she was listening, too. And there was a fierce kind of pride in her voice, just as there was in Mrs. Fickletint's, as she explained how Crackledawn made the Faraway's sunlight.

"Marvels," she said, "are droplets of sunlight in its purest form grown over in the kingdom of Rumblestar and carried here by dragons, the only creatures who can cross the divides between the Unmapped Kingdoms. They take the finished sun scrolls on to the Faraway, too, because after phoenixes, dragons are the most powerful of all magical beasts."

Zeb knew the Unmapped Kingdoms were real—he was *in* one, after all—but unraveling every single thing he'd ever learned about his world's weather was extremely confusing. Even if it did involve music. "*I've* never seen a dragon back in the Faraway," he said curtly.

The little spikes on Mrs. Fickletint's throat bristled. "Of course you haven't. Dragons leave the sun scrolls inside the hollows of your trees, under your largest rocks, and between the branches of your most unclimbable trees. Then, soon after they arrive, they vanish, giving you the sunlight your world needs for the day."

"Well, that was what *used* to happen," Oonie sighed. "Before the fire krakens started sniffing out sunchatter and cursing it, and the ogre eels started drowning Sunraiders and their ships. And it all makes sense now," she said grimly. "These Midnights have no doubt been growing in power as the phoenix magic faded, because they sensed the harpy's return."

Mrs. Fickletint nodded. "Of the barrels of sunchatter that *do* make it back to Wildhorn, many now contain cursed sounds. But it can take weeks before the water surrounding sunchatter turns black, and Sunsmiths *must* keep sending sun scrolls to the Faraway. The cursed sunchatter that makes it there is what's affecting your climate, and it's why the Lofty Husks asked Oonie here to captain a boat well before her time. She might be the youngest Sunraider in the kingdom, but she has a knack for finding pure sunchatter."

Oonie reddened. "We really should be getting back to—"

Mrs. Fickletint held up an adamant paw. "No matter how deep the ocean, no matter how tall the waves, and no matter how little sunchatter there is left, Oonie will find it. Even when I tell her not to because the voyage looks unforgivably dangerous. She hears little snatches of melodies from the sunchatter, you see. Even if it's miles off and no one else can hear a thing! And she's been able to do this ever since she can remember."

Oonie blew out through her lips. "Finished, Mrs. Fickletint? Can we get back to business now?"

Mrs. Fickletint wrapped her tail around Oonie's arm and smiled proudly. "I remember hearing about you diving off the *Jolly Codger*, aged five, because you insisted there was sunchatter some thirty feet below the surface, which there indeed was! And you were the talk of Wildhorn that time you hauled in the biggest catch of the month!"

Oonie shook the chameleon off. "I have to ask for help untangling the nets, though, don't I? And putting the sunchatter into the barrels for the Sunsmiths . . ." She fiddled with her braid, and for the first time, Zeb saw a flicker of vulnerability in Oonie. She had the presence of someone completely in control of things, like an undersized dentist or a very young doctor, but beneath all this, he recognized something fragile.

"Accepting help isn't a crime," Mrs. Fickletint replied. "If you weren't always so hard on yourself, you'd realize that." She paused, and then said, very quietly: "And you'd make a lot more friends."

Oonie plopped the chameleon back in her jug, then set the crockery down at the other end of the table. "You can come back when you stop nagging."

Mrs. Fickletint nipped Oonie on the hand, but it was a playful gesture, and she turned to Zeb. "Despite being outrageously stubborn and having a tendency to hurl herself at danger whenever the opportunity arises, Oonie here is the finest Sunraider Crackledawn will ever know. It is an honor to have been chosen by the Lofty Husks to chaperone her aboard the *Kerfuffle* as—"

"Chaperone?" Oonie said sharply.

Mrs. Fickletint corrected herself. "*Accompany* her aboard the *Kerfuffle* as we sail out each morning to find sunchatter to bring back to Wildhorn." The chameleon rose to her feet as she reached her crescendo. "What I'm saying, boy, is that not all without sight are blind."

Oonie looked up from her maps. "Crackledawn's Unmappers are born from the sea—washed ashore on the island of

Wildhorn as babies in large shells called conches. We don't have parents like you do in your world." Zeb flinched at the assumption, but Oonie carried on. "We're just one giant family here."

Mrs. Fickletint wagged a claw. "A family you would do well to lean on from time to time."

Oonie ignored her and carried on speaking to Zeb. "My shell opened a little earlier than it was meant to, before my sight formed more than blurred shapes and hazy colors, so you're right: I can't see. Not with my eyes anyway." She paused. "What's your name?"

"It's Zeb," he said, sitting down carefully on the edge of a trunk. And before he could stop himself, he added: "And I don't have parents either. I don't even have a home."

He sank a little lower on the trunk as his sadness crept in. What was he doing spilling his story to strangers? He waited for Oonie or Mrs. Fickletint to say something horrid—he was their prisoner, after all. But neither did.

Instead, Mrs. Fickletint climbed out of her jug, and when she was standing at the edge of the table in front of Zeb, she said, in a voice so gentle Zeb thought he might cry: "I'm sorry to hear that, Zeb. And Oonie's sorry too. Aren't you, dear?"

"Hmmmm," the girl replied, feeling her way over another map.

"Oonie!" Mrs. Fickletint snapped. "You're a captain in charge of a crew here, and showing a little kindness now and again wouldn't hurt."

"He's our prisoner!" Oonie retorted. "Not a member of our crew."

"I think we might be moving past that now," Mrs. Fickletint replied sternly. She turned back round. "Though, Zeb, if you *do* try anything funny, please know we will not hesitate to feed you to a fire kraken." She clasped her paws. "If we're going to stand a chance against Morg, I'm beginning to realize we need to start working together."

Zeb picked at his jeans. He was done with others, wasn't he? And it wasn't as if Oonie looked enthusiastic about joining forces.

"Don't mind Oonie," Mrs. Fickletint whispered to Zeb. "She takes a while to thaw. Took me months to convince her I was sticking around when the Lofty Husks first paired me with her." And then, in an even quieter voice so that only Zeb could hear: "I'm the only friend she has. She's pushed away everyone else who's tried to get to know her: classmates, Sunraiders, even the Lofty Husks don't exactly get a warm welcome. She's touchy about having to rely on others, you see. Hates the idea of accepting help because she thinks it makes her look weak." Mrs. Fickletint rolled her eyes. "But chameleons are brilliant at nagging. And there's only so much nagging an eleven-year-old can take before they give up and let you in."

The chameleon smiled at Zeb, and against his better instinct, he found himself smiling shyly back before he quickly wiped his smile away. He appeared to be on a slippery slope—who knew where spilling stories and smiling could lead. . . .

Oonie lifted up a piece of parchment. "The ripplemaps I use to navigate the seas have bumps instead of markings, and this one here suggests it'll be a few hours yet to the Blackfangs. We should reach them by midnight."

Mrs. Fickletint nodded, then sprung from the table onto a lamp via a barrel, before darting onto the stove and flicking it on. The only chameleons Zeb had ever seen on nature documentaries had been slow-moving things, but Mrs. Fickletint rushed about the cabin like an escaped balloon letting out air.

"So much to do, so little time," she muttered. "We'll need a four-course meal at the very least to give us strength for the Blackfangs. And we'll be wanting multiple cups of tea and the fire turned up a notch to dry out Zeb's clothes. And I really should ask the hurtle to iron a fresh set of sheets so that bedtime's not a disaster." She thrust a pan onto the stove, emptied a can of soup into it, then began frantically stirring while her scales switched from purple to blue to green. "You'll have to excuse the colors, Zeb. When I get in a fluster, I lose complete control of my scales. It's mortifying, but there it is." She glanced at Oonie. "Oonie, darling, do you think I'll have time to knit us all a quick scarf in case the ocean gets chillier down south?"

Oonie laughed and, to his horror, Zeb felt himself giggle too. It was such a strange feeling, having not had much to laugh about in such a very long time, that Zeb felt as if he'd completely lost control of his mouth. He shoved a hand over it in case any more mistakes slipped out. And yet as he sat in the cabin of the *Kerfuffle*, safe for a while from Morg and her Midnights, he realized that he was almost glad to have company.

Was this bustling about alongside other people what being in a family felt like? He imagined his new world and the amazing house he'd live in, if all went well. It *would* be rather quiet without any people—but then he remembered the pianos in every room and pulled himself together. People were, after all, not to be trusted and neither, he suspected, were chameleons.

Chapter 11

Mrs. Fickletint was a very good cook. She whipped up a four-course meal in no time: seaweed crisps and dip, followed by Oonie's favorite—sizzlebud's soup (a delicious soup that made everyone's tongues change a different color with each mouthful). Pasta twirls came next, a dish Mrs. Fickletint revealed was FuSilly, which, upon eating, made your face contort into hilarious expressions. Zeb had to pinch his thighs to stop himself getting completely carried away laughing. Then, finally, came dessert: a chocolate brownie called mudface that was so incredibly gooey, it was impossible to eat it without getting it all over your face.

While the hurtle washed up, Oonie talked through who would be doing what up on deck when they reached the Blackfangs and what their plan was should Morg show up. But as dusk drew in around the *Kerfuffle* and the ocean fell away beneath the boat to dark and hidden places, Mrs. Fickletint brought the conversation to a close.

"Ships have been sunk and battles have been lost because of sloppy bedtimes." She began heaping pillows and quilts onto one of the armchairs for Zeb. "You're guaranteed a good sleep in a threadbear. They only growl through their rips when they're unsure of you, but these two seem to know that beyond wild talk of building new worlds, you're probably all right."

Zeb thought about scowling, but there didn't seem to be much point. Mrs. Fickletint had treated him a lot better than Morg had. Better even than the Orderly-Queues and Derek Dunce . . .

The chameleon settled herself at the end of Oonie's cubbyhole bed and began knitting up a storm. "If you need anything," she called, "just holler for me. I love to be woken up in the middle of the night. It gives me a sense of purpose." She glanced at Oonie, who was sitting up in her bed, chiseling at a piece of sunchatter with her knife.

"Almost finished, dear?"

Oonie laid her knife down and held up what she'd carved. "Enough to fool Morg, do you think?"

Both Mrs. Fickletint and Zeb smiled then. Because Oonie had come up with an idea over dinner to hoodwink Morg. She'd carved the sunchatter into an almost exact copy of the Stargold Wings she'd felt when holding the pouch. Now they just had to hope that if they did run into the harpy, they could throw her off their scent with a bit of trickery.

Zeb snuggled down into the threadbear, and within minutes, it sprouted brown fur and started purring. It was quite comfortable, and from where he lay, he could see all sorts of extraordinary creatures drifting past the windows of the boat: a squid that squirted rainbow ink, a shoal of luminous jellyfish with feathered tentacles, a transparent octopus, and—most spectacular of all—an enormous silver whale with a song so low it shook the boat.

But Zeb couldn't shake the thought of the Blackfangs ahead. He felt sick with nerves, because even if the *Kerfuffle* made it past those perilous rocks, they then had just three days to find the Final Curtain and avoid being ambushed by Morg and her Midnights.

Zeb glanced toward the cubbyhole. How would Oonie cope if Morg's dragon found them and she couldn't see? It was one thing captaining a boat she'd learned her way around but quite another facing down Morg and her followers out in unchartered territory. The harpy would finish her and Mrs. Fickletint off in minutes. Zeb turned back to the hearth. Oonie wasn't his problem, nor was Mrs. Fickletint, however kind she seemed. They'd have to fend for themselves. Just like he had all his life. With these thoughts fighting one another, Zeb tried his best to go to sleep as the *Kerfuffle* sailed closer to the Blackfangs.

Had Zeb known that Fox Petty-Squabble was bent on keeping her promise to him—that she had used the fifth phoenix tear to open the theater's trapdoor and find her way into Crackledawn—he might have felt a little more inclined to trust the girl and the chameleon. But he fell asleep unaware that at this very moment, Fox was hastening into a candlelit cave as big as a cathedral with an organ that stretched the height of it.

Before Fox had found this cave, she had feared she would be lost in the darkness of Morg's underground tunnels forever. But after a while, the phoenix magic in her hand had sparked into life. It could sense that it was in the possession of good, not evil, and every time Fox came to a crossroad in Hollowbone, it tugged her one way or the other to show her exactly where to go. Fox had heard waves crashing all the while, as if she was on the brink of an Unmapped Kingdom but couldn't quite get there. And this was because the phoenix magic wasn't leading her out into Crackledawn's open seas after Morg. It was leading her on into the heart of the kingdom through a far more convenient portal. One that led into the biggest cave on Wildhorn.

The moment Fox left the never-ending tunnels of Hollowbone and crawled through a hole in the rocks into Cathedral Cave, she knew she had crossed over into an Unmapped Kingdom. She could feel the magic hanging in the air—half-afraid, half-hopeful—just as it had been when she'd arrived in Jungledrop all those years ago. There were sounds now, though, too. Sobs and whimpers somewhere up ahead.

Fox ran on through the cave, past a giant organ and alcoves lined with huge cauldrons, for she had encountered a kingdom in the grips of Morg's dark magic before and she could tell that Crackledawn needed her help urgently.

It wasn't until she burst into a candlelit chamber filled to the brim with terrified Unmappers and elves so weak they could barely stand, that she realized the scale of Morg's power. Beyond the cave, the ogre eels surrounding Wildhorn hissed and the skeletons banged their spears, desperate for the elves' magic to fade so that they could storm into Cathedral Cave and finish the Unmappers off.

But Morg was not among them. She sat astride her bone dragon as it beat on above the sea, following the lead of a fire kraken who was closing in on the Stargold Wings.

Chapter 12

Zeb woke to a loud croaking noise. It was coming from what looked like a crocodile skull on the bedside table next to Oonie's cubbyhole.

Oonie rolled over, bashed the jaws shut, and sat up. "That's the Alarm Croc, Mrs. Fickletint. We're here."

The chameleon shot out of Oonie's bed at record speed, flashing a multitude of colors before turning to the Alarm Croc again, which was now coughing up small blue sweets.

"Watergums!" Mrs. Fickletint cried. "I thought Crackledawn had seen the last of these several years ago, what with the phoenix magic running out."

She placed one in Oonie's hand, then chucked another to Zeb. "We don't have time for breakfast now—I'll sort food out once we're past the Blackfangs—but you'll want to eat one of these."

Oonie chewed hard. "Watergums help you to breathe, talk, sing, laugh, whistle, and, if need be, burp underwater."

"One sweet lasts a lifetime," Mrs. Fickletint said between nibbles. "So, if I were you, Zeb, I'd stop looking at yours as if it were a pair of dirty underpants and eat it. Because if we're hurled overboard in the middle of the Blackfangs, you're going to want that watergum's magic."

Zeb placed the sweet in his mouth and sucked nervously. The watergum was chewy, like toffee, but it was salty instead of sweet, and there was a lingering aftertaste of seaweed. There was no time to complain, though, because Oonie was already making her way up the stairs.

They emerged from the trapdoor to find a sky full of stars and the moon beaming down on the silver sea. There was no sign of Morg or her Midnights, but Zeb stiffened as he took in the Blackfangs. He had been expecting a single line of rocks stretching the width of the ocean. But what lay before them was a sprawling maze of daggered shards rising up out of the sea like mountain peaks. The rocks were black, many were studded with barbs, and each one glinted in the moonlight like a warning.

"The Blackfangs are taller than our boat!" Zeb cried. "And spiked! If we hit one, we'll be smashed to pieces!"

Oonie took a deep breath. "Not if I can help it, we won't."

Mrs. Fickletint grabbed the inkpot below the bench and drew out the quill. She handed it to Oonie, who wrote THE FINAL CURTAIN onto the sail.

"But—but you can't see the rocks," Zeb whispered to Oonie. "They're *terrifying*!"

Oonie clambered over the benches to the stern. "Sometimes it's easier not to see."

The sail shimmered in the moonlight, then the boat nosed its way toward the first of the Blackfangs. It knew, as Oonie had hoped it would, where to find the Final Curtain and that it lay somewhere beyond the southern boundary.

The *Kerfuffle* eased through a corridor of rocks, and Mrs. Fickletint perched herself on the Bother-Ahead Beacon at the bow, as planned. A dragonhide sail, Oonie had explained, could carry a boat for miles and miles over the open sea, but if there were obstacles in its path, which the beacon's amber glow signaled there were, it might need a little help steering a way through.

"Left a bit, Oonie!" the chameleon shouted. "Now a swift right before we're knocked unconscious by a spike!"

Zeb watched, amazed, as Oonie steered the boat without

seeing a thing. She guided it past the upturned remains of another boat jammed between two rocks, which, Zeb realized with a grimace, must have tried, and failed, to cross the Blackfangs. But Oonie's expression was calm, and her eyes, though unseeing, seemed to fix at a point ahead—as if she could see an invisible finish line, rather than the rocks themselves, and had all her hopes pinned on it. Not only this, but the bond between Oonie and the chameleon was watertight. They seemed to trust each other in a way Zeb had never really seen before, and he wasn't altogether sure what to make of it.

"Keep going here, Oonie—straight ahead!" Mrs. Fickletint called. "Now take us left—sharp—to avoid a quick gorge through the heart! Excellent, my dear! You'll see us through in no time!"

Zeb buried his head in the bucket he'd been instructed to use to bail out water if things got rough and let out a few whimpers.

But though the boat veered to the side and swerved round corners, with Oonie at the helm and Mrs. Fickletint at the prow, it slid on through the Blackfangs without any bother. Then a cloud closed over the moon, and out of nowhere, a wind picked up. Zeb heard it in the sail first, a few flaps against the dragonhide. Then the gusts began, whumping at the leather and tugging the rigging.

"Not a storm," Mrs. Fickletint squeaked. "Oh, please not a storm . . ."

The sky darkened further, a roll of thunder sounded, and the Blackfangs suddenly looked even more frightening, a forest of splinters every which way Zeb turned.

"This is Morg's dark magic!" Oonie yelled as the first of the rain began to fall. "Her fire kraken must have caught the scent of the Stargold Wings! She can't be far away now, and she'll be doing everything she can to stop us in our tracks. So, keep those instructions coming, Mrs. Fickletint! We have to clear the Blackfangs and get going!"

But storms care little for instructions. Especially storms conjured from dark magic. When Mrs. Fickletint yelled "right," the wind buffeted the boat left, and when Mrs. Fickletint screamed "straight ahead," the rain came crashing down, grinding the *Kerfuffle* to a halt.

"We have to keep going!" Oonie roared. "If Morg finds us in the Blackfangs, there's no way we'll escape!"

Zeb threw bucket after bucket of rainwater back into the sea while Mrs. Fickletint clung on to the beacon for all she was worth. The boat inched onward again while the thunder pealed and lightning split the sky.

"Where next, Mrs. Fickletint?" Oonie shouted. "We can make it if we hold our nerve!"

The chameleon steadied herself against the wind. "Hard right!"

But as the boat turned, a fork of lightning split a shard of rock, sending splinters of stone toward the boat.

"DUCK!" Mrs. Fickletint screamed.

Oonie and Zeb ducked, and the rocks sailed past. Then the channel between the rocks widened and the Bother-Ahead Beacon began flashing green.

Zeb blinked into the rain. "What does green mean?!"

Oonie tensed, and Mrs. Fickletint flashed several colors at once. Then the chameleon shrieked: "WHIRLGHOUL! Keep right at all costs, Oonie!"

Zeb watched in horror as the *Kerfuffle* approached a spinning vortex with two watery arms reaching up out of the middle. The arms reached through the storm toward the boat, trying to drag the vessel into its hold.

"Keep her steady, Oonie!" Mrs. Fickletint cried. "You can do this!"

The storm raged on, slamming into the boat and shunting it closer to the whirlghoul. Everyone screamed, but then Mrs. Fickletint was shouting commands again, Oonie was gripping the rudder, and Zeb was bailing water out of the boat as fast as he could. The *Kerfuffle* wobbled, swerved, then careered on past the whirlghoul and burst out into open sea.

"We—we did it!" Zeb cried. "We sailed through the Blackfangs!"

Mrs. Fickletint cheered and Oonie smiled. The *Kerfuffle* had several large dents in her side and everyone was drenched, but they were alive. And not even the storm could dampen their spirits. Zeb couldn't stop grinning. He had doubted the crew aboard the *Kerfuffle*, and yet by working together they had survived the Blackfangs, a feat only the legendary Nefarious Flood had done before them!

"To the Final Curtain!" Zeb found himself yelling as he punched the air in triumph. "Wherever that may be!"

He blushed suddenly, because this sort of optimism was most unlike him, but there had been something unexpectedly enjoyable about being part of a crew. The joy vanished as soon as he saw that the Bother-Ahead Beacon was flashing red. Before anyone on board the *Kerfuffle* could react, the

Blackfangs behind them exploded. Shards of rock flew into the storm, water sprayed everywhere, and heaving its mighty body out of the sea was a beast with pulsing suckers and red skin that shone with slime.

Chapter 13

"Fire kraken!" Mrs. Fickletint yelled.

Zeb swayed. The kraken was vast, and it was advancing through the ocean at terrifying speed. Tentacle after tentacle slammed down onto the sea as it propelled itself forward—and soaring through the lightning above it came the bone dragon. Morg sat astride it, her own wings juddering in the wind, her skull-mask fixed on Zeb.

"To the trapdoor!" Oonie shouted. "We've got to trust the *Kerfuffle* to take it from here!"

Zeb and Mrs. Fickletint scrambled over the benches toward Oonie, who was yodeling and nodding as she yanked the trapdoor open. But the kraken was faster still, and Zeb screamed as it drew up alongside the *Kerfuffle* like a raging fire. Its bulging head loomed close, and a swarm of red tentacles wrapped themselves around the boat, squeezing the wood so hard it creaked. Then the whole deck tilted, and Zeb, Oonie, and Mrs. Fickletint tumbled down its length, slamming against the prow.

From up above, the harpy laughed. "*Zebedee Bolt!*" she screeched. "You dared to steal my Stargold Wings!"

The kraken held the *Kerfuffle* upturned, and the slime from its suckers spattered down into the boat. Zeb, Oonie, and Mrs. Fickletint huddled together as the dragon circled above.

"Plan B!" Oonie panted. "Because it doesn't feel like hiding's an option!"

Morg unfurled her wings, and Zeb felt her dark magic throbbing with the storm.

"W-what if it doesn't work?" Zeb stammered.

"It's *got* to work!" Mrs. Fickletint cowered into Oonie's side. "It's our only chance!"

The dragon cried out, and Zeb's throat tightened. Would Morg realize that what she wanted more than anything wasn't in the pouch around Zeb's neck? Would she see through their trickery? Or was there a chance that a runaway boy, a blind girl, and a talking chameleon could defy the odds and hoodwink the harpy?

Black sparks fizzed around Morg, and she cackled as a pair of gold wings slid out of the pouch around Zeb's neck. Zeb thought of the real Stargold Wings, hidden inside the cabin. He hoped that the copy would fool Morg. They didn't flutter as they rose into the sky, drawn to the harpy by the pull of her dark magic, but the rain was lashing down and the storm was swirling, so Morg couldn't have seen that.

"The Ember Scroll will be mine!" the harpy roared as the sunchatter drew closer still.

The kraken sniffed the air and, sensing something was amiss about the object rising toward the harpy, loosened its grip on the boat for a second. The *Kerfuffle* crashed back onto the sea. Mrs. Fickletint raced over the deck toward the trapdoor, Oonie fumbled after her, and Zeb, hardly daring to believe his eyes that their plan might have worked, scrambled behind. But as Morg closed her fist around the sunchatter, the fire kraken changed tack.

It swung a tentacle toward the deck and seized Zeb, yanking him off the boat and holding him up in the air. Zeb screamed as the kraken's suckers curled around him, but no matter how hard he thrashed, he couldn't escape. Morg screeched with rage as she realized that what she was holding was not what she wanted. And Zeb felt his limbs go slack. Oonie and Mrs. Fickletint were safe inside the cabin. They'd even shut the trapdoor. And though they had talked of backup plans and being a crew, that was before an encounter with Morg. Now they had the Stargold Wings and a chance to flee if the harpy and the kraken were distracted with Zeb. He felt tears rise inside him. They had been so close. But it was over now. The *Kerfuffle* would race away, and when Morg realized Zeb didn't have the Stargold Wings, the kraken would finish him off.

The beast raised Zeb up toward Morg and her dragon, and though Zeb had wrestled his arms free, he couldn't force his body out of the kraken's grasp.

"Give me the Stargold Wings, boy!"

The harpy's mask swam before him as the dragon beat its boned wings against the rain. Zeb's heart hammered against his ribs. This was it: the moment the *Kerfuffle* shot away, leaving him alone in the storm with Morg's dark magic.

Only that didn't happen.

There was a thump down on deck as the trapdoor of the *Kerfuffle* burst open. Then, there, wielding a lasso, was Oonie.

She spun the lasso round and round in the air to the cries

of Mrs. Fickletint on her shoulder. "Left a bit, Oonie! Right a touch! That's it! Now THROW!"

Zeb blinked in disbelief. They'd come back for him! They hadn't abandoned him, as he'd thought. They'd been mustering up a plan C!

The lasso shot out and fixed around the kraken's tentacle, drawing it and Zeb back toward the boat. And Zeb knew then that this was no ordinary lasso. This was an object filled with magic. It couldn't free Zeb—the fire kraken's hold was unflinching—but little by little it was pulling the giant tentacle back on deck.

"No!" Morg screeched, hurtling down. "You will not escape this time!"

But Zeb was in the boat now, his legs scrabbling beneath the kraken's hold.

"Give me your hand!" Oonie shouted.

"You'll never manage to pull me out!" Zeb cried as he bucked and twisted. "Go on to the Final Curtain without me and find the cave that has never been found!"

"Just hold out your hand!" Mrs. Fickletint screamed as Morg swooped closer still.

"NOW!" Oonie yelled. "Trust me!"

Morg was just meters away from Zeb now, so he flung out a shaking hand toward Oonie, and when their palms met, all hell broke loose.

There was a loud clank and dozens of portholes appeared in the sides of the *Kerfuffle*. The cannon, which had been innocently blowing bubbles below deck before, suddenly emerged from a new trapdoor. And then, the boat's hidden phoenix magic began to pour out, red-hot fireballs exploding from the portholes and cannon into the night. They tore through the kraken's tentacles and blasted Morg and her dragon backward. Zeb, Oonie, and Mrs. Fickletint huddled together as the sky around them blazed red, and Mrs. Fickletint shrieked a running commentary so Oonie could navigate what was going on.

Fireballs pummeled against the kraken again and again, and the creature writhed and roared, its skin sizzling until eventually it sunk, lifeless, into the sea. Morg was steering her dragon back toward the *Kerfuffle*, and now that the kraken was no more, the cannon swung round to face her. It hurled a lobby of fireballs out, shattering a part of the dragon's tail and sending it, and Morg, plunging into the sea. They rose up at once, but the fireballs kept coming, pinning them down among the waves.

"What next?" Zeb cried. "The *Kerfuffle* can't hold Morg here forever!"

As if in reply, the *Kerfuffle* unleashed the last of its phoenix magic. The Bother-Ahead Beacon shattered, and in its place stood the carved head of a dragon. Next came the sound of wood splitting, and Zeb and Mrs. Fickletint watched, open-mouthed, as two enormous red wings burst out from each side of the boat.

"Wings, Oonie!" Zeb cried. "Your boat has wings!"

They were leathery, like the sail, and in one whumping motion, they carried the *Kerfuffle* up into the sky. Still the fireballs fell from the portholes, raining down on Morg and her dragon, so that no matter how hard they tried, they couldn't approach the boat.

"I know where you're going"—Morg shrieked after them—"thanks to *you*, Zebedee Bolt, when *you* told *your* pathetic friends to go on to the Final Curtain without *you*!"

Zeb winced. In his panic, he'd given away a part of the message from the Stargold Wings.

"And there I was thinking the Ember Scroll was up by the sun, when all along it was a cave that has never been found that I needed to reach!" She cackled. "I will get there before any of you, and the Ember Scroll will be mine!" The harpy and her dragon thrashed against the fiery sea. "The Stargold Wings won't come willingly to me now that they've clearly sided with you, but it will be a different story when I bring the Ember Scroll to them. My Midnights will find you, and I will write my ending and begin my rule!"

The *Kerfuffle* flew on through the storm, away from the harpy and her dragon. Zeb, Oonie, and Mrs. Fickletint were too exhausted to say a word, but one thing had been proven that night: They were a small but mighty crew. Against the odds, they had sailed past the Blackfangs, they had outwitted Morg, and they still had a chance of finding the Ember Scroll.

Chapter 14

The *Kerfuffle* sped through the night over the glistening sea. The storm had fizzled out, the cannon had slid back below deck, and Morg's cries were now long gone. Only the *whrum* of beating wings could be heard as the *Kerfuffle* flew through a star-filled sky toward the Final Curtain.

Zeb sat on a bench beside Oonie and Mrs. Fickletint. "How on earth did we pull that off?" he said eventually.

Oonie turned what was left of the lasso over in her hands. "Luck mostly, but also this Hope-Rope. The hurtle found it in a trunk last week, and because it's woven with a hidden strand of sunlight, the person wielding it can bring down almost anything if he or she hopes hard enough." She paused. "And, well—"

"Go on, Oonie," Mrs. Fickletint urged. "You know as well as I do that Zeb played a key part in that escape."

Zeb frowned. "Me?"

Oonie pretended to be fascinated by the Hope-Rope all of a sudden.

"Oonie . . ." Mrs. Fickletint poked a claw into her side. "You can't just pretend it didn't happen."

Oonie chewed her lip, and then she took a deep breath and said: "I think, maybe, possibly, somehow you activated the *Kerfuffle*'s hidden magic, Zeb."

Zeb shook his head. "Oh no, I definitely didn't do that. During the lasso episode, I was almost certainly crying."

Mrs. Fickletint smiled up at him from the bench. "I beg to differ, Zeb. Crackledawn's dhow boats are enchanted, but only a handful of them have ever released magic on this scale. It's said only the deepest trust can work such a miracle. And you stretched out your hand. You trusted Oonie and me." She laughed wearily. "Portholes! Explosions! WINGS! What a kerfuffle indeed!"

Zeb considered this as the boat flew on through the night. He had vowed not to trust other people, and yet it had sort of happened without warning. One minute he had been getting ready to meet his doom at the hands of Morg, the next minute he was holding Oonie's hand and things were looking infinitely less depressing.

He shrugged. "Probably just a coincidence that the *Kerfuffle*'s magic kicked off when I stretched out my hand."

"Yeah," Oonie said hastily, "could well have been."

Mrs. Fickletint rapped her knuckles. "You and I were helped by Zeb, and you might as well admit it, young lady, or this is going to be a very tedious voyage indeed."

Oonie was still for a moment, and silent, as if she was struggling with something Zeb couldn't see. Then she turned to Zeb and nodded. "You did good." There was a pause. "For a Faraway boy."

Zeb blinked. It wasn't much of a speech—only seven words, actually—but those words landed close to Zeb's heart. He suddenly found himself thinking of Fox's promise back in the Faraway. He had blocked it out, especially since the harpy had told him she had betrayed her own brother. But he had trusted Oonie and Mrs. Fickletint just now—so perhaps he'd been too quick to write Fox off. What if she'd kept her word after all?

Mrs. Fickletint cleared her throat and turned to Oonie.

"That was a terribly moving speech, darling, even if it *was* on the short side. And I was just wondering whether—after eleven long years of you pushing everyone around you away—you might be able to extend your trust beyond me for a while, to include Zeb, too."

Zeb hardly dared breathe, because he couldn't help feeling he and Oonie were on the cusp of something important and, in a heartbeat, either one of them might blow it completely.

Mrs. Fickletint leaned a little closer to Oonie. "You know this boat like the back of your hand, but this voyage is going to be bigger than anything we've taken on before. What if the *Kerfuffle* goes under and we have to find another way to the Final Curtain, a way you're not used to at all? What if you and I get separated and you find yourself alone in unfamiliar territory? What then?"

Oonie scooped the chameleon up and clutched her to her chest. "Don't you ever say anything like that again, Mrs. Fickletint. We'll always be together."

But Oonie's brow was furrowed and her nose was scrunched up tight. She was thinking hard, Zeb could tell.

"It's time, Oonie," Mrs. Fickletint whispered. "If you're serious about saving the Unmapped Kingdoms and the Faraway, you need to start acting like a *real* captain. You need to take the one risk you're afraid of taking."

Oonie didn't move for a little while longer, then she raised her head. "I'll trust you, Zeb." She paused. "But *only* because Crackledawn needs me to."

Mrs. Fickletint kissed Oonie's cheek, then she hopped down onto the bench again. "So, Zeb? Can *you* trust *us*?"

Zeb picked at his jeans. "I tried that back home. Again and again I trusted grown-ups to find a foster home for me. And every time they let me down." He paused. "There was *one* person I met just before I came here, but then Morg—" He broke off, confused.

"Grown-ups often get themselves into a pickle with these things," Mrs. Fickletint replied. "But girls and chameleons? We're not going to let you down. When the fire kraken held you prisoner, we didn't sail away, even though we had the real Stargold Wings down in the cabin. You're part of our crew. And crews stick together. They *have* to if they want to save the world in just three days."

Zeb, who had never been part of a family or a friendship group, let alone a crew that vowed to stick together, felt so unexpectedly cheered by the prospect, he almost toppled off the bench. And there was something else, too. Seeing Morg and her dark magic up close again had confirmed that what was happening here in the Unmapped Kingdoms was bigger than him. However much he told himself the Faraway didn't matter, he was beginning to see that it did.

Zeb looked first at Oonie and then at Mrs. Fickletint. "I'm not quite sure about my original plan," he said slowly. "I think I need a bit more time to think about what happens to the Faraway if we find the Ember Scroll."

Mrs. Fickletint was beginning to smile.

Zeb plowed on. "I'm going to give you and Oonie a trial run in trust." He looked at them nervously. "But just so you know, I'm expecting to be disappointed."

"Hooray!" Mrs. Fickletint cried. "Oh, it *is* nice not to be loathed by you, Zeb."

And Zeb noticed even Oonie managed a smile then. A small one, at the very edge of her lips, but it lingered as she faced the moonlight and let the night breeze sift through her hair.

Zeb looked at the moon as Mrs. Fickletint settled down for a snooze in Oonie's lap. It was so big and bright, he felt he could almost reach out and touch it. And far below, shining like foil, was the sea. The *Kerfuffle* flew on above tiny islands dotted here and there, not much more than a scrap of sand and a handful of palm trees. Zeb felt a sudden pang that Oonie—smiling up at the sky—couldn't see the wonder of Crackledawn laid out beneath her.

"I don't see the world the way most people see it," she said quietly, as if reading his thoughts. "I notice things others miss. Even if the sunchatter's miles and miles away, I can still hear little snippets of its music—tiny snatches of sunrises and sunsets—as if it's calling just to me."

Zeb nodded, knowing how it felt to hear melodies wherever you were and realizing with a jolt that this thing they had in common—their connection to music—might have been part of the reason he'd decided to trust Oonie.

She went on. "The Crackledawn in my mind is as crystal clear as if I *could* see it." She paused. "I can tell you what stars smell like and what moonlight tastes of."

"What *do* stars smell like?" Zeb asked.

Oonie leaned forward and sniffed. "Like wild mint. Fresh and cool and fierce."

Zeb gave the air a big long sniff, but no matter how hard he tried, he couldn't unlock the secrets of Oonie's world.

"And the moonlight?" Zeb asked. "What does that taste of?"

"Moonlight?" Oonie smiled as the *Kerfuffle* soared on over the sea. "Moonlight tastes of adventure."

When Zeb awoke the next morning, the hurtle was tidying up the mess left in the wake of the kraken's attack, Mrs. Fickletint was darning Oonie's ripped tunic (while stirring a pot of porridge with her toe and writing a to-do list with a pen in her mouth), and something in the direction of the staircase was making a strange crackling noise. Zeb pulled the Stargold Wings out from beneath his pillow. They were still glowing but not as brightly as before. Mrs. Fickletint had mentioned last night that their magic was running out. They had helped Zeb on the dragon's back and revealed a message to the crew. But eventually their magic would fade completely, and only being reunited with the Ember Scroll could restore their power.

Zeb sat up in his threadbear. The crackling noise was coming from a plaque nailed to the wall halfway up the stairs that held a large conch. Zeb watched in surprise as the opening to this conch moved, just like a mouth.

An old, and very frightened, voice sputtered out: "Calling all those aboard the *Kerfuffle!*"

Mrs. Fickletint spat out her pen, threw down her needle, abandoned her porridge, and charged toward the conch. "Greyhobble!"

"A message from the Lofty Husks?" Oonie murmured as she clambered out of her cubbyhole. "Then Morg hasn't quite managed to strip them of their magic yet!"

The crew huddled on the stairs around the conch.

"I don't have much time," the voice inside the shell was saying. "We are still hiding inside Cathedral Cave on Wildhorn, and the Sunsmiths here are using the last of the sunchatter to compose symphonies for the Faraway's sun scrolls. But Morg's skeletons surround the cave, and every hour that goes by they draw out a little more Lofty Husk magic, weakening our protection charms so that, one day soon, they will be able to rush inside, finish us all off, and claim Crackledawn for Morg."

Mrs. Fickletint nibbled at her tail. "If only this conch allowed us to speak back! I could send a message to Greyhobble to pass on to dear Mr. Fickletint and our children, just to tell them that I love them in case—in case—"

Oonie shook her head. "Don't think like that, Mrs. Fickletint."

Greyhobble went on. "We thought all was lost yesterday. Timberdust, Crumpet, and I assumed we had a matter of minutes before our magic left us. But then something extraordinary happened."

Zeb, Oonie, and Mrs. Fickletint leaned in closer.

"Morg left Wildhorn, screeching about stealing back the Stargold Wings, and as she did so, something—*someone*—hurtled into Cathedral Cave. A woman from the Faraway clutching a phoenix tear!" There was a pause. "Fox Petty-Squabble is here in Crackledawn!"

Zeb felt something new and unforeseen rise up in his chest. Fox was *here*, in Crackledawn?

"The phoenix tear helped Fox to break back into the Unmapped Kingdoms, and its magic has not only granted me the strength to send you a message now, but it has also strengthened the protection charms around Cathedral Cave, so, for the time being, we remain safe from Morg's Midnights. But Morg is still looking for the Ember Scroll. If she finds it and writes her ending, then the world will crumble! The *Kerfuffle* is our only hope. You *must* find the scroll before Morg and bring back a phoenix to save us all!"

Oonie nudged Mrs. Fickletint. "Like I told you all along . . ."

The chameleon rolled her eyes.

Then Greyhobble spoke again. "I can sense the presence

of a Faraway child aboard the *Kerfuffle*, so before the last of my magic leaves me completely, there is one more thing that needs to be said."

There was a crackling, shuffling sort of sound, then another voice sounded from the conch. "Zebedee Bolt," it said. "I told you I'd come back for you, and I want you to know that I intend to keep that promise. I *will* find you. And I *will* show you that you are worth crossing worlds and kingdoms to find."

Oonie gasped, Mrs. Fickletint gaped, and Zeb felt the air slide from his lungs. The promise Fox had made to him back in the Faraway hadn't been broken. Not yet anyway.

"If Morg overheard our conversation back in the theater," Fox said, "then she will have poisoned you against me. She will have told you that I betrayed my brother in Jungledrop."

Zeb stiffened.

"I did betray Fibber, but I was wrong to. And I did everything in my power to set things right." She paused. "I'm not perfect. Nobody is. But that doesn't mean we should stop trying to make the world a better place. You *will* save the Unmapped Kingdoms and the Faraway, Zeb, even if right now you're not sure whether they're worth saving. And you will come to realize that people can be trusted and promises can be kept. Until then, I want you to have this."

The conch belched, and then, to Zeb's surprise, a little black purse tumbled out.

Zeb picked it up, but when he tried to draw back the silver zipper to see what was inside, he realized he couldn't open it. No matter how hard he tugged, the zipper wouldn't budge.

"An Unopenable Purse," Mrs. Fickletint gasped. "Not even knives can break the zipper or tear the velvet it's made from. It's said there are only a handful of these left in the whole of the Unmapped Kingdoms."

Fox spoke again. "Greyhobble told me that if someone holds an Unopenable Purse and hopes hard upon it, it will fill with enchanted objects and, when the time is right, the purse will open and these objects will be revealed." She paused. "I do not know what you will find in this purse, Zeb, but I do know that I poured every hope I have for you upon it. So, good luck, and know that I'm rooting for you every step of the way."

The conch crackled, then fell silent.

"*You* know Fox Petty-Squabble?" Oonie said incredulously.

Mrs. Fickletint flashed several colors at once. "*The* Fox Petty-Squabble who rescued a Lofty Husk, freed Jungledrop's

Unmappers, saved a glow-in-the-dark rainforest, restored rain to the Faraway, *and* became best friends with her brother?!"

Zeb shifted. This did *not* sound like the woman Morg had told him about.

"I—I met her once," he mumbled. "Just after I ran away from my foster home. But then Morg kidnapped me."

"I heard she rode on the back of a golden panther," Oonie said, her face full of awe.

"I heard she took on a forest full of cursed trees and a troop of demon monkeys, all in the space of a single night." Mrs. Fickletint turned to Zeb. "What miraculous thing did she do when you met her in the Faraway?"

"She offered to take me out for a milkshake." There was an awkward silence. "And—and she made a promise to me. She told me she'd come back for me."

Mrs. Fickletint smiled. "Well, it looks like she's doing just that."

Zeb turned the Unopenable Purse over in his hands. This was something someone from his world had held, and now he was holding it. But not only that. This was something filled with hope, a reminder that there was someone rooting for him after all. He realized that he was smiling because the truth of things was, finally, starting to sink in. Trust might start small. An outstretched hand or a promised milkshake. But it could grow.

"If a promise can cross worlds," Zeb said quietly, "do you think it can battle past fire krakens, ogre eels, and harpies, too? Or does it run out of steam eventually?"

Oonie guffawed. "I don't think a promise by Fox Petty-Squabble would ever run out of steam."

"So, you could say this was an unbreakable sort of promise," Zeb said, slipping the Unopenable Purse into his pocket.

Mrs. Fickletint nodded.

Through a porthole, Zeb glimpsed a silver whale with a little calf tucked under her fin. Then he glanced at the sunchatter in the barrel behind them. It was glittering, like thousands of gold coins. All this magic, Zeb thought, tucked away in the Unmapped Kingdoms, and yet the Unmappers here worked hard to share it with his world so that the Faraway would be filled with beauty too. He was starting to understand the extraordinary balance of it all.

He stood up to face Oonie and Mrs. Fickletint. And, with the Stargold Wings clasped tight in his hands and the Unopenable Purse firmly in his pocket, he said: "Let's give saving the world a go, then."

Chapter 15

There wasn't time for Mrs. Fickletint to shower Zeb with kisses, because suddenly the boat began to drop down toward the sea. The crew rushed to the porthole in the kitchen and looked out just as the *Kerfuffle* splashed down onto the water and its wings slid back into the slats of wood as if they'd never been there.

Zeb gulped. The water here was black, like oil. And drifting on the surface, lifeless, was a shoal of butterflies the size of dinner plates.

"Butterflips," Mrs. Fickletint gasped. "Underwater butterflies are said to live in the most remote parts of the ocean. Even *they* have been killed by Morg's dark magic!"

"There's sunchatter in these parts," Oonie murmured. "Lots of it. But it's not singing I can hear—it's sobbing.

Which means the whole lot is cursed." She bit her lip. "The Bother-Ahead Beacons, what color are they?"

"Yellow," Zeb replied firmly.

Mrs. Fickletint nodded. "If there were Midnights in these parts, they've gone now."

"But what if it was Morg who was here?" Zeb cried. "What if the Final Curtain is close by and she's already found the Ember Scroll?"

Oonie shook her head. "We'd know if she had the scroll because it's said the Unmapped skies will shake with fear and the sun will hide if she finds it."

Mrs. Fickletint grimaced at the sea. "This will be her Midnights patrolling the ocean looking for us and the Stargold Wings. . . ." She glanced at the Bother-Ahead Beacons again. "For now, though, we're safe."

The *Kerfuffle* eased on through the dark water, and Zeb caught a glimpse of a lifeless squid covered in hearts, which Oonie explained must once have been a squidge—a rare breed of squid fond of hugs. Zeb shivered. Morg's dark magic was everywhere. . . . Then the crew felt the unmistakable sensation of sand slide up beneath the hull, and the *Kerfuffle* ground to a halt.

Mrs. Fickletint scampered up the stairs and pushed the trapdoor open a fraction. "It's a large island," she whispered. "And even though the water around it is pitch-black, the island itself seems to be untouched by Morg's dark magic! Beyond the bay there's a sandy beach, a wild-looking jungle, and"—she frowned—"a rock goblin asleep in a hammock. . . ."

"Rock goblin?" Zeb braced himself. "Should we take the cannon?"

Oonie shook her head. "The rock goblins are on our side. They run the Cheeky Urchin back home on Wildhorn—a food and drink shack specializing in exotic fruit juices that make *your* bottom wiggle."

"What a goblin is doing all the way out here beats me," Mrs. Fickletint said, shaking her head.

Oonie took a deep breath. "Let's go and investigate, because if the *Kerfuffle* has come to a stop, there must be a reason for it."

The crew inched out of the trapdoor, tiptoed across the deck, then Zeb and Mrs. Fickletint peered over the prow of the boat. A cluster of small creatures were sobbing in the shallows. Some were pale blue with pointed ears, others gold with wings.

Zeb eyed them. "Are *you* *sure* we shouldn't just grab the

cannon? We could give the surrounding area one quick blast before we get off the boat?"

"They're water pixies and sand sprites," Mrs. Fickletint replied. "And they look as miserable as us about Crackledawn's magic fading. They're nothing to worry about, Zeb. Unless you've got a secret stash of puddleberries in your pocket. In which case you'll be mobbed the minute you step off the boat. Water pixies are obsessed with them."

The *Kerfuffle* had nosed up onto a large semicircle of golden sand, and just before the jungle of trees began, there was a little wooden shack. All this Mrs. Fickletint relayed to Oonie.

"Palms cover the roof, pans hang down from hooks below, and dangling from the counter is a sign that says: WELCOME TO RICKETY GRAMPS."

Oonie nodded firmly, but Zeb noticed her shoulders were bunched up and she was gripping the prow of the boat so tight her knuckles were white. Brave, risk-taking, adventure-seeking Oonie was scared.

"What's the goblin up to?" she whispered.

"To the side of the shack, there's a hammock strung between two palm trees," Mrs. Fickletint explained, "and he's asleep in there."

"He's really green," Zeb added.

"I know what a goblin looks like," Oonie hissed.

Everything from the goblin's clothes—palm-leaf shorts and a seaweed waistcoat barely covering his potbelly—to his nose, which was big and bulbous and looked very much like a pear—was green. In fact, the only thing that wasn't green were his dreadlocks, which were gray and matted, like a bundle of old rope.

"Should we wake him up?" Zeb asked.

Oonie nodded. "We've only got two nights until the full moon. We don't have time for afternoon siestas."

Zeb was used to the way Oonie moved aboard the *Kerfuffle*—swiftly, decisively—but she was hesitating now. And it wasn't until Mrs. Fickletint scrambled up onto her shoulder that she began to look like the Oonie that Zeb knew.

"A short drop off the boat, then you're in the shallows," Mrs. Fickletint whispered as Oonie swung a leg up onto the side of the *Kerfuffle*. "After that, it's a couple of strides to the beach. Then the goblin's hammock will be straight ahead."

Zeb watched as Oonie lowered herself into the blackened sea, slowly and carefully. Sliding over the prow after her, he flinched as his own legs slipped into cursed waters and his feet touched the sand. Oonie stumbled in the shallows ahead and Zeb charged through the water after her. He arrived, breathless, by her side.

"Is everything okay?" Oonie whispered.

Zeb shook himself. "Er—yes. I just didn't want to be late."

Mrs. Fickletint said nothing but smiled knowingly.

Ignoring her, Zeb walked up onto the beach. The sand between his toes felt comforting, his first time on land since arriving in Crackledawn.

It was only when the crew were standing right in front of the hammock that the goblin awoke. He opened one eye, then the other, before hoisting himself upright, falling off his hammock, and landing flat on his face in the sand. He got up, dislodged a shell from his enormous nose, and gasped.

"Visitors! An Unmapper, a chameleon, and"—he rubbed his eyes—"a Faraway boy! Well, I never. . . . What with all the dark magic skulking around, Rickety Gramps hasn't had a single customer in over a decade! Not since the Lofty Husks stopped by all those years ago to wish me a Merry Christmas and check in to see how my retirement was going. And then you lot come along! Well, now you're here, I'd best fix you up a juice. I, Dollop, did used to be the head chef at the Cheeky

Urchin, after all—before I realized that I needed to escape the rat race and have a bit of me-time. Now it's all yoga, bubble baths, and vegetable smoothies, which is just as well because it's pretty hard to keep relaxed when the ocean around you turns blacker each day. . . ."

Dollop reconfigured his body into a yoga pose: a one-legged, palm-meeting, knee-bending balancing act, which Zeb thought looked both painful and perilous (mainly on account of the goblin's potbelly, which threatened to unbalance the whole maneuver).

Dollop wobbled a little, then a lot, before collapsing in a heap.

"So relaxing," he said, spitting out sand. "Now, what can I get you all?"

From Oonie's shoulder, Mrs. Fickletint cleared her throat. "We're looking for the Final Curtain."

Dollop frowned. "This is a tropical island, not an interiors shop."

"I'm not sure we're looking for a curtain exactly," Oonie said. "We're looking for the Ember Scroll, but the Stargold Wings sent us a message saying we should sail on south to the Final Curtain, step beyond all we know is certain, seek a cave that has never been found, and claim the scroll before the moon is round."

Dollop flipped himself up into a handstand that came crashing down when his belly collided with his nose. "Before the moon is round . . . Why the rush?" He staggered up, panting. "Why not stay a while and enjoy some inner peace?"

"BECAUSE MORG IS HERE IN CRACKLEDAWN!" Zeb spluttered. "AND WE DO NOT HAVE TIME FOR INNER PEACE!"

Mrs. Fickletint patted him on the back. "Well said, dear."

"MORG IS HERE?!" Dollop yelped. He did several very fast, very unrelaxing yoga poses to try and calm himself down. "She's come to steal the Unmapped magic once and for all, hasn't she?! This is the end! We're all doomed!"

"Not if you can help us, we're not," Oonie said firmly.

"Inner peace, inner peace, inner peace," Dollop chanted with his eyes closed. He opened them nervously. "Gah! You're still here. It's really happening, then. I'm not dreaming!" And then he squinted at Oonie. "Don't I recognize you?" He paused. "Yes, you're the Unmapper whose conch opened early. The girl who can hear sunchatter miles away . . ."

Oonie nodded.

"I remember the Lofty Husks back on Wildhorn saying you were destined to become a brilliant Sunraider." Dollop lowered his voice, as if he was afraid he might be heard. "But to take on Morg—are you *sure* that's wise?"

"Of course it's not wise," Mrs. Fickletint snapped. "But it's happening. The Lofty Husks and all the other Unmappers are imprisoned on Wildhorn. So, as much as it pains me to say that two children and a chameleon are in charge of saving the world, that's the state of the matter. We're all Crackledawn's got! And for a reason I'm finding very hard to fathom, the *Kerfuffle* has insisted we stop off here on our quest to write a hopeful ending for the world."

Dollop did a shaky sun salutation, then several elaborate breathing exercises. "I don't know what the Final Curtain is or where you'll find it. But if the Stargold Wings told you to step beyond all you know is certain and seek out a cave no one else has found, then I know what you need."

The crew leaned in hopefully and Dollop took a deep breath. "You, my friends, need a Crackledawn dragon."

Chapter 16

The crew sat on stools outside the shack while Dollop handed three blue juices, garnished with pineapple, over the counter.

"Blueberry swigs," he explained to Zeb. "My speciality at the Cheeky Urchin, but I haven't added wigglewort this time—the herb that makes your bottom shake—because now is *not* the time for wobbling bottoms. It is the time for pancakes and planning."

While they tucked into fluffy pancakes laden with exotic fruit, Dollop gave a hurried explanation of the island. It was called Rickety Gramps because it was the island where the spirits of the Faraway's grandparents went to rest. And on the surface of things, it appeared slow-moving and uneventful. But on closer inspection it was—much like grandparents themselves—intensely magical, which was why it had withstood Morg's dark magic so far. Footprints known as footglints appeared, out of nowhere, in the sand. There were calm trees instead of palm trees, which whispered soothing stories when you couldn't get to sleep. And while the shore looked perfectly ordinary, it was, in fact, a seasnore, which snored every time the tide drew back. Zeb concluded that, given everything he had faced so far in Hollowbone and Crackledawn, he could probably handle Rickety Gramps without needing to go back to the ship for the cannon.

"Why do we need a dragon to find the Ember Scroll?" Zeb asked. "I've only met one before, and it's not an experience I'm keen to repeat . . ."

"Dragons," Dollop replied, "are the wildest of all the magical creatures in the Unmapped Kingdoms. They scatter moondust each night to keep what is left of the Unmapped magic going because they are loyal to the very first phoenix, but they bow to no one. Not even the Lofty Husks."

"Unless they're a dragon conjured from bones," Mrs. Fickletint murmured, "in which case they're loyal to Morg. . . ."

Dollop shuddered. "When the Unmapped dragons swoop by in the dead of night to collect scrolls for the Faraway, they're rarely seen. They can travel vast distances without tiring, they can fly through the fiercest blizzards, they can burn entire cities with one blast of fire."

A few days ago, Zeb would have scoffed at the idea of dragons racing over New York, but he was getting a little better at taking magic in his stride.

"They don't speak and they don't abide by our rules," Dollop added. "Theirs is a world we don't fully understand, though it's said that if one dragon kills another dragon, that dragon will be banished from the Unmapped Kingdoms forever." He took a slurp of his swig. "Unmapped dragons can be any color, but you can tell which kingdom each dragon is from because they have distinctive quirks. Rumblestar's dragons have giant, star-studded wings so they can fly higher than the moon. Jungledrop's dragons have tails as long as rivers so they can trail rainforest magic in their wake. Silvercrag's have icicle teeth so they can breathe jets of ice."

"And Crackledawn dragons?" Zeb asked nervously.

"I've never been lucky enough to see one," Mrs. Fickletint said, "but according to Terrence Talonswipe, author of *The Dragonfiles*, they have gills and webbed talons so they can swim incredibly fast underwater."

"You're right," Dollop said. "They can race beneath the waves, but they can't breathe fire there."

"And their eyes are flecked with sunlight," Oonie said.

Dollop nodded. "The thing that might interest you lot most is that Crackledawn dragons have a notoriously good sense of smell, particularly when it comes to sniffing out magic."

"Better than fire krakens?" Zeb asked.

"Infinitely better. So, if the Ember Scroll is in unchartered territory, you're going to need a dragon to sniff it out." Dollop glanced at the *Kerfuffle*. "Your enchanted boat has taken you this far, but now it's time for an upgrade."

"But how can we call a dragon to us when they're the wildest beasts in the kingdom?" Zeb cried.

"He's right," Oonie said. "It would be like trying to call in the wind."

"You can summon almost anything if you know how," Dollop said eagerly. "And while I don't recall anyone ever *successfully* summoning a dragon before, that doesn't mean you won't." He rummaged about beneath the counter before emerging, moments later, with a leather-bound book. The words "*Mustering Up Magic*, edited by Enora Nattermuch" ran along the spine. "It's like a phone book. Only for magical creatures. The Lofty Husks dropped it off, in case I ever want to summon a lift back to Wildhorn." Dollop opened it and began scanning the pages. "To summon a cockle imp, sneeze four times. To summon a silver whale, whistle with an item of silver under your tongue." He ran a finger down the page. "Ah yes, here. To summon a dragon—"

Zeb winced. It was bound to be something impossible *and* dreadful, like tap dancing on the ocean floor while juggling sea-hoppers and fending off a fire kraken.

"—play the Faraway's very first sunrise."

Music lay at the heart of calling a Crackledawn dragon? Zeb's surprise was quickly replaced with gloom because the very first sunrise would've happened way, way before any of them were born, so what Dollop was suggesting was impossible!

Oonie snorted, clearly thinking the same thing. "There would have been a symphony for the first sunrise here in Crackledawn once—the earliest Unmappers would have played it on the organ in Cathedral Cave before sending the sun scroll on to the Faraway—but it would have been sent centuries ago."

Mrs. Fickletint tutted. "I think that swig has gone to your head, Dollop."

"And how can we *play* anything?" Zeb asked. "I don't see any instruments lying around."

"We're getting carried away with the impossibles," Oonie said. "Maybe we need to focus on the possibles first. Somehow, we need to find someone very, very, very old who remembers the symphony of the first sunrise. Then we can work out how to play it."

Dollop said nothing for a while and then his eyes lit up. "Trampletusk . . . Of course!" He hopped excitedly from one foot to the other. "*She's* why your boat led you here! It knew you needed a dragon to reach the Final Curtain, and it knew only Trampletusk would remember the sunrise needed to summon it!"

Zeb braced himself. "Who or what is Trampletusk?"

"There's an old saying," Dollop went on, "that perhaps you have in the Faraway, too: *An elephant never forgets*. And in the deepest part of the jungle here lives the last enchanted elephant in Crackledawn. Trampletusk remembers every little thing that has ever happened in this kingdom: what your first words were, Oonie, and what you ate for dinner on your sixtieth birthday, Mrs. Fickletint."

"How dare you," Mrs. Fickletint muttered. "I'm not a day over fifty-nine."

"Then she can remember where the phoenix hid the Ember Scroll!" Zeb cried. "And maybe she can let us into the harpy's memories too, so we can keep track of her!"

"Alas," Dollop said, "Trampletusk only recalls the memories of Crackledawn's inhabitants: the Lofty Husks, the Unmappers, and the magical creatures here. I've only ever seen her at night, because in the day she takes herself off into a cave to absorb all the memories fizzing away in the kingdom. But if you're after the first sunrise, she's *your* best bet."

Oonie stood up. "We need to start looking for her straightaway—we've only got two more nights, then the full moon rises. We *have* to find the Ember Scroll before Morg."

Dollop nodded. "And before the Midnights I've seen snooping around these parts come back and find you . . ."

Mrs. Fickletint eyed the jungle beyond the shack. "What can we expect in there?"

"Mostly it's just feather-tailed monkeys, prattleparrots, and the odd silkbat." Dollop paused. "But there *are* one or two suzukis."

Zeb nibbled his nails. "Suzukis?"

"Enormous black flowers with silver speckles and very tall

stems," Dollop explained. "Ninety percent of the time they sing sweetly when you pass by."

"And the other ten percent?" Zeb asked.

Dollop gulped down the last of his swig. "They swallow you whole."

After a few frenzied yoga moves, Dollop led the way on through the jungle. There were trees laden with bananas, jackfruit, coconuts, and some sort of magical fruit that looked like a mango but was blue. There were monkeys with rainbow-colored tail feathers darting through the branches. And there were prattleparrots on vines who chattered nonstop about pointless things: *"Do you think it's going to be sunny or rainy fourteen Fridays from now?" "I'm not sure, but I love rectangles." "I wonder what silence is."*

There was no sign of the suzukis at first. Mrs. Fickletint was on guard on Oonie's shoulder all the same, whispering instructions to navigate the route. And though back in the shallows, Zeb had told himself that rushing after his captain to check she was okay was a one-off, now he found himself anticipating her every move to make sure she didn't come to any harm. Unseen by Oonie, Zeb yanked fallen branches out of her path so she didn't trip up, pushed thorny undergrowth aside so she wouldn't graze her legs, and even snapped a low-hanging vine in half because it was blocking her way. But when Oonie bumped into Zeb heaving away a rock (which was covered in moss, so definitely slippery), she flinched.

"You'd better not be helping me, Zeb."

For a second, Zeb didn't know how to respond, then he gave up worrying about it and simply said: "Don't worry, I'm making things as difficult for you as I possibly can."

Oonie's mouth twitched. She hadn't been expecting that. And when, after an hour of walking, they came to a river, she let Zeb hold her arm to guide her across.

They clambered up the bank on the other side together to find a whole grove of black flowers. The suzukis were taller than Zeb and Oonie, their petals were like open clams, and they were humming.

"Phew," Dollop panted. "The suzukis appear to be in a good mood today."

"You said there'd be one or two of them!" Mrs. Fickletint hissed. "Not a forest full!"

"There's been so much dark magic afoot, it's been hard to juggle inner peace with household chores," Dollop said.

"Gardening here on Rickety Gramps has been rather put on the back burner. And you should see my ironing pile. . . ."

He strode on through the flowers, and despite one hairy moment, when a particularly large suzuki stopped singing and snapped its petals shut inches from Zeb's sneaker, the little group made it out the other side of the grove.

Zeb looked up. The canopy blocked the sky, but he reckoned it was probably past midday now. He thought of Morg astride her bone dragon. How long before she found the Final Curtain? Would they make it there ahead of her if they managed to call a Crackledawn dragon? His mind jumped to Fox. She had faced Morg and her Midnights in Jungledrop, and beaten them, so he told himself that it would be no different now, that she and the Lofty Husks' protection charms would be enough against Morg's skeletons and ogre eels.

But what Zeb did not realize was that Morg was stronger than ever now that she had a lead on the Ember Scroll. And though Fox Petty-Squabble had a phoenix tear, the magic inside it was slipping away fast. As its glow dimmed, the Midnights surrounding Cathedral Cave grew in power: The skeletons found another crack in the cave walls to jab their spears through, and the ogre eels stirred up waves so big they sent rocks tumbling.

Again and again, the Lofty Husks recast their protection charms to seal the cave, but time was running out. Everyone inside that cave knew that unless a phoenix was summoned very soon, the end would surely come.

The crew paused a while to eat some nuts Dollop had brought along with him, then the goblin hastened on again, deeper and deeper into the jungle. When the light began to fade, the trees parted a little way to reveal dozens of waterfalls rushing down from the rocks and undergrowth into a shimmering blue lagoon. And there, at the far end of this lagoon, stood an elephant.

But this was no ordinary elephant.

Trampletusk's ears were so large they stretched down to the ground. And they weren't gray and wrinkled, they were silver and wafer-thin, like butterfly wings, her tusks silver too. She was one of the most spectacular things he'd ever laid eyes on. Even the Stargold Wings around his neck seemed to flutter with anticipation. Oonie's face shone with awe too. She couldn't see the elephant like Zeb could, but she could taste the wonder; she could smell the magic hanging in the air.

"Like breathing in a rainforest," she murmured.

The elephant looked up, and in a voice that seemed to be made of velvet, she said: "You've come for a memory, haven't you?"

Dollop led the group around the lagoon. "I'm sorry to disturb you, Trampletusk. I know you're not a people person as such, but, well, the world is falling apart, and we need your help."

The elephant nodded. "Morg is back. I have seen the fear and panic in the memories of the Unmappers and Lofty Husks."

"We might be able to beat her," Oonie said, "but we're going to need a Crackledawn dragon."

"A well-behaved one," Zeb cut in. And then, to ensure the enchanted elephant didn't get any ideas about Zeb being weak or anything, he added: "Because Mrs. Fickletint here is fifty-nine, and she doesn't want a bumpy ride."

The chameleon threw him a haughty glare.

"So, you need to play the Faraway's first sunrise," Trampletusk said.

The crew nodded hopefully. They were so close to the elephant now, Zeb could see that her ears were actually transparent and it was the markings on these ears—glittering swirls and dots and flecks—that were silver. Zeb glanced at the trees behind Trampletusk. They were different from the others they had seen so far. These trunks were vast, and thousands of glass bottles hung down from ribbons wound round the branches. Zeb peered closer. Each bottle contained a wisp of silver light.

Trampletusk followed Zeb's gaze. "I am the guardian of Crackledawn's memories. My ears are so large I hear everything that goes on in this kingdom." She dipped her head toward the trees. "And each night, the memories drop from my ears into these bottles here."

Zeb watched the memories swirling, like curls of smoke, under the trees.

"I can give you the memory you want," Trampletusk said, "but I will need a memory to replace it to ensure the magic beneath these trees is not unbalanced. Because if you were to take away a memory as important as the very first sunrise, which gave light and life to the Faraway, and forget to replace it, then *all* the memories would vanish. A kingdom with no memories is vulnerable. It is easier to destroy. And with Morg in Crackledawn, we cannot take any chances."

Mrs. Fickletint cocked her head. "What sort of memory are you looking for?"

But Trampletusk wasn't looking at the chameleon. She was looking at Zeb. "You, boy from the Faraway. You have a memory as powerful as the very first sunrise."

Zeb was starting to feel distinctly uncomfortable, because there was truth in the elephant's words. He knew the memory Trampletusk meant. It could stop him in his tracks when walking to school. It could bring on an Outburst in seconds. But he never spoke about it. Not to Derek Dunce or the Orderly-Queues or any of his teachers at school. Looking up at Trampletusk, he couldn't speak. He knew they needed to summon a dragon—and fast—but it had been ages since his last Outburst, and he knew talking about this particular memory would only bring on the tears.

"Come, boy," Trampletusk said as she turned toward the trees. "Walk with me."

Oonie took a small step forward. "If he goes, I go too."

Zeb's skin tingled. He had kept Oonie safe in the jungle and now she was doing the same for him. Being in a crew, he thought, was a bit like wearing a shield.

"Very well," Trampletusk said. "But the Memory Trees won't permit anyone else. Not even the chameleon. Too many newcomers and they'll tighten their hold on the memories, and the one you want will never be released."

Mrs. Fickletint flashed a multitude of colors from Oonie's shoulder. "But—but I go everywhere with Oonie!"

"She can rest a hand on my side," Trampletusk said. "I give you my word that until the sun rises and you have the memory you want, I will not let either of these children come to harm."

"They'll be away *overnight*?" Mrs. Fickletint cried.

Trampletusk nodded. "You cannot rush a memory out." She glanced at Zeb. "Not when it's as powerful as the first sunrise."

Mrs. Fickletint rung her paws. "Oh, Oonie. If I'd known you were going to wander off without me for a whole night, I would have made you a packed supper, I would have knitted you some emergency bed socks, I would have written you a goodbye card, I would've—"

Oonie stroked the chameleon, then set her down on the ground. "Don't fuss, Mrs. Fickletint. I'll be fine."

"They're in good hands with Trampletusk," Dollop said. "And to take our minds off Morg while they're away, we can indulge in a bit of treetop yoga."

Mrs. Fickletint shot the goblin a withering look. "The end of the world is looming, Dollop. Now is *not* the time for yoga."

"You must think of a way to conjure a piano," Trampletusk said. "For when the Faraway boy returns, he'll need one to play the first sunrise."

Zeb's heart quickened. Up until this point, he had been trying his very best to believe it was simply a coincidence that *he* had been the one the harpy dragged into the Unmapped Kingdoms. But now there was a task opening up in front of him, one that seemed almost *made* for him. He felt for the Stargold Wings around his neck. Oonie had wondered whether the phoenix magic inside these wings had searched out her and Mrs. Fickletint for a reason. Was the same true for Zeb? Had the phoenix magic known about him all along? Had it been secretly believing in him when he thought there was no one in the world who seemed to care?

Dollop turned to Zeb. "Can you even play the piano?"

Zeb snapped out of his thoughts. "Yes," he replied. "As a matter of fact, I can." He looked at the others. "I mean I can't read music or anything, but I can play tunes from memory. It was the one thing I enjoyed in the Faraway."

"Not quite the heights of optimism I was hoping for," Dollop muttered, "but it'll have to do."

Mrs. Fickletint, meanwhile, was having trouble controlling her scales. They were flashing so frequently, she looked more like a police siren than a chameleon. "Be careful, Oonie. One hand on Trampletusk's side—at all times." She turned to the elephant. "And do be gentle with Zeb. He tends to fall apart under extreme magical pressure."

But as Zeb walked off into the trees with Trampletusk and Oonie, he knew that it would not be magic that made him fall apart that night. It would be the memory—the one he kept locked inside the tightest chamber of his heart, the one he knew he had to share if they wanted to find the Ember Scroll.

Chapter 17

Zeb and Oonie walked on either side of Trampletusk as they made their way beneath the Memory Trees. The feather-tailed monkeys and prattleparrots were quiet now. Just the waterfalls sounded, spilling over rocks dotted between the trees and lapping gently against the banks of the lagoon.

Zeb watched the memories flickering inside the bottles. Had Trampletusk stored the conversations between Zeb, Oonie, and Mrs. Fickletint on the *Kerfuffle* inside them already? Was yesterday's victory against the fire kraken now tucked beneath the trees?

Trampletusk led them on, one heavy footstep after another. And though Zeb was frightened, he realized there was something comforting in the way the elephant walked, her steady plod like the thuds of a giant heartbeat. Zeb craned his head round to look at Oonie.

"Cover your ears," he said. "Only Trampletusk gets to hear the memory."

"What?!" Oonie hissed. "I can't see, and you want me to cover my ears as well?! I think I've got enough to be dealing with."

"Nonsense," Zeb replied. "You're great at multitasking."

"Fine," Oonie sighed. "I'm not listening."

But she very much was. Because Oonie was beginning to realize that she and Zeb had something in common: What they *said* wasn't necessarily what they *meant*.

Zeb spoke, very quietly, into Trampletusk's ear: "I think I know the memory you want. But it's—it's stuck inside me. All sorts of people have tried to make me talk about it. Foster parents, social workers, that kind of thing. But it hasn't worked. The memory won't budge." He paused. "I think there might be something wrong with my windpipe."

Trampletusk considered this. "Memories can weigh a lot," she said. "In fact, some can be so heavy they sink down into our toes. But we can always bring them up again. If we want to."

Zeb scuffed his sneakers through the undergrowth. The

elephant was wise. Zeb knew that his memory wasn't really stuck—whatever he told himself. He was just scared of bringing it up. He had always managed to pull himself together after an Outburst. A brief stint of blubbing and then on he went. But if this particular memory came out, he worried the Outburst that followed might never end. . . .

Trampletusk turned her large head toward Zeb. "Memories can sting, especially if they're filled with love. And it's a searing kind of pain that makes you want to howl, like when you whack your elbow."

Oonie, who had given up pretending not to listen, piped up at this. "Elephants have elbows?"

"Unfortunately so. I knocked mine against a rock last week, and the pain was so intense I very nearly fainted." Trampletusk stepped beneath a tree and under the light of a hundred memories, she lowered herself to the ground. Zeb and Oonie sat down on either side of her, and the waterfalls rippled around them. "What if I told you that you can tell me the memory locked inside your toes and that you can fall apart afterward, but that falling apart won't last forever. The tears will stop. And Oonie and I will be here, ready to pick up the broken pieces."

Zeb felt the Outburst swell inside him.

"And then every time you think of the memory in the days, weeks, and years afterward," Trampletusk said, "you will know that falling apart isn't the end. It's the beginning. Because that's where courage starts."

Zeb was doing everything he could think of to stop the tears from coming: jaw clenches, balled fists, and moody eyes. But they had already begun to fall now. He tried to brush them away, but then more came. And still more after that. It was time, at last, to let the memory out.

He took a deep breath. "My mum died when I was a baby," he sniffed, "and I never knew my dad. The welfare agency gave me a photo of my mum, something to remember her by, but it got left in the Faraway, in my rucksack, when Morg stole me away. It was never the photo that brought her back to me, though." The tears rolled down Zeb's cheeks. "It was the music. A tune that used to come to me every time I thought of her. And when I taught myself to play the piano, I found myself playing that tune. Because my memory"—Zeb swallowed—"is of my mum singing it to me over and over again." He thought back to the piano in the theater. "I've no idea how I remembered the tune, because I was only a baby when she died, but whenever I play it, the rest of the world fades away, because I can see her: a smiling face with sparkling blue eyes." He sobbed harder. "And I—I remember then that once upon a time I was loved."

Zeb cried and cried, and though she knew she wasn't meant to be listening and she was still very much on a trial run, Oonie felt her way round to Zeb and clasped his hand tight.

Trampletusk wrapped her large ears around the children. "Let it all out, Zeb," she whispered. "Let it all out."

And Zeb did. All the pain and the hurt and the disappointment that he had buried inside him for so long. Oonie didn't move. Neither did Trampletusk. They simply held Zeb tight as he wept for everything he'd lost.

Zeb had no idea when the tears had stopped and sleep closed in. But when, eventually, he opened his eyes again and Trampletusk unfurled her mighty ears, he saw that night had passed and the twilight before dawn—when the world is neither dark nor light—had arrived. Zeb sat up and rubbed his eyes. The Outburst had passed. Oonie and Trampletusk were still there. And he hadn't, as far as he could tell, fallen apart completely. He thought of his mom. The sadness hadn't gone, but he noticed it didn't weigh quite as heavily inside him as it had before.

Zeb looked up at Trampletusk. "My memory—it's not in my toes anymore, is it?"

Trampletusk shook her head. "It's in your heart now, Zeb. And hearts are bigger than toes. Memories can breathe a bit more easily in there."

"But don't you need to *take* Zeb's memory?" Oonie asked.

Trampletusk smiled. "I take the echoes of memories. To strip a person or a kingdom of their past would be to erase them altogether." She looked at Zeb. "And you don't deal with a difficult memory by getting rid of it. You deal with it by learning to live alongside it." She tapped Zeb's chest with her trunk. "In here."

"Hearts seem to require quite a lot of work," Zeb said cautiously. "And up until now, I've been mostly focusing on my biceps."

Oonie snorted. "REALLY?"

Zeb scowled at her. "You're still on a trial run, Oonie. Despite the hand holding. So please try to remember that."

Trampletusk smiled. "It is your heart, not your biceps, that is your strongest feature, Zeb."

A tickling sensation was sliding over Zeb's chest now. He gasped as a silver wisp, just visible in the twilight, drifted out from his T-shirt. It floated up toward a bottle hanging from the branch above them, then it slipped inside it. There was a fizzing sound, then a crackle, and the memory that had been stored in that bottle squeezed out past Zeb's memory and hung in the air beneath the trees.

"That's it, isn't it?" Zeb whispered. "The very first sunrise in the Faraway?"

Oonie smiled. She couldn't see it, but she could hear sounds tinkling.

The memory drifted down toward Zeb and settled, weightless but shining with magic, in his palm. The Stargold Wings flickered inside their pouch as Zeb bent his ear to the wisp. He had been expecting to hear the whispers and giggles that he had heard in the sunchatter back aboard the *Kerfuffle*, but perhaps they would have been used to conjure a small amount of sunlight, like a single sunbeam. This, though, was different. This was a melody full to bursting and one so pure and clear it could have been spun from glass.

Then, just like that, the melody stopped and the wisp vanished.

"Where's it gone?" Zeb cried. "We need that memory to summon the Crackledawn dragon!"

Trampletusk nodded. "It is inside you now, Zeb. And if my ears do not deceive me, I think that's the rest of your crew calling."

Zeb and Oonie couldn't hear what Trampletusk could, but they hurried back, on and on beneath the trees toward the lagoon until, finally, they arrived to find Mrs. Fickletint hopping up and down on Dollop's head.

"You're back!" the chameleon cried. "And all in one piece, too!" She looked at Zeb. "So, did you do it? Did you get the very first sunrise in the Faraway?"

"Of course he got it!" tutted Dollop. "Just look at the boy! He's positively basking in inner peace!"

Zeb grinned.

"Then there's not a moment to lose!" Mrs. Fickletint called. "Because Dollop and I have conjured a piano!"

Chapter 18

After a hasty breakfast of bananas filled with chocomelts (chocolate balls with gooey middles, which seemed to grow in abundance on Rickety Gramps's sweet-tooth trees), Mrs. Fickletint and Dollop led the way up a winding path to a clifftop looking out over the sea.

The sun hadn't risen yet and the sky was a dusky pink, but in the dawn light Zeb could see the ocean stretching on and on—black like a pool of ink. There was no land in sight to the south of the island, but the Final Curtain was out there, somewhere. And watching over all of this, from the clifftop, was a piano.

It was nothing like the sleek instrument Zeb had played in the theater. This one was smaller, upright, and it was made out of twisted wood. Zeb took Oonie's proffered hand and led her, excitedly, toward it.

Oonie ran her fingers across the keys, then she stroked the chameleon on her shoulder. "How did you manage to conjure this?"

"After a brief spot of meditation"—Mrs. Fickletint arched her brow in Dollop's direction—"we realized we needed a DIY tree."

Dollop pointed proudly to the only tree on the clifftop. Zeb noticed that instead of leaves dangling from the branches, there were all sorts of practical objects like wrenches, nails, scissors, and duct tape.

"A Dream It Yourself tree," Dollop explained. "Once we'd plucked off the essential parts of a piano—a hammer, some string, and a few keys—we simply closed our eyes and dreamt up the real thing!"

Mrs. Fickletint nodded. "It didn't seem to matter that the keys were very obviously house keys and the hammer was meant for bashing nails—the magic seemed to know exactly how to iron all that out!"

"Well done!" Oonie cried as Zeb high-fived Dollop.

It was Trampletusk who moved the celebration on. "With

just one more night until the full moon rises, you need to press on and find the Ember Scroll." She looked at the piano. "Zeb must play—now—if you are to summon a Crackledawn dragon in time."

Zeb took a deep breath, then he sat down on the wooden stool. He looked up over the piano and across the sea. He'd never played for anyone else, and for a moment he felt painfully shy. What if he played the melody wrong and no dragon appeared? It wasn't as if any of the others had managed to summon one before. . . . But if he did nothing, Morg would win, and Fox and Oonie and Mrs. Fickletint, and even Dollop and Trampletusk, would be no more.

Zeb raised his hands to the keys, tried to ignore everyone watching him, and played. The melody came to him instantly, and it was one of the most beautiful tunes anyone on the clifftop had ever heard. Fluttering, higher notes at first, and then the melody grew into something big and full, something that seemed to hold in all the possibilities of a new day dawning.

Closing his eyes, Zeb imagined the music stirring the Faraway into life. He thought of mountains rising and trees appearing, of animals stretching and people awakening. The tune swelled, and the melody that rang out was so impossibly beautiful it brought a tear to Mrs. Fickletint's eye. Only Zeb knew, though, that there were parts of this tune that echoed the one his mother had sung to him as a child, and he found himself wondering whether it was possible that he had been born for this very moment. He opened his eyes, and as he played, he watched the pink sun inching above the horizon, streaking the sky with gold.

And then it came.

Just a speck on the horizon, at first. But moments later, it was a silhouette. A silhouette with wings and a great forked tail. Zeb squinted into the sun as the melody grew bigger and louder and the Stargold Wings around his neck danced. Then the silhouette swooped down to the sea, raking talons through the waves before soaring up into the sky again and letting out a cry. The noise rose with Zeb's melody until it seemed that the whole of Crackledawn rang out with the sound of hope.

Oonie gasped. Mrs. Fickletint gave in and wept. And Dollop and Trampletusk smiled.

"A dragon!" Zeb breathed. "We—we summoned a Crackledawn dragon!"

The dragon was more magnificent than anything Zeb could

have imagined. It was the color of emeralds and peacocks, and its wings beat like the sails of a mighty ship. It wheeled above them, its scales aglitter in the sunlight, and Zeb stopped playing then and watched, spellbound. This was the wildest magical beast in the Unmapped Kingdoms, and at *his* call, it had come to help them.

The dragon circled the clifftop before gliding down toward the group. Its webbed talons crunched onto the cliff in front of the piano, and as it folded in its wings and settled back on its hind legs, Zeb gaped. The dragon had looked large in the sky, but now that it was right there in front of them, it seemed outrageously big. Even its teeth, razor-sharp and snaggled, were the size of tusks, and large spikes ran from its neck to its tail. In a single swipe, this dragon could send them all tumbling off the clifftop.

It watched the group warily, its large amber eyes, flecked with sunlight and split down the middle with a black dash, resting on Zeb. It wrinkled its snout as it gave him a good long sniff, and Zeb didn't move a muscle because he knew from Dollop that dragons didn't follow rules, which meant this one could blast fire at any moment.

"You—you answered my call," he whispered, hardly daring to believe it.

The dragon dipped its head in reply, and Zeb found himself smiling. A creature this huge and wild and magnificent had come for someone as unimportant as him.

Trampletusk stepped forward. "It was good of you to answer our call, Snaggle. From the memories I have collected over the years, I have seen that you are one of Crackledawn's most loyal dragons."

Snaggle growled, but the growl had a softness to it. The kind of noise a bear might make when going about its business undisturbed. And somehow Zeb could tell from this growl that the dragon was male and that he was old enough to have a few wrinkles round his eyes but probably young enough to hurtle through the sky without complaining of a sore back or a stiff leg.

"Can—can you lead us to the Final Curtain?" Zeb asked. "And then on to the cave that has never been found?"

Snaggle considered this for a moment. Then he dipped his head again.

Oonie approached tentatively until she was level with Zeb on his piano stool. Then Zeb stood up too, and, hand in hand, both children edged closer and closer to the dragon.

They stood before Snaggle, swallowed by his shadow. He

smelled of pine trees and bonfires, and Zeb jumped as the dragon swung his head round so that it was level with him, Oonie, and Mrs. Fickletint. Then Snaggle blinked once, very slowly, before lowering his body down to the ground. Zeb felt a rush of panic at what lay ahead: a journey on the back of the wildest creature in the Unmapped Kingdoms!

He leaned toward Oonie. "I think it's best if you get on first. You're the captain, after all."

"If I didn't know you better," Oonie replied, "I'd think you were scared."

"I'm not scared. I'm just incredibly polite."

Before anyone could say anything else, Snaggle clamped his jaw on the scruff of Zeb's T-shirt, yanked him off the ground, then set him down again between the spikes on his back.

Zeb's eyes widened as he placed his hand on the dragon's scales. They were smooth to touch—and warm—like resting a palm on a rock that has soaked up the sun. But he could feel the dragon's wildness pulsing beneath its scales. Oonie settled herself between the spikes in front of Zeb, and Snaggle snorted, rising up on all fours and flexing his muscles.

"Takeoff already?" Mrs. Fickletint braced herself. "Oh, I *do* wish I'd packed us all some altitude tablets."

Dollop tossed a red-feather quill up to Zeb, who caught it and frowned.

"It's an omniscribble," the goblin explained. "There was a bush of them growing on the way up here, and given that these quills can write on any surface and never need ink, I thought it might come in handy for when you write a hopeful ending onto the Ember Scroll." He looked at Oonie. "Until then, I'll look after the *Kerfuffle* for you."

Zeb shoved the omniscribble into his pocket next to the Unopenable Purse. "Thank you, Dollop."

Then Trampletusk reached her trunk up to Zeb and wrapped it around his hand. "Remember to feed Snaggle from time to time. Dragons fly better when their bellies are full."

Zeb balked at Snaggle's enormous teeth. "What does he eat?"

"Some dragons eat badly behaved children," Trampletusk replied. "Some, but not nearly enough, eat prattleparrots. And some eat unbroken snow. But Snaggle?" The elephant's ears twitched. "I believe he eats secrets." She smiled. "Goodbye, Zeb. Go bring us back that phoenix."

Then, without warning or ceremony or any sort of safety briefing whatsoever, Snaggle launched into the air. Zeb's stomach lurched, his palms filled with sweat, and he felt absolutely sure that for the second time in Crackledawn he would topple off a dragon's back. But the Stargold Wings weren't yanking him about this time. They knew, as the crew did, that this dragon was worth holding on to.

"Thank you, Trampletusk!" Zeb yelled. "For giving us the memory we needed and—and for everything else, too!"

Trampletusk lifted her trunk and Dollop waved as Snaggle turned and soared out over the ocean. His enormous wings beat on either side of them and Oonie flung out her arms, threw back her head, and whooped.

"We're riding a dragon, Zeb!"

Mrs. Fickletint shrieked from her lap. "Oh, *do* be careful, Oonie! Why can't you just sit still like Zeb?!"

But Zeb, despite feeling wary about the drop to the sea, seemed to have completely lost control of his arms too. He watched, aghast, as they flung out on either side of him. Riding a Crackledawn dragon was like riding the wind, and although it *was* mildly petrifying, it was also the most exciting thing that had ever happened to him.

Chapter 19

Snaggle hurtled through the sky above an ocean that looked black as far as the crew could see. Morg's Midnights had been everywhere, it seemed, draining the kingdom's sunchatter and searching for the Stargold Wings. But there was no sign of Morg, and gradually the tropical waters returned.

Zeb gasped as a pod of silver whales surfaced beneath them. They were huge, as big as church spires, and the spray from their blowholes hung in the air in the shapes of castles, mountains, trees, and stars before melting into the sea. The whales disappeared from sight, then, without warning, Snaggle tucked in his wings and dived down toward the water. Zeb and Oonie clung on to the dragon's spikes as Snaggle shook his head and gills appeared behind his ears.

"Oh, heavens!" Mrs. Fickletint wailed. "We're going under!"

Snaggle plunged beneath the waves, and after a brief, and very spluttery, panic, Zeb realized that the watergums he, Oonie, and Mrs. Fickletint had swallowed back on the *Kerfuffle*, did actually work. They could breathe and talk and even laugh underwater!

It was like another kingdom down there. Zeb had seen various sea creatures drifting past the *Kerfuffle*'s portholes, but being in among them was altogether different. Within touching distance, there was a golden stingray, a cluster of multicolored seahorses, *and* a shoal of puffer fish swimming backward. But what hit Zeb most were the sounds. All the times Zeb had swum underwater back home, the noises around him had seemed muffled. Here, though, sounds were crystal clear, and they were *extraordinary*. The golden stingray was humming, the seahorses were giggling, and the puffer fish were whistling.

This underwater world was teeming with life and noise, and it made Zeb wonder what the rest of Crackledawn must have looked like before Morg's Midnights moved in. He thought of Fox Petty-Squabble and how she might have felt when she explored the glow-in-the-dark rainforest of Jungledrop as a child. Had she felt the same bone-tingling wonder that he did now? Maybe, if everything went to plan and he saw her again, he could ask her about the weird and wonderful magical creatures she'd discovered. Zeb hoped hard that the magic in the phoenix tear Fox had brought to Wildhorn could keep her, the Lofty Husks, and the Unmappers safe just a little while longer, until he and his crew found the Ember Scroll.

Snaggle swam fast beneath the sea. One push from his back legs and they raced past a striped octopus with hiccups. Another push and they glided alongside a jellyfish the size of a tractor wheel. The sunshine poured down from above, and a coral reef—every color of the rainbow—spread out below them, encrusted in parts by bright gold jewels that sang and sneezed and snored.

"Sunchatter," Oonie laughed. "Untouched by Morg's Midnights!"

Every now and again, Snaggle turned his head round to check on the crew. And Zeb got the feeling that it wasn't simply that the dragon was curious now. It felt like Snaggle was watching over them in case they came to harm. Zeb thought of Trampletusk's words about Snaggle's loyalty. Dragons didn't follow rules or bow down to anyone, but it seemed as if this dragon had made a pledge with himself to keep the crew safe. And Zeb felt the invisible shield around him grow a little bigger.

Snaggle swam on down, past a shoal of leopard-print fish and a striped eel that slunk out of a crack in the reef and yawned so loudly it made Zeb jump. But as Snaggle descended into deeper water, the sea creatures began to drift away, the ocean grew quieter, and the coral faded until the reef was nothing more than a stretch of gray. The crew tensed, and Snaggle picked up more speed, his eyes darting here and there as they made their way on.

Suddenly the water around them filled with the smell of rotten fish.

"Sea witches!" Mrs. Fickletint blurted from Oonie's lap.

Zeb clung on to Oonie's waist, because through the gloom he could now see a cluster of women with barnacled skin, seaweed hair, and webbed hands and feet reaching out grappling arms toward them. They opened their mouths wide, but in that second, Snaggle raised his wings to form a cocoon around the crew, and his wings blocked out everything: the reef, the sea witches, and any sound they might have made.

Oonie's voice was a whisper in the dark: "Sea witches roam

the ocean for drowned Sunraiders, and if their cry finds its way into your ear, you fall into an eternal sleep."

"Thank goodness for Snaggle," Mrs. Fickletint said.

Zeb shuddered at the thought of the sea witches, but tucked beneath Snaggle's wings, he felt safe from all the menace the ocean could throw at him. Snaggle kept swimming, and though Zeb knew he should probably let go of Oonie's waist, he couldn't quite bring himself to and she didn't seem to be shrugging him off. Perhaps this far down in the ocean, Oonie was just as out of her depth as he was.

After a while, Snaggle peeled back his wings, and the ocean, with all its sounds and creatures, returned. The reef and the sea witches were gone, and the water was altogether darker, and colder, now. Snaggle sniffed the crew, one by one, as if double-checking that they hadn't come to any harm, then, satisfied, he swam on.

Remembering that they hadn't yet fed Snaggle and there could be worse than sea witches ahead, Mrs. Fickletint whispered a few secrets into his ear to keep his belly full: "*Sometimes, when I'm in a filthy mood, I snack on chocolate before breakfast.*" "*Once, when my to-do list got completely out of control, I ate it in protest, and I didn't stop burping for a week.*" Snaggle swallowed, as if gobbling down the words in delight. Then he licked his lips and swam on.

Eventually, the seabed came into view, and Zeb glimpsed a patch of sunchatter on the ocean floor. But the jewels were glittering darkly. Any magic they had once possessed was now long gone.

"How do we know the Midnights who cursed this sunchatter have moved on?" he asked. "What if this part of the ocean is filled with fire krakens and ogre eels? There are no Bother-Ahead Beacons to help us now. . . ."

"We've got to trust Snaggle," Oonie replied.

And Zeb could have sworn he heard the dragon purr then, as if he had heard Oonie's words and was acknowledging that trust. Snaggle hastened on over the ocean floor, his ears cocked. He could sense something ahead that the others couldn't. Even Oonie couldn't seem to hear what the dragon could. Zeb kept listening until he came across a noise at the furthest point of his hearing—a low rumbling that seemed to be coming from somewhere ahead.

"Can you hear that?" he whispered to Oonie and Mrs. Fickletint.

"I'm afraid so," the chameleon replied.

"But I can't think what it could be." Oonie frowned. "It

sounds like an engine whirring, but that doesn't make any sense. All the boats in Crackledawn are sailboats, and I thought it was just Dollop living out past the Blackfangs."

The rumbling grew louder and louder until it became a roar—a deafening, thundering roar. Snaggle showed no sign of stopping.

"What about a little pause here?" Mrs. Fickletint shouted over the roar. "A brief chat about what's ahead?"

But Snaggle only swam faster, thrusting his back legs again and again through the water. And then, suddenly, the roar made sense. Up ahead, stretching the width of the ocean as far as they could see, was an underwater waterfall.

Zeb gasped. "It's like we've reached the end of the world!"

The waterfall was a wall of white water, blocking the way on, but Zeb saw a glimmer of silver behind the water, hinting that there was something beyond it. Perhaps this wasn't the end of the world but the start.

Oonie, it seemed, could sense something similar. She ran her tongue over her top lip, then shouted: "The sea here—it tastes of mysteries!"

Mrs. Fickletint buried herself in Oonie's tunic. "I am not in the mood for a mystery!"

"But Snaggle led us here," Oonie cried. "He knows what he's doing."

Zeb blinked, because the Stargold Wings were glowing through the pouch—fainter than when they'd shone down in the *Kerfuffle*'s cabin, but a light nonetheless, a sign that something promising lay ahead.

"What if this waterfall is what we've been trying to find all along?" Zeb shouted. "What if *this* is the Final Curtain?! The Stargold Wings said we'd have to sail on south and step beyond all we know is certain. Maybe this is as far south as the ocean goes and that's why the waterfall is called the Final Curtain—because it's the end of Crackledawn as you know it! Maybe the cave that has never been found lies beyond!"

"Hold on tight!" Mrs. Fickletint yelled as Snaggle hurtled on toward the waterfall, clearly not planning to stop.

Zeb clung to Oonie and buried his head in her hair as Snaggle charged into the waterfall. He waited for the pummel of the extra water hammering against his skin, but what he felt instead was a cool sort of tingling, like electricity rushing through his bones.

"We're passing through an enchantment!" Oonie cried.

Mrs. Fickletint yelped. "Let's hope it's a good one!"

They burst out the other side of the waterfall. The ocean was crystal clear again, and it was quiet. As if someone had turned the volume on the waterfall right down. There was no sign of a cave, but there was something else. Something large and carved from silver stone that rose up before them into dizzying heights.

"An underwater palace?" Zeb whispered in disbelief. "All the way out here?"

The building was a glistening jumble of turrets, domes, and spires, like something out of a fairy tale.

"Steepledoor is *real*," Oonie murmured.

"And there we were assuming that it just existed in Petronella Piffle's *Fabulous Fables*," Mrs. Fickletint said. "But it exists! An underwater palace, ruled by merglimmers, at the edge of the kingdom!"

"Merglimmers?" Zeb asked warily.

"Mermen and merwomen with mirror-skin tails," Mrs. Fickletint explained. "No one I've ever known has seen one, but the stories claim they were the first magical creatures conjured by the phoenix, so they've always been on our side."

Zeb frowned. "But we want a cave, not a palace ruled by merglimmers."

"He's right, Oonie," Mrs. Fickletint said. "Isn't he?"

Feeling the weight of the crew's expectations upon her, Oonie wriggled. "I'm finding it hard to work out *what* we want with you squeezing the life out of me like this, Zeb. . . ."

Zeb whipped his arms away.

"Petronella Piffle never mentioned the Final Curtain in her book," Oonie said. "What we just passed through was an enchantment, and enchantments change the whole time. It's a wall of water—a bit like a curtain—today, but when Petronella visited Steepledoor, the enchantment could have been anything: a reef, an underwater cave, a shipwreck. . . . So, this *could* still be the Final Curtain and the cave could still be here somewhere." She leaned forward to Snaggle's ears. "What do *you* think, Snaggle? Was the waterfall the Final Curtain, and are there merglimmers here who might know something about the cave that has never been found?"

The dragon dipped his head almost immediately, and the crew grinned then, and cheered. With Snaggle's help, they had reached their first milestone! They had found the Final Curtain with a night still to go before the full moon rose! And judging by the fact that the palace was still in one piece, it seemed they had made it here before Morg. Snaggle swam a little closer to

Steepledoor. Then he stalled before the steps leading up to the palace, his nostrils flared, his amber eyes roaming.

"What is it, Snaggle?" Mrs. Fickletint asked. "What can you see?"

The dragon backed away from the palace and skirted round the side of the building instead. The palace went on and on—a vast clutter of spiral towers and domes—but all around it there was nothing. Only crystal-clear water and golden sand.

"It feels too quiet . . . ," Zeb murmured. "Where are the merglimmers?"

"There are no sea creatures either," Mrs. Fickletint whispered. "Not so much as a single fish."

"*And* no sunchatter," Oonie added nervously.

Snaggle rounded yet another cluster of towers, and that's when the crew heard what the dragon's ears must have caught before: moaning. And it was growing louder as Snaggle swam on.

"There!" Zeb pointed to a lone tower set back from the palace. "I saw something moving behind the bars across the window at the top."

"Merglimmers?" Oonie asked.

Mrs. Fickletint followed Zeb's gaze. "Yes! It's them! I can

see their mirrored tails shining. But why are they locked up inside their own tower?"

The answer, which had been lying in wait beneath the silt, exploded out of the sand in front of them: a long, thick purple body—even bigger than Snaggle's—with flickering gills, row upon row of razor-sharp teeth and a single bloodshot eye in the center of its forehead.

"Ogre eel!" Mrs. Fickletint screamed.

"Turn back, Snaggle!" Zeb roared. "Turn back!"

But then something even more horrifying happened. Snaggle began bucking his legs and thrashing his tail until one by one the crew tumbled off his back onto the sand. The dragon took one last look at them, then he turned away and hastened back toward the Final Curtain.

Chapter 20

Zeb's mind was a blur. Snaggle was meant to be on *their* side. He had been leading the crew toward the Ember Scroll, keeping them safe all the way here. Had Trampletusk been wrong about where this Crackledawn dragon's loyalties lay? Had he always planned to lead the crew into the hands of Morg's Midnights?

The ogre eel rose before them, its forked tongues quivering. It was used to disloyalty in magical beasts; dark magic thrived on it. And now it had the Faraway boy and the Sunraider girl exactly where it wanted. Swinging its tail round toward them, it scooped them into its grasp and hissed.

Mrs. Fickletint was buried from sight in Oonie's pocket, but Oonie and Zeb screamed because the eel's tail was wrapped around them, tight as a noose. And though they kicked and screamed and Zeb tried to wriggle his hand into his pocket to grab the Unopenable Purse, the ogre eel held them fast. So there was nothing they could do when it slithered round the back of the palace and flung them down into a large stone pit.

Stretching out into the shadows, it was lined with seaweed and slime. Zeb grabbed Oonie's hand and made a wild attempt to pull himself up the seaweed, but the eel was already closing the mesh of stone bars down over the top of the pit.

"A dungeon," Zeb panted. "We're trapped in a dungeon!"

The eel used its tail to turn a large key in the padlock. Then, to Zeb's horror, the eel lifted this key up and dropped it into its mouth. Its gills flickered as it swallowed the crew's escape route whole, then it slithered away toward the tower that held the merglimmers.

"Where's—where's Snaggle?" Oonie asked as Mrs. Fickletint tiptoed out of her pocket. "Where did he go?"

Zeb rounded on her. "He's gone, Oonie! Don't you understand? He was never on our side! He was just bringing us here so that the ogre eel could hold us prisoner until Morg came back with the Ember Scroll to claim the Stargold Wings!"

Oonie shook her head. "But—"

Zeb clambered up the seaweed and gripped the bars. He

shook them again and again, but they wouldn't budge, so he slid back down into the slime and yanked out the Unopenable Purse instead. Heart hammering, he pulled on the zipper. But still the purse remained stubbornly shut. Zeb thought of the Stargold Wings suddenly, and he lifted them out of the pouch in the hope that they might work some magic to free them from the pit. But the wings neither moved nor glowed; whatever magic they still possessed they didn't share. Then the weight of Snaggle's betrayal hit home. Zeb had wept under the Memory Trees for the Crackledawn dragon. He had summoned him with the very first sunrise. He had trusted him. And look where that trust had got them.

"I made a mistake," Zeb muttered, stuffing the Stargold Wings back into the pouch. "You can never trust anyone, because no matter what happens, they always let you down."

Mrs. Fickletint hopped onto Zeb's leg. "Don't stop trusting just yet, Zeb. Now more than ever we need to pull together and—"

But Zeb was done with pulling together. He was hurt—ragingly hurt—because the Crackledawn dragon had made him feel safe for a while, and hopeful, too. But none of that mattered anymore.

He pushed the chameleon off his leg, and she tumbled into the seaweed. "The world is as ugly as I thought it was, and I do *not* need you telling me otherwise, Mrs. Fickletint." The anger rose inside Zeb. "If you hadn't decided to make us all a crew, none of this would've happened! I could've given the Stargold Wings a bit more time, then maybe they'd have yanked me off your wretched boat to find the Ember Scroll alone! But no no no, you had to get in there first and start banging on about trust!" He threw up his hands as his rage spilled out. "How on earth did I let myself get taken in by a silly little reptile?"

Mrs. Fickletint's face fell.

Oonie felt around for the chameleon and lifted her up into her lap, then she turned a furious face in Zeb's direction. "If you speak to Mrs. Fickletint like that again, I'll punch your lights out. And as for you speeding off to find the Ember Scroll alone . . ." Oonie snorted. "You wouldn't have lasted two minutes!"

"Says you?" Zeb snapped. "The captain who gets her crew trapped by a rotten dragon?"

Oonie's nostrils flared. "*You* were the one who summoned a rotten dragon! Maybe if I'd given it a shot, we'd have got a decent one!"

"Steady on, you two," Mrs. Fickletint warned.

Zeb ignored her. "I'd like to see *you* summon a dragon, Oonie! You're too scared to do anything without Mrs. Fickletint's help!"

Oonie made to swing a punch in Zeb's direction, but Mrs. Fickletint flew up into the air and wrapped herself around Oonie's fist. "Save the fighting for the ogre eel!"

But Oonie's temper was unraveling fast now. "At least I've got Mrs. Fickletint, Zeb. Who've you got, hmm? Not a single person cares about you here or back in the Faraway! You're a nobody, and we should never have let you into our crew, because now the voyage is over and the Unmapped Kingdoms and the Faraway are doomed!" She threw her head back. "I wish I'd never met you!"

The chameleon dropped to the ground, then she looked from Oonie to Zeb and shook her little head sadly.

Zeb was breathing fast, but there were tears in his eyes too. Because it was one thing assuming nobody in the world cared about him; it was another to hear that fear spoken aloud by someone else. He had started to believe in the trust trial as he helped Oonie through the forest on Rickety Gramps, after she'd held his hand under Trampletusk's ears, and when they whooped together on Snaggle's back. But here they were, back to square one.

What did that mean for Fox Petty-Squabble and her world-crossing promise? Oonie had just said it—he was a nobody. He slammed a fist into the seaweed. His great escape was scuppered for good all because he'd started trusting other people. He waited for the Outburst to come, but he realized he was beyond that now.

"I'm done with saving the world," he muttered. "The trust trial is well and truly over."

Chapter 21

Zeb sank back against the pit. Oonie huffed, then did the same. And they sat like that, angry and quiet, for a while.

Mrs. Fickletint, however, gathered herself up. "You two ought to be ashamed of yourselves." She put her paws on her hips. "Carrying on like that when we have a world to save and just one more night until the full moon rises!"

Zeb and Oonie continued to sulk in silence.

Mrs. Fickletint looked at Oonie. "One day, you will understand what it means to be a captain." She turned to Zeb. "And one day you will learn some manners. Until then, both of you need to listen in close because Morg could swoop by any time—and Mrs. Fickletint has got a backup plan."

Zeb pretended not to listen, and Oonie plucked idly at a piece of seaweed.

The chameleon went on nonetheless. "I stayed hidden in Oonie's pocket when the ogre eel grabbed us. Partly out of fear, I admit, but partly because I was thinking seventeen steps ahead, as women often do." She paused. "I'm small, so I can slip through these bars easily—more than easily, actually, because I've lost at least half a pound this week due to chronic stress. And I can change color, too. So, I can use my size to get out of this dungeon and my camouflage to sneak past the ogre eel—then I can creep inside the tower holding the merglimmers—"

Oonie raised her head then. "—and if you speak with the merglimmers, maybe you can free them, and they can tell us what they know about the cave that has never been found. . . ." A smile hovered over her lips. She was meant to be moping, but Mrs. Fickletint's plan was too good to ignore.

Zeb considered the chameleon's idea. It wasn't totally terrible, but he was far too hurt to start hoping in a future all over again. "What if the ogre eel sees you?" he asked glumly. "What if Morg arrives before you manage to speak with the merglimmers?"

"That, dear Zeb, would be most unfortunate indeed. But *what ifs* can go two ways." Mrs. Fickletint drew herself up as tall as she could go, which wasn't very tall at all. "What if the ogre eel doesn't see me and I reach the tower? What if Morg doesn't come back and the merglimmers tell me where the cave is? What if we find the Ember Scroll and save the world?"

"What if it's not a world worth saving?" Zeb muttered.

Mrs. Fickletint rolled her eyes. "It's getting rather exhausting dealing with such low levels of enthusiasm, Zeb. If you can't say anything positive at all, please bury yourself in the seaweed and let Oonie and me get on with things."

Zeb watched as Oonie took a deep breath, as if pushing all thoughts of the fight to one side for a moment. Then she gave Mrs. Fickletint a little kiss before feeling her way up the seaweed and setting the chameleon down by the bars.

"Good luck," Oonie whispered. "You're the bravest chameleon I know."

Mrs. Fickletint eyed the ogre eel skulking behind the tower in the distance. Then she squeezed herself between the bars, changed her scales to the color of sand, and raced off toward the merglimmers.

Zeb sat in the pit, brooding, while Oonie waited, crouched

in the seaweed by the bars. For a while Zeb said nothing, then curiosity got the better of him, and he clambered up the side of the pit to look out beside Oonie.

It was hard to spot Mrs. Fickletint at first. But when Zeb screwed up his eyes and really looked, he could just make out a sand-colored shape scuttling over the ocean floor toward the tower of merglimmers. Then Mrs. Fickletint stopped suddenly and looked back toward the palace.

"Uh-oh," Zeb mumbled.

Oonie flinched. "What's happened?"

"She's not moving," Zeb found himself saying, even though he'd been thinking, just moments before, that he would make a pact with himself never to speak to Oonie ever again. "Mrs. Fickletint's stopped right out in the open, even though the ogre eel is still lounging around behind the tower. Why doesn't she press on while she's got the chance?"

Then Zeb gasped. Because now Mrs. Fickletint's camouflage was fading and she was materializing, in all her purple glory. And before Oonie could ask for an update, Mrs. Fickletint's cross little voice shouted: "COME AND GET ME, YOU GREAT BIG BULLY!"

A look of horror washed over Zeb's and Oonie's faces.

"What on earth is she doing?!" Zeb spluttered. "This wasn't part of her backup plan!"

The ogre eel shot out from behind the tower and went straight for Mrs. Fickletint, who screamed and began running for her life back toward the dungeon.

Oonie seized the bars. "What's going on, Zeb?"

Zeb was so glued to the ogre eel charging after Mrs. Fickletint that he didn't see the large, scaled shape dart out from the side of the palace and race toward the tower. Seconds later, though, there was an almighty crash.

"The tower full of merglimmers!" Zeb cried. "It's—it's falling down!"

He watched, openmouthed, as thousands of stones crumbled to the ground. There were cheers next, and a wild hiss from the ogre eel as it spun back round toward the tower to try and contain the merglimmers. But hundreds of armored mermen and merwomen were now swarming around it. And then—Zeb's heart skipped a beat—bursting out of the rubble came something huge and scaled. Something Zeb had thought was long gone . . .

"IT'S—IT'S SNAGGLE!" he yelled, clutching Oonie's arm, all thoughts of anger suddenly forgotten. "HE'S COME

BACK! And—and"—Zeb watched as the Crackledawn dragon swooped down and flicked the little chameleon onto his back—"he's rescuing Mrs. Fickletint!"

Snaggle sped on toward the dungeon with Mrs. Fickletint on his back.

"Never underestimate the backup plan!" the chameleon yelled as merglimmer after merglimmer set upon the eel, and it fell, with a ground-juddering thump one last time, onto the sand.

Snaggle screeched to a halt outside the pit, and Mrs. Fickletint slid off his back and rushed into Oonie's arms.

"Oh, Mrs. Fickletint!" Oonie laughed. "You're a wonder!"

"There I was, nipping over the sand like a demon," the chameleon panted, "when I glanced back and saw Snaggle hiding in the shadows of the palace. I could tell from the way he was crouching there, all ready to pounce, that he was waiting for a chance to free the merglimmers. But he couldn't have done that with us on his back, because even a Crackledawn dragon can't fight an ogre, protect a crew, and bring down a stone tower all at the same time!"

Snaggle looked away then, embarrassed by the attention. But his ears were pricked, and every now and again he glanced back at the crew as if he understood that he was a part of something now, even though he was a dragon, and dragons usually kept to themselves.

Mrs. Fickletint chattered on. "I thought fast when I saw Snaggle hiding, and I put my life on the line! And while I was being incredibly heroic, and the ogre eel was getting incredibly cross, Snaggle swam full tilt at the tower!"

Zeb stared from Mrs. Fickletint to the dragon in disbelief. But before he could try and make sense of things, Snaggle bent his head down to the bars in front of Zeb. He watched the boy carefully, twisting his head this way and that. Wrinkling his nose, he poked his snout through the bars and let it rest against Zeb's cheek. For a few seconds, Zeb stayed absolutely still, and then something surged inside him and before he could stop himself, he stretched his hands through the bars and wrapped them around the dragon's neck.

"I—I thought you'd left us," Zeb whispered. "I thought you weren't coming back."

The dragon purred—a sound that rumbled deep inside Zeb's ear. Then he blew a string of bubbles from his nostrils, as if to suggest the very idea of him not returning was ridiculous. He was wild to the core, this dragon, but there was a warmth about him too, a kindness buried behind the teeth and talons.

Zeb held on to him with eyes pressed shut. "You're sticking around, aren't you?"

Snaggle dipped his head, and as Zeb drew back from the Crackledawn dragon and looked into his amber eyes, he realized that he had been wrong to give up on trust. He thought of the Unopenable Purse in his pocket and a faith in Fox flickered into life again. And for the first time since meeting Morg, he allowed himself to imagine what his life in the Faraway might look like if they went back there together. He didn't know *how* Fox would find him, or what their future might look like, but he knew now that he had to keep on hoping. There was no going back this time. If Crackledawn's creatures were working together to save their world and his, he needed to stay in this fight too. He needed to bring a phoenix back to the Unmapped Kingdoms.

Zeb placed his palm on the dragon's snout. "Thank you for coming back, Snaggle."

He turned to look at Oonie. There were things he wanted to say. But Oonie was trying to speak too.

"I'm sorry, Zeb," she said quietly. "I never should've

said those things about you. You're not a nobody. You're—you're . . ."

Her words trailed off, but Mrs. Fickletint urged her on.

Oonie swallowed. ". . . You're my friend."

Zeb felt so happy in that moment, he thought his heart might burst. "I was wrong about something, too," he said. "I told you that you were too scared to do anything without Mrs. Fickletint's help. But you just rebuilt a crew. All on your own." Zeb smiled. "And that's not bad, captain."

Oonie was smiling, too, now. And then they were laughing together, just like they had done when they first rode on Snaggle. But it was the hug that Zeb knew he would remember most that day. He and Oonie holding on to each other so tightly, not even an ogre eel could pry them apart.

"Oh, we're a crew again!" the chameleon cried, squashed merrily in between Oonie and Zeb. "I am so deeply proud of both of you! It is *such* a weight off my mind knowing you don't want to throttle each other anymore!"

As they drew apart, laughing, even Snaggle's teeth bunched into a smile. Then they watched as a single merglimmer broke away from the throng behind, who were building the fallen tower back up again, and swam up close to the pit. On the top half, she wore armor: a sparkling breastplate and a silver helmet over her long, blue hair. But her tail was covered in mirrored scales, and she might have looked serene had she not been rummaging frantically through her handbag.

"Where *have* the spare dungeon keys got to?" she muttered, drawing out a hairbrush, a pack of tissues, and four leather-bound books. "So, that's where *The Complete Works of Monotonous Snore* is. Honestly," she tutted, giving her handbag a short, sharp shake, "this guzzlebag has a lot to answer for. . . ."

She looked down through the bars at Zeb, Oonie, and Mrs. Fickletint. "I'm Perpetual Faff, by the way. The gatekeeper here at Steepledoor. And I am *so* sorry about the shoddy welcome. No one at the Final Curtain to greet you after you successfully passed through the barrier enchantment, then an altercation with an ogre eel who stormed the palace last night and locked everyone up!" She looked at Zeb a little closer and her eyes widened. "A boy from the Faraway. Now, that *is* interesting. . . ." This was followed by more rummaging in the guzzlebag until, thoroughly flustered now, Perpetual Faff drew out a pocket mirror and a pair of reading glasses. "Oh, where are the spare set of keys?!"

Mrs. Fickletint laid a paw on her arm. "Breathe, dear. I had a bottomless handbag once, and it was very nearly the undoing of me."

Perpetual Faff took a deep breath and then she did, fortunately, bring out the key she was looking for. She slotted it into the padlock and it clicked open. Then Snaggle hauled the grate away and Zeb, Oonie, and Mrs. Fickletint clambered out.

"Thank you," Oonie said. "But now we need your help again. Morg is back in Crackledawn, and as you can see, her Midnights are everywhere. But Zeb here has the Stargold Wings, and they gave us a message to find the Ember Scroll, which—"

Perpetual Faff cut in. "Is that right, Faraway boy? Are you really in possession of the Stargold Wings?"

Zeb opened the pouch around his neck, and under the merglimmer's gaze, the Stargold Wings gave a weak shimmer.

Perpetual Faff smiled. "We merglimmers have been waiting for you for a long time, Zeb. We swore to the very first phoenix that when the Faraway boy came with the Stargold Wings, we would show him the way on to the Ember Scroll."

Zeb frowned. "But how could the very first phoenix know I would end up here? I didn't even know about the Unmapped Kingdoms until a few days ago!"

"When it comes to choosing someone to save the world," Perpetual Faff replied, "magic likes to think ahead."

Zeb swayed. The phoenix magic really *had* known about him all along! And it had singled him out to save the world!

Oonie grinned. "Told you you're not a nobody."

Mrs. Fickletint looked at Perpetual Faff. "You said you could show us the way on," she said eagerly. "The Stargold Wings told us to sail to the Final Curtain, then we'd find the Ember Scroll inside a cave that has never been found. And if Morg hasn't been here yet, then we still have a chance of finding the scroll before her and before tomorrow's full moon!"

Perpetual Faff shook her head. "I'm afraid there is more than one Final Curtain in Crackledawn."

Mrs. Fickletint flashed yellow, then blue, then a rather sickly color of green. "I'm not sure I understand."

The merglimmer looked at the group. "I think you'd better come inside while I explain. And be quick about it." Perpetual Faff began a frantic fumble through her guzzlebag. "I just need to find the right key."

Chapter 22

After much flapping, Perpetual Faff drew out the strangest key Zeb had ever seen. The handle was studded with rubies, and the key itself was as long as a walking stick. Seconds later, the merglimmer was ushering the group onto the back of their dragon and racing round to the front of the palace. Zeb, Oonie, and Mrs. Fickletint rode Snaggle through an arch, into a huge marble hallway. There was no furniture inside. And no merglimmers, either; they were still busy rebuilding the tower. The only thing inside this room, positioned at the top of a small flight of marble stairs, was a very large door. Large enough that even Snaggle could fit through it without having to stoop. It was domed in shape, and it had been carved from silver stone.

Snaggle swam around the door, sniffing this way and that, as he took it in.

"But—but there's nothing on the other side," Zeb stammered. "The door doesn't *go* anywhere . . ."

Perpetual Faff hung back at the foot of the stairs. "When magic's involved, there's always *something* of note behind a closed door." She looked from one member of the crew to the next. "No one from Crackledawn has ever been through this door. No Unmapper. No Lofty Husk. No magical beast. Even I have never been beyond it—and that's not simply because I can't keep track of my keys. We merglimmers were ordered by the very first phoenix to keep it locked until the day the boy from the Faraway came, holding the Stargold Wings." She looked at Zeb. "And now here you are."

Mrs. Fickletint frowned. "But you said there was more than one Final Curtain in Crackledawn. Does that mean there are more doors like this one?"

Perpetual Faff nodded. "According to the very first phoenix, there are three. And the other two are portals, each one guarded by an enchantment called a Final Curtain, which was conjured by the very first phoenix."

Zeb bit his lip. "Then this door here could be a portal too?"

"Perhaps," the merglimmer said. "The portal in the north of the kingdom belongs to the dragons. Rumblestar's dragons use it to carry the marvels here for the sun scrolls, and Crackledawn's dragons use it to take the sun scrolls on to the Faraway. The other portal belonged to the phoenixes. It was said they simply needed to stand before it and the portal would sense where they wanted to go and open up a way there." Perpetual Faff's face darkened. "Morg will know where that second portal is because she used it thousands of years ago to enter Crackledawn from Everdark."

Oonie hung her head. "Morg heard Zeb saying we were off to the Final Curtain, and she said she'd get there first. But if she wasn't heading for this door, she must have been speeding off to the portal belonging to the phoenixes. And if she just had to stand in front of it and will on the cave that has never been found for it to appear, she could be miles ahead of us!"

Perpetual Faff raised a blue eyebrow. "She might have reached the phoenix portal. And she might have sent her Midnights to guard the other two doors in case you lot showed up. But you are standing before a third door, built at the beginning of time just for Zeb. For this very moment." She took a deep breath. "It's time to find out what's on the other side."

Zeb slipped down from Snaggle's back, then Oonie and Mrs. Fickletint followed.

"We'll go through together," Oonie said. "That way if something dreadful happens, me and Mrs. Fickletint will be right there beside you."

"And Snaggle will be right behind us?" Zeb asked, turning to the dragon.

Snaggle nodded firmly.

Zeb found himself squeezing Oonie's hand then, and had they not been so pressed for time, he wondered whether he might have even managed another hug.

Zeb took the key from Perpetual Faff. It was heavy, but he hauled it up the stairs and, with a little help from Snaggle, heaved it into the keyhole. Placing both hands on the key, he turned it, and the door creaked open to reveal what was beyond.

Snowflakes.

They were utterly unlike the ones Zeb had seen falling in the Faraway. These were black. Small, glittering crystals that drifted down from the sky like stencils cut out of the night. Zeb wondered, for a moment, whether it *was* night beyond this door and that's why the snowflakes looked dark. But when he peered through them, he saw a sun glowing behind the clouds and a valley boxed in by mountains covered in thick, black snow.

Zeb blinked. He could feel water all around him on this side of the door, but beyond the threshold it was like another world entirely. The mountains ran down to a sprawling forest, split through the middle by a frozen river. The ice there was black, too, as were the icicles hanging from the branches of the trees and the frost beneath them. Zeb inched backward as Mrs. Fickletint relayed the scene to Oonie. Something about this didn't feel right.

The water grew colder suddenly, and, as if the doorway somehow had breath of its own, a flurry of black snowflakes fluttered over the threshold and Steepledoor's hallway emptied of water.

Oonie turned her face up to the snowflakes. "The cold—it feels like how I imagined standing in Silvercrag might feel like, where the snow scrolls are made for the Faraway. And if this *is* somehow Silvercrag, then the message in the Stargold Wings makes sense! *Step beyond all you know is certain.* We were never searching for a cave in Crackledawn. It was in Silvercrag all along. . . ." She frowned. "Only this doesn't feel like the kingdom I learned about on Wildhorn where the very wildest magic spins in every snowflake."

Perpetual Faff nodded. "This is Silvercrag all right. Now that the door has been opened, I can tell we're on the fringe of another Unmapped Kingdom. But for the snow and ice to be black? That doesn't sound right at all. . . ." She swallowed. "That sounds like Morg used the phoenix portal to break into Silvercrag and is now unleashing her magic there."

Zeb felt sick with worry at the thought of the harpy brewing curses on the other side of this door. Then he felt something else: a familiar tingling over his skin, just like he had when passing through the Final Curtain. An enchantment was stirring, and it seemed to be happening inside his pocket. He rummaged around in it, and when his hand met with the Unopenable Purse, he realized it was wriggling—as if something within the purse was trying to get out. Zeb pulled the purse into the open just as the little silver zipper slid back of its own accord and all sorts of things that couldn't possibly have fit inside came spilling out.

Brown fur jackets and trousers, together with sealskin boots and thick woolen mittens that looked just the right size for him and Oonie. Miniature knitted leg-warmers and a tiny bobble hat came next, which Mrs. Fickletint beamed at, followed by flasks of water, food parcels, and a bag labeled SECRETS for Snaggle. Zeb marveled at it all. Fox couldn't have known they'd end up in Silvercrag, but she'd poured all her hopes for him into the Unopenable Purse, and the phoenix magic inside it had delivered. Just as marvelous, though, was the knowledge that someone was watching out for him, even if Fox was miles and miles away.

The purse spat out three final objects and when Zeb saw what they were, he frowned. "A ruler? A whistle? And a tiny pair of scissors? We're trying to save the world, not have an afternoon of arts and crafts!"

Oonie reached out, and Zeb placed the items, one by one, in her hands. She shook her head. "I heard about a few magical objects in the lessons I went to, but I can't say I ever heard about these things being magical. Any ideas, Mrs. Fickletint?"

"No," said the chameleon. "I can imagine very few scenarios in which whipping out a ruler would help us against Morg. . . ."

Even Snaggle, who sniffed each item in turn, withdrew with a crumpled brow.

"And yet an Unopenable Purse is powered by phoenix magic," Perpetual Faff said, "and that magic is on your side, so you've got to hope the objects will make sense soon enough." She turned to Zeb. "Zip them into the purse, even if the ruler seems completely the wrong size—I, of all people, know how much space there is inside magical bags." She stroked her guzzlebag fondly. "Keep that purse safe, Zeb. Now it's unlocked, you can open it any time though it won't be conjuring up any more objects." The merglimmer looked at Oonie and then she took a deep breath. "Unmappers cannot travel between kingdoms, but as gatekeeper here, I give you my permission to accompany Zeb on into Silvercrag and save the world from Morg."

Oonie smiled, clearly half-excited, half-afraid by what might lie ahead. The crew thanked Perpetual Faff for her help and gobbled down half of the food parcels (hard-boiled eggs, which were purple, and something that looked like a sausage roll but tasted much nicer). Oonie stored the rest for later in the enormous pocket of her fur jacket, along with a flask of water, while Snaggle scoffed the secrets. And as the merglimmer began shaking out the contents of her guzzlebag in an attempt to find a handkerchief to wave them off, Zeb and Oonie changed into their furs and Mrs. Fickletint tugged on her leg warmers and bobble hat.

Zeb placed a foot on the first step leading up to the door.

Oonie joined him, as did Mrs. Fickletint on her shoulder, then Snaggle nudged them forward.

Zeb paused at the threshold. "What if we can't go back again? We might step across into Silvercrag and get stuck there—with Morg." He turned to Oonie. "What if you and Mrs. Fickletint never find your way back to Wildhorn? And I never find Fox Petty-Squabble?"

Oonie was hesitating now too. "It's—it's not going to be easy, making my way through snow and ice and a whole kingdom's worth of unfamiliar creatures and places."

From Oonie's pocket, Mrs. Fickletint winced. "No, it's not going to be easy at all."

But there was one member of the crew who didn't seem afraid. Snaggle breathed in the icy air, and everything from the spikes lining his back to his talons and forked tail suddenly glittered with frost. And it was white frost, the way it was meant to look. As if the old Silvercrag knew that hope was coming. Zeb gazed at the silver-white icicles now hanging from Snaggle's chin. He looked magnificent. He also looked ready—for winter and for Morg.

And spurred on by their Crackledawn dragon, the crew of the *Kerfuffle* took a deep breath and stepped into the swirling snow.

Chapter 23

All trace of Steepledoor disappeared the moment the crew stepped through the portal. They were standing on a hill covered in black snow. Ahead of them lay the valley, with the forest and the river running through it, while behind them plains of dark snow stretched for miles until the land built up once again into mountains, icicled trees, and frozen waterfalls. Through the falling snow and clouds, Zeb could still see the hazy glow of an afternoon sun. But it was as quiet as midnight.

"It's like looking at a photograph," he said. "Nothing's moving. Shouldn't there be Unmappers in Silvercrag? Or at very least some magical beasts or Lofty Husks?"

Oonie chewed her lip. "I read a book a few months ago called *Silvercrag: A Complete History* by Wilbur Shivermitten, and it said the Lofty Husks here are snow eagles and the Unmappers are Scavengers and Storytellers who live in igloos on the ice plains near the Impossible Peaks, mountains so high no one has ever scaled them." She paused. "But it doesn't sound like there's anyone nearby. And you're all *sure* you can't see anyone either?"

"I'm afraid not," Mrs. Fickletint said. "Maybe it's got something to do with the black snow. If it's cursed, then perhaps Silvercrag's inhabitants are hiding because it's dangerous."

"But *we're* all right," Zeb replied as a black snowflake fell into his palm.

"Maybe Morg's curse only works on Silvercrag's inhabitants," the chameleon replied. "We're free of her dark magic, for now. . . ."

Zeb shifted uneasily. "But what if the Unmappers and Lofty Husks here aren't hiding? We might be too late and they're already dead."

"We can't think like that," Oonie said. "The Unmappers here are strong and brave. Their Scavengers travel in chariots pulled by frost giants, and they roam the ice looking for magical crystals to help write their snow stories." She clenched her jaw. "We *have* to believe we still have a chance of finding the Ember Scroll."

Snaggle turned a full circle, his nose to the ground, nostrils twitching. Looking up at the valley ahead of them, he grunted. Somehow, in this wintry wilderness, it was clear that the dragon knew where the Ember Scroll was.

"Right," Mrs. Fickletint said, adjusting her leg warmers. "I think we should have a quick debrief before we set off. We could establish a few onboard rules for riding Snaggle perhaps—Zeb, for one, could work on his posture. And we could come up with some key battle tactics in case we're ambushed by Morg."

"We don't have time for all that, Mrs. Fickletint," Zeb said. "That's an afternoon sun up there. We've only got until the full moon rises tomorrow to stop Morg!"

Snaggle, who wasn't one for debriefs or rules anyway, flipped the chameleon onto his back. Mrs. Fickletint straightened her hat and began barking orders to Zeb as he helped Oonie up onto the dragon. Zeb settled himself in front of Oonie this time, because he got the impression Crackledawn dragons did not like being mothered by overprotective chameleons. And since that moment Snaggle poked his head through the dungeon bars, Zeb had felt a strange kind of bond grow between them. On the outside, he and the Crackledawn dragon were very different, but both of them had faced the world alone, until now. Both of them were learning to trust.

Snaggle launched into the air, and the icy wind gusted through Zeb's lungs as they soared over the valley. At first, Snaggle's talons knocked clumps of snow from the treetops, then they were higher than the trees, soaring on through the valley toward the Ember Scroll.

Zeb glanced down at the forest below. The trees were bigger and taller than those back home, and the branches here looked different too. They looked more like frozen feathers than boughs covered in leaves.

Mrs. Fickletint followed Zeb's gaze. "I believe they're Flyaway Trees. Or they were before they got coated in cursed snow."

"According to Wilbur Shivermitten, if you cut down a feather from one of those trees you can fly on it, like a broomstick, for a full ten minutes." Oonie's face fell. "But Morg will have stolen their magic by now."

Mrs. Fickletint pointed to a huge humpbacked bridge, made entirely of black icicles, arching over the frozen river. "That looks like the famous Brittle Bridge!"

It was clear that Oonie had an image of the bridge locked

inside her mind from the stories she had read. "If you'd grabbed an icicle from the Brittle Bridge before Morg came, you'd have been able to run faster than the wind until it melted!"

Zeb felt Snaggle tense suddenly. He scanned the valley until he found what the dragon had seen. Several upturned chariots beside a frozen lake and the body of something enormous sprawled out close by. It was wearing armor carved from frost, and it had a long white beard tied in thirteen knots.

"A frost giant!" Mrs. Fickletint breathed. "Killed by Morg, no doubt."

"Oh, the poor creature," Oonie murmured.

Snaggle growled as he flew on past, then he beat his wings faster still until they burst out of the valley, leaving the hills and the forest behind. In front of them stretched glittering black ice plains, broken only by a frozen river. But Snaggle didn't slow. He flew on and on, over iced lakes that Oonie claimed would grant you invisibility for a day if you were brave enough to cross them. And they soared above dozens of caves that Zeb guessed were full of the magical crystals Scavengers collected, if Morg's curse hadn't already snuffed them out and drained their magic. . . .

Eventually, igloos appeared. Hundreds of them, all shapes

and sizes, cluttered into some sort of camp around the river. Some were small, no bigger than a garden shed, while others were so large they had room for towers and multiple chimneys. Some were triangular in shape with staircases leading out of the roof up to small turrets, while others still were built on stilts and had elaborate flumes winding down to the river. But each one shone black like a polished shadow.

Many of the igloos had been flattened, the firepits dotted about the place had been knocked over, and strewn on the ground like discarded puppets were men and women dressed in furs, giants clad in glinting armor, and huge birds with snow-white feathers.

Mrs. Fickletint clutched Oonie's arm. "Silvercrag's Unmappers, its frost giants, *and* its Lofty Husks—*dead*! What has Morg done here? Has she wiped out a whole kingdom in her quest to find the Ember Scroll?"

Snaggle narrowed his eyes, then swooped down to get a better view, and as the crew raced over the camp, Zeb noticed the enormous chests of the frost giants were still rising and falling.

"Wait—they're alive!" he cried. "I can see the frost giants breathing!"

Snaggle circled the igloos, and Mrs. Fickletint breathed a

sigh of relief. "It's the same with the Unmappers and Lofty Husks! They're not dead—they're *asleep*!"

"A cursed sleep," Oonie murmured. "Maybe that's what this snow does to Silvercrag's inhabitants. It stops them in their tracks—"

"—and opens up the way for Morg to find the Ember Scroll," Zeb finished.

"We might be able to break this curse if we can find the Ember Scroll first," Mrs. Fickletint said. "But that doesn't change the fact that there will be no snow scrolls for the Faraway now that the Scavengers and Storytellers are asleep. Your snowy lands were already melting, Zeb, but without snow from Silvercrag, they will vanish in days!"

Zeb tried to imagine a Faraway without snow. The Arctic and the Antarctic would disappear. As would the polar bears, beluga whales, and narwhals. And once an animal was extinct, there was no going back.

He leaned forward over Snaggle's neck. "How long until the cave that has never been found? Are we close yet?"

Snaggle snorted and a plume of mist shot out from his nostrils, and Zeb knew that there was a long way to go yet. But the dragon sped on, leaving the camp behind, as more foothills began to spread out below them. They started small enough, just rolling hills, black on black. And then they began to build into something bigger, mountains with crags and peaks and jutting ledges. Zeb bent his neck back to see how far up they went and almost toppled off Snaggle's back. The mountains rose to such dizzying heights they were lost, eventually, in the clouds.

"The Impossible Peaks," he murmured.

Mrs. Fickletint paled. "The Unmappers haven't scaled them, because apparently nothing, let alone magical snow crystals, can survive up there, so there's little point trying. And I heard even Silvercrag's dragons have never made the summit because it's a part of the kingdom that's just too wild to conquer."

"Morg must have scaled them," Oonie said quietly.

Mrs. Fickletint inhaled sharply. "I don't think she can have gone over these mountains, because if you look closely at that ledge there"—she pointed—"chunks of rock have crumbled away, and there are black feathers jammed into the cracks." She shivered. "Morg knows how to dig through rock better than anyone—that's how she escaped the never-ending well in Jungledrop and found her way to Hollowbone—and I think she might have conjured a tunnel *through* the Impossible Peaks."

Zeb scanned the mountain face. "If there *was* a tunnel, it's closed up now."

"And from the way Snaggle is flying," Oonie said, "it doesn't feel like he's going to hang around to try and open it back up." She took a deep breath. "Hold on, crew: Our Crackledawn dragon's heading for the summit."

Snaggle climbed up into the sky, circle upon circle as he searched for a way over the mountains. But they kept rising. An impassable face of rock.

"Surely they'll end soon?" Zeb cried.

But Snaggle beat on, heaving himself and the crew higher and higher into the sky. They were so far up now, Mrs. Fickletint had covered her eyes, and even Oonie was gripping Snaggle so tight her mittens were shaking. The air was thinning the higher they went, and, before long, the crew found themselves gasping for breath. Even Snaggle seemed to be struggling, each puff a labored grunt, and icicles hung from his lashes. The dragon slowed a fraction, and Zeb felt a knot of panic twist inside him. If Snaggle backed down now, they'd never save the world. Going over the Impossible Peaks was the only option, no matter how scared it made Zeb feel. He bit his lip as Snaggle struggled on and then he remembered how Mrs. Fickletint had fed the dragon after the sea witches to keep his energy up. Maybe a secret would give Snaggle just a little more strength to reach the summit.

Zeb bent forward over Snaggle's neck. "All my life I've felt lonely," he whispered, "but when I'm with you and my crew, I feel like"—he paused before letting the last part of his secret out—"like I'm a part of something at last."

The snow fell harder, but the dragon turned then, and his wide amber eyes blinked slowly, as if he understood a little about what it meant to feel alone. Then he turned back to the sky, and, fueled by the strength of Zeb's secret, he pushed up on through the snow.

The Impossible Peaks showed no sign of coming to an end. But Snaggle was showing no sign of backing down. Mrs. Fickletint, though, had begun to cough. A small, spluttery cough that squeezed her breath into short, sharp gasps.

"Too high," the chameleon squeaked from Oonie's pocket. "Too much for Mrs. Fickletint now."

"Don't you go talking like that, Mrs. Fickletint!" Oonie said through chattering teeth. "We're going to reach the summit soon. You'll see!"

Zeb risked a look behind him. Mrs. Fickletint was blue and shaking, and at the sight of her like that, a lump slid into his throat. The chameleon was bossy and she fussed over everyone far too much, but she was what kept this crew together.

"Don't give up, Mrs. Fickletint!" Zeb cried. "Stay with us! Snaggle will keep you safe!"

But the higher they rose, the weaker Mrs. Fickletint's breathing became. Oonie's furs were crusted with black ice now, Zeb could no longer feel his toes, and even though Snaggle was trying to roar fire so that Mrs. Fickletint might be warmed, all that came out were clouds of glittering ice. And then the snow closed in around them and Zeb could no longer see which way was up or down.

"We should turn back!" he cried. "We're not going to make it after all, and Mrs. Fickletint is on her last legs!"

Oonie lifted the little chameleon up to her chest and tucked her into her coat, where it was warmer. But she didn't order Snaggle to fly down to safety. She was the captain of this crew and knew what was at stake if they gave up now. "We have to keep going!" she shouted into the blizzard. "We're the only ones left who can beat Morg!"

Snaggle thrust his wings on up through the snow, even though Mrs. Fickletint's eyes were closed now and Zeb's head was growing dizzy with lack of air. On and on he went, through the driving snow and past the point the fiercest Silvercrag dragon had ever dared to go. The blizzard raged, pinning Snaggle back, but he forced his way on, his wings juddering against the wind and snow.

And then, when Zeb felt sure that his lungs couldn't possibly take any more, the Crackledawn dragon burst out of the blizzard, and the crew realized that he had done something remarkable. They were above the clouds now, and not only was it no longer snowing, but the mountain peaks below them were glittering white instead of black. The snow here was whiter than paper, whiter than bedsheets, whiter even than the moon. They must have risen up above Morg's curse! Snaggle had achieved what nobody else in the kingdom had been able to: He had conquered the Impossible Peaks.

Chapter 24

"You did it!" Zeb gasped in astonishment. "You actually did it!"

But Snaggle wasn't celebrating. He was racing over the first ridge, because the peaks dropped away a little after that—a sea of summits piercing the clouds all the way on to the setting sun—he *had* to get lower if Mrs. Fickletint was to stand a chance.

The air began to grow thicker, and as soon as Zeb was able to breathe more easily, he twisted his whole body round until he was facing Oonie. "Is she okay?"

Only the chameleon's head showed, poking up out of Oonie's coat, and Zeb could see that Mrs. Fickletint's eyes were closed and her scales were still blue.

"Tell me she's going to be okay!" Zeb panted.

But Oonie said nothing. She was bent over Mrs. Fickletint, whispering the chameleon's name over and over again. "Her heartbeat's so slow and faint—it's almost not there at all!"

Zeb felt his own heart quicken. Surely this wasn't the end for Mrs. Fickletint? Surely she was going to wake up and start bossing them about again? Snaggle tried again to breathe fire, but only ice appeared. He swung his head round and his eyes—usually so full of fight—looked tired and sad. And it was only then that Zeb realized all that the little chameleon had come to mean to him.

"Don't—don't leave us, Mrs. Fickletint!" he stammered. "Oh, please don't leave us!"

Snaggle flew on, and Zeb felt the Stargold Wings around his neck flutter and then grow still. He drew the wings out into the open and they glowed a bit before the light sputtered out. The phoenix magic inside them was almost gone now, but they seemed to be trying to tell Zeb something. And then he remembered the objects inside the Unopenable Purse. Still facing Oonie, Zeb tugged the purse out into his lap.

"Think back to everything you know about magic, Oonie. How can a ruler, a whistle, and a miniature pair of scissors help us? The very first phoenix knew I'd come along one day, so maybe it also knew that Mrs. Fickletint would need its help! Maybe one of these objects could make all the difference!"

"But I didn't even finish my first year of lessons!" Oonie cried. "I missed out on tons of stuff about magical objects." She stopped suddenly. "Hang on, I could have *sworn* I overheard a crew of Sunraiders talking about a rule-breaker they'd found over in the Sighing Caves last month—an object that looked like an ordinary ruler but had magical powers."

Zeb stuffed the Stargold Wings back into the pouch and took out the ruler while Oonie cupped her mittens and blew on Mrs. Fickletint to try and warm her. But the chameleon showed no sign of moving. And up ahead of Snaggle, the Impossible Peaks showed no sign of ending.

Zeb frowned at the ruler. There were dashes to mark the different lengths and a word at the start of the ruler to denote the type of measurements used. "Pinches?" he murmured.

Clutching Mrs. Fickletint close to her chest, Oonie racked her brain. Then she gasped. "I remember! It's all about rhyme: The ruler is measured in pinches instead of inches, and if you pinch it in the right place, you're given something to treasure rather than measure! And what we'd treasure more than anything right now is something to warm Mrs. Fickletint up!"

Zeb lifted a hand out of his mittens, and the cold clawed at his fingers. He ran his thumb over the dash marked 1 PINCH. "Words are appearing, Oonie!" And then he raised an eyebrow. "It says: *Greybobble's golden sink.*"

"What?!" Oonie cried. "That makes no sense!"

Zeb placed his thumb over the next dash. "*Timberdust's velvet pantaloons.*"

Mrs. Fickletint's head drooped to one side. "No!" Oonie gasped. "Don't go! I've—I've got this, I'm going to work the rule-breaker out, I promise!"

But Mrs. Fickletint's scales were slipping from blue to white now and she was ice-cold.

"What if—"

"Quiet, Zeb!" Oonie barked. "I'm trying to think!"

But it was obvious Oonie had stopped thinking and was panicking. Tears rolled down her cheeks, and she started to sob. Her first friend, the only creature she had relied on for so long, was fading. "I can't remember," Oonie sobbed. "I can't save her!"

"No," Zeb replied, "but maybe I can." He paused. "If you let me."

Oonie raised her tear-streaked face and sniffed as her pride fell away. "Please help, Zeb."

Zeb looked at the rule-breaker and thought fast. "It's giving us the names of Lofty Husks," he panted. "They're *actual* rulers, and the words seem to be spelling out things that belong to them. Their most treasured items maybe?" His mind whirred. "You said the rule-breaker gives you something to treasure rather than measure, so maybe it's listing the Lofty Husks' most treasured items, and one of them will be something we could use now!" He passed a thumb over the third dash. "*Wrinklestoop's marble chess set.*" Then the fourth, and his eyes lit up. "*Crumpet's eversnug hot water bottle*. This is the one we need, Oonie!"

Zeb pinched—hard. The rule-breaker trembled, shook from side to side, and then, to Zeb dismay, it broke in half. His hopes plunged, and even Snaggle let out a long, sad sigh. What could they do now for poor Mrs. Fickletint?

But sometimes magic just needs a moment to get going. Especially the magic of a rule-breaker, which—as Oonie and Zeb were about to find out—only really springs into life when the ruler is broken. Sparks burst out of the ends of it, there was a loud bang, the rule-breaker disappeared, and in Zeb's hands lay a hot water bottle lined with the softest fur.

"We've got it!" he cried, thrusting the hot water bottle into Oonie's arms.

She slipped Mrs. Fickletint down inside the fur so that the chameleon was pressed up close to the warmth. Oonie, Zeb, and Snaggle held their breath. For a full, terrible minute, nothing happened. Then, very slowly, Mrs. Fickletint opened one eye. The other followed, and she blinked. Her scales changed from white to blue before flashing red, then settling purple once again. She looked up to see Oonie and Zeb on either side of her.

"My crew," she said quietly. "My precious little crew."

Oonie cuddled the chameleon, while Zeb and Snaggle exchanged a relieved look.

"You gave us such a scare, Mrs. Fickletint," Zeb said. "I don't know what we would have done if we'd lost you."

Mrs. Fickletint smiled weakly. "I know exactly what you would have done. Stayed up far past your bedtime and got yourself into an awful spin about Morg." She snuggled into the fur lining the hot water bottle. "That Fox Petty-Squabble is doing a good job of keeping her promises."

Mrs. Fickletint smiled again, and then, exhausted by the ordeal, she fell asleep, safe and warm at last, leaving Zeb to wonder how Fox and the Unmappers were faring on Wildhorn. How much longer could they ward off Morg's Midnights before the skeletons broke into Cathedral Cave and finished everyone off?

Oonie stroked Mrs. Fickletint, then she looked up at Zeb. "When I first met you, I thought you were a selfish little scaredy-cat, but you're not. Not at all."

Zeb blushed.

"You're brave. You think fast. And"—Oonie paused—"you're kind."

Zeb felt pride rise up inside him. He had saved Mrs. Fickletint, and big biceps hadn't featured at all. He belonged to a crew who believed in him, and this was the greatest happiness he had ever known. He looked at Oonie. "You did good, too, you know."

"Me?" Oonie laughed. "I just panicked and started crying."

"You asked for help," Zeb said. "And that means you're strong. Strong enough to make room for a miracle."

Mrs. Fickletint slept on as the sun dipped beyond the peaks, and Snaggle flew into the night. Zeb shivered as the darkness crept in. Before long, the sun would rise and they'd only have a few hours left to find the Ember Scroll and stop Morg from destroying *everything*. . . .

The crew shared what was left of the food parcels—wafers

filled with caramel goo and crisps that crackled inside their mouths. Snaggle ate a handful of secrets from Oonie that involved her admitting she hadn't brushed her teeth for at least a week and couldn't remember the last time she had had a bath. Then Zeb and Oonie thanked him so many times for scaling the Impossible Peaks that eventually he grew so embarrassed, he nipped their boots to move the conversation on.

After a pause, Zeb said shyly: "Snaggle, have you ever thought about being part of a crew?"

The dragon raised a frosted eyebrow.

"I know, I know," Zeb said. "I was dead set against the idea when I arrived in Crackledawn. But crews are actually quite good news."

Oonie nodded. "We'd love to have you in ours, if you wanted. And if you have time, of course. We appreciate you've got a lot on your plate what with finding the Ember Scroll, scaling mountains, and keeping us safe."

Snaggle dipped his head and carried on flying. Zeb and Oonie grinned—their little crew was growing.

The first stars appeared above them, bright white like specks of ice, and something began to emerge from the clouds below. Zeb watched nervously. He had thought that everything in

Silvercrag was under Morg's curse and that no other creature had scaled the Impossible Peaks. If that was the case, then why were there two dappled horses rising up on wings toward them? Snaggle didn't seem disturbed and bent his head in greeting.

"Winged horses!" Zeb whispered to Oonie. "Two of them. Good news, right?"

Oonie gasped. "Skystallions! Wilbur Shivermitten wrote about them being extinct in Silvercrag, but they must have been living up here! The only creatures, apart from Snaggle, to have secretly scaled the Impossible Peaks! Up here, they've stayed well clear of Morg's curse. . . ." She laughed. "Skystallions are said to grant Unmappers safe passage through Silvercrag. I read they only stay for a night, but so long as they're with you no harm will come your way."

"Then we can sleep and not worry about falling off Snaggle and being speared on a mountain peak!" Zeb breathed a sigh of relief. "If Mrs. Fickletint was awake, she'd be *so* pleased."

He watched as the skystallions drew up, one on either side of Snaggle. Their manes and tails trailed through the dark and their wings reached right over the crew, so that Zeb felt nothing, not even Morg and her Midnights, could harm them. Safe, at last, from the harpy's dark magic, Oonie and Zeb drifted off to sleep.

Chapter 25

At sunrise, several hours later, Snaggle shook the crew awake. The skystallions were gone, but the Impossible Peaks were still there, and Snaggle was still flying above them. Zeb remembered Dollop's words about Crackledawn dragons traveling vast distances without tiring. It was just as well, because they had a world to save and only until moonrise to do it, but Zeb could tell that Snaggle was beginning to flag.

Mrs. Fickletint wriggled out of the fur lining the hot water bottle and began bossing Oonie and Zeb around straightaway. "Empty the hot water bottle, Oonie; it's lukewarm now. But remember to pop it back in the purse afterward, Zeb; that's a genuine eversnug fur and they're extremely hard to come by."

The snow clouds below them had gone, and now that the

sun was up, Zeb could see the mountains in all their glory. Towering peaks and overhangs as well as crags and gullies—and everything was coated in snow and ice. But Snaggle hadn't woken them for the views. There were shapes in the sky ahead that looked like birds. A dozen of them, with long necks and black feathers flying straight toward them.

"What—what are they?" he whispered to Mrs. Fickletint.

The chameleon, now nestled in Oonie's pocket, craned her neck to get a better look. "Oh, heavens," she muttered. "That's not good. Not good at all."

"What is it?" Oonie asked.

Mrs. Fickletint tugged on her hat. "That, my dears, is a flock of nightswans. And as you'll recall, Oonie, Wilbur Shivermitten was *far* from positive about them. Apparently they—and Silvercrag's winterwolves—are drawn to dark magic, if given the chance. Morg laid a curse on this kingdom to stop it fighting back, but maybe she can sense our presence here because we're not bound by her curse." The chameleon gulped. "She'll have filled those nightswans with enough magic to scale the peaks and come after us and the Stargold Wings."

But Snaggle didn't turn around at this. He knew the Ember

Scroll was beyond the birds, and he needed to press on to find it.

"What's a nightswan?" Zeb asked warily.

"I think they look a bit like swans," Oonie replied, "but they're black, and they can breathe webs made from shadows."

Oonie leaned down to pat Snaggle. "We'll find somewhere to rest soon, but do you think you can fend off the nightswans until then? The sun's up now, so maybe its warmth will mean you can blast them with fire, then we can—"

Her words were cut short by an almighty crash. The kind of sound a mountain might make if someone split it in two and left it to fall. The air juddered; the Impossible Peaks swayed. And then the sky flashed black.

Zeb cowered into Snaggle's neck as the crash rang out through all of Silvercrag. Then the din stopped and the sunlight returned. But its echo sent a chill through the crew.

"'The skies will shake with fear and the sun will hide.' . . . It's happened, hasn't it?" Zeb whispered. "Morg has found the Ember Scroll!"

Oonie nodded. Mrs. Fickletint nodded. Even Snaggle dipped his head.

Then the advancing nightswans screeched in celebration as they sensed Morg's dark magic growing in strength. The harpy was just moments away from victory, because if the nightswans imprisoned them, it would not be long, at all, before Morg came by to claim the Stargold Wings. Then it would all be over. No phoenix would rise up to save things. The Unmapped Kingdoms would vanish, his world would go too, and he would never see his crew or Fox Petty-Squabble ever again.

Oonie, though, was gripping Snaggle's spikes with a new determination. "We must *not* lose hope. Morg might have won the race, but she hasn't won the battle. We're still alive. We've still got the Stargold Wings *and* a Crackledawn dragon. So, there's a chance—a very small one—that we can still catch Morg before she writes her ending and somehow save the world."

Spurred on by Oonie's courage, Snaggle narrowed his eyes and ground his teeth as he flew on toward the nightswans. Despite his exhaustion, he threw open his jaws and let out a roar. And this time, he breathed fire, not ice. Great bursts of flames that sent the nightswans reeling in all directions. Snaggle kept flying, drawing breath again and again to keep the fire coming and the nightswans away. But Zeb and Mrs. Fickletint could see that the flames were petering out. Snaggle couldn't fly *and* wield flames after everything he'd been through. They had to help him out.

Full of panic, Zeb yanked the whistle out of the Unopenable Purse and blew it hard. But the nightswans only screeched louder as they spread out in a line across the sky, blocking the way through. Summoning the last of his strength, Snaggle prepared to make a charge through the nightswans.

Sensing something ominous ahead, Oonie's buried her head in her coat. Then Zeb closed his eyes, and Mrs. Fickletint screamed a last-minute instruction: "HOLD ON!"

Surging faster and faster toward the line of nightswans, Zeb thought for a moment they were going to make it, but in the nick of time, the nightswans reared up. And from their beaks came dark webs that hung in the air briefly before joining together to form one large black net. It flashed in the sunlight. And then it plunged, as if it had a mind of its own, wrapping its sticky shadow-string all around the Crackledawn dragon.

The crew bit and tore and punched at the web. And Snaggle roared. But he didn't have the strength for fire now. Nothing, it seemed, could break the web. And now the nightswans were closing in. Snaggle tried, in vain, to beat his wings, but they were plummeting through the sky toward the peaks. And hot on their heels, squealing with delight, came the nightswans.

"We're done for now!" Mrs. Fickletint yelled.

"Not if we can pull all our thoughts together and work out how the whistle and scissors can help us," Zeb shouted. "Come on! The phoenix magic must have sent them for a reason—we've got about ten seconds to figure them out!"

Oonie chewed her lip. "Magic is unpredictable. And mischievous."

Zeb nodded. "Magic plays with words and messes with ideas, it jumbles sense upside down. . . ."

"People—people usually blow whistles hard," Mrs. Fickletint stammered. "Like you did a moment ago. But nothing happened." Her eyes lit up. "So, what about blowing it gently?"

Zeb could barely move for the panic and the web and the fact that Snaggle was falling blisteringly fast. But he inched his hand up through the net to his mouth, wiggled the whistle between his lips, and blew so softly it was as if he hardly used any breath at all.

Snaggle, Oonie, and Mrs. Fickletint were suddenly absolutely still. They were no longer hurtling down through the sky, and the nightswans that had been careering toward them seemed stuck in the air too. Still screeching, they were completely unable to beat their wings or breathe their webs. Whatever spell the whistle had conjured, it held them and everyone but Zeb—whose hands were shaking around the whistle—in its grip.

Mrs. Fickletint managed a few squeaked words, though she couldn't move the rest of her body. "A whistle*slower*! I thought the last one sunk to the bottom of the sea in Crackledawn during an ogre eel attack, but we had one all along! And it has slowed the whole ghastly situation down!"

"Well done, Mrs. Fickletint!" Oonie cried.

Even Snaggle managed a quick sigh of relief.

"But we're still trapped inside the web." Zeb gulped. "And you guys can't move! It won't be long before Morg comes along."

"Unless . . ." Oonie gasped. "The scissors!"

"They won't be able to cut a web like this!" Mrs. Fickletint spluttered. "They're miniature, remember?"

"But what if it's just like Zeb said: 'Magic plays with words and messes with ideas.' Could the miniature scissors be a *short-cut*?"

"You mean they could literally cut us out of the problem?" Zeb asked.

The nightswans screeched.

"There's only one way to find out," Oonie cried.

Zeb wriggled his hands into the purse and set the scissors to the web. Then, hoping hard, he made one small cut, which sliced straight through the shadow web. It fell away, and though the whistleslower's spell kept the nightswans bound, the phoenix magic in these objects was on Zeb's side, and it released the crew. Snaggle shot up into the sky again, revived by the short rest, and rocketed past the shrieking nightswans.

"It worked!" Oonie exclaimed as the squawks of the nightswans petered out. "We're almost overflowing with miracles now!"

Mrs. Fickletint whooped, Zeb cheered, and Snaggle bent his head round and nuzzled Zeb's leg.

Zeb went to tuck the scissors and the whistle back into the purse, but the scissors vanished into thin air and only the whistle remained. Zeb stashed it away carefully in case he needed it again. Then he looked out over the Impossible Peaks, shining in the midday sun. His eyes widened, because the mountains were, at long last, coming to an end. And where they stopped—still many miles in the distance—the sea began. There was no sign of Morg yet. She had the Ember

Scroll, but it seemed she was lying low. Perhaps she could sense the nightswans had been beaten and was waiting for the Stargold Wings to come to her.

An hour passed, and then the sea came into view, a dazzling blue that held icebergs as big and as bright as fallen pieces of moon. This was a place untouched by Morg's curse. A pebbled beach crusted with ice stretched for as far as the eye could see in both directions, but jutting out into the sea in front of them was the last of the mountains—a vast and craggy peak gleaming with ice. As Snaggle beat on toward this mountain, Zeb's knees shook. Even from the height they were, Zeb could see a great yawning opening in this mountain. It loomed like a giant mouth and was fringed with icicles the size of spears, lit blue inside, and ringing with the sound of the harpy's laughter.

Zeb swallowed. Mrs. Fickletint swayed in Oonie's pocket. And even Oonie's courage wavered here.

"It's the cave, isn't it?" she whispered. "Only it's no longer the cave that has never been found. It's the cave *Morg* found."

Zeb nodded. "A place so remote Morg hasn't even needed to lay her curse here. There are no Unmappers or magical beasts now. It's just the harpy. . . ."

Snaggle soared closer, and Mrs. Fickletint shook with fear. "I—I thought I'd be brave enough for this, but we don't even have a plan. How are we going to steal the Ember Scroll from under the nose of the most evil creature in the Unmapped Kingdoms?"

Morg's laugh rang out again.

It was then that the Stargold Wings inched out of Zeb's pouch and hung before the crew. They only had a drop of phoenix magic left inside them now, but what they had, they gave to the crew that had risked everything to get here. Gold sparks danced in the air, and though the odds were against them and time was running out, sometimes all you need to save the world is a dusting of courage.

Chapter 26

Snaggle swung round the last mountain, past the sinking sun, and down toward the entrance of the cave. The wind buffeted Zeb's and Oonie's furs, and the salt air stung their cheeks, but Snaggle kept going, his talons raking the icy sea, his wings smashing through the icicles as he charged into the cavern.

It was vast inside the cave, as if the entire mountain had been scooped out to make room for ice. It glittered from the walls, rose up in places like frozen waves, and from the roof hundreds of meters above, it glowed blue.

Zeb's face drained of color, because there, on a jutting ice ledge snaking into the middle of the cave, was Morg. Her wings were outstretched, and in her hands she held a piece of parchment so intensely gold it made Zeb squint. *This* was the

Ember Scroll, and though the magic inside the Stargold Wings had vanished, the scroll seemed to be straining toward them, as if it could tell that a part of it was nearby.

Morg clutched the scroll tighter. "You have come!" she cried. Her wings rippled with pleasure, and the bone dragon skulking on the ground below her screeched. "I did not come after you when I found the Ember Scroll because I could sense the nightswans had been beaten and knew that you would be foolish enough to think that you could come after me and steal the scroll. But that is not how this works." She raised her skull mask. "Give me the Stargold Wings."

Zeb, Oonie, and Mrs. Fickletint said nothing, though their hearts were pounding. But the fourth member of their crew was readying himself for a fight. Snaggle lowered his head and growled.

The harpy smirked, then she glanced at her bone dragon. "Kill the Crackledawn dragon. I'll deal with the rest."

Snaggle shook his crew off, ushering them behind him. Then he sent a flash of fire toward Morg and her dragon. But they dodged the blast and then the bone dragon was roaring back at Snaggle, and Morg was laughing from the ledge.

Zeb grabbed Oonie, and they scampered behind an ice

boulder. Mrs. Fickletint wailed from Oonie's pocket because Snaggle and the bone dragon were locked in fight now—talons tore, tails smashed, and fire raged—and the crew knew that if they didn't come up with a plan fast, they'd lose their most powerful ally.

Oonie gripped Zeb's hand and whispered, "When the time's right, use the whistleslower. Then move fast, because Morg is *much* stronger than the nightswans. . . ."

Before Zeb could reply, she was off—running blindly across the ice toward Morg, with Mrs. Fickletint screaming directions in her pocket.

"Oonie!" Zeb yelled. "Mrs. Fickletint!"

But Oonie kept moving, stumbling on toward Morg while the dragons fought on. The harpy cackled as Oonie tripped over a ledge of ice, and Zeb started forward. But Oonie picked herself up again and carried on. The harpy tucked the Ember Scroll under her wings so that she could use both hands to sculpt the air into a ball of black, fizzing sparks. Then, as she raised the ball in both hands, ready to hurl at Oonie, Zeb realized what Oonie wanted him to do.

He snatched the whistleslower out of the purse, then blew gently. And at the very moment the ball of dark magic should have shot out from Morg's hand and snuffed the life out of Oonie and Mrs. Fickletint, everything stopped. The ball hung in the air at Morg's fingertips, the dragons froze, and Oonie and Mrs. Fickletint came to a grinding halt.

But Zeb moved. Faster than he had ever done before. Morg *was* stronger than the nightswans, and she and her ball of terrible magic were already edging out of the whistle-slower's hold. Zeb raced across the cave and clambered up to the ledge Morg stood on. The ball fizzed and gathered momentum toward Oonie and Mrs. Fickletint, and the harpy inched a hand toward the Ember Scroll tucked beneath her wing. But in the nick of time, Zeb darted in and grabbed the scroll.

It was warm to touch and the words on the parchment—the story of how the world began—rippled gold. Zeb flung himself off the ledge, yanked Oonie and Mrs. Fickletint out of the line of fire, then the whistleslower and its powers vanished completely, and the cave burst into life once again.

The dragons fought, the ball of dark magic shot out and exploded against a tower of ice where Oonie and Mrs. Fickletint should have been, and before Zeb had even a second to grab the omniscribble to write an ending onto the Ember Scroll, Morg screeched. The cave trembled and then the ice began to creak and giant cracks split down the walls.

The crew screamed as shards of ice rained down, then boulders broke away, smashing all around them. And in the commotion, the bone dragon changed tack. It tore away from Snaggle and charged through the falling ice toward Zeb, Oonie, and Mrs. Fickletint.

"Burn them all!" Morg yelled. "The Ember Scroll will outlive fire!"

Zeb, Oonie, and Mrs. Fickletint clung to one another as the bone dragon raised its horned skull and opened its mighty jaws. And then Snaggle blasted through the falling ice. He charged toward the bone dragon, and the jet of fire that stormed from his mouth tore Morg's dragon apart until it was nothing more than a heap of bones.

Snaggle drew back, panting amidst the crumbling cave, as he and the rest of the crew saw what he'd done. He'd broken the one rule dragons kept: *Never kill another dragon*.

"You fool!" Morg roared. "Now even if you win, you will be banished from the Unmapped Kingdoms forever!"

But there wasn't a moment to think about consequences, because the cave was tumbling down, and even Snaggle couldn't fight a falling mountain. He scrambled toward his crew and threw himself over them and the Ember Scroll.

Zeb's ears rung with the sound of shattering ice. Then there was silence for a second before the howling began. Snaggle drew back his wings, and Zeb's whole body shook with fear. The cave was gone; it was a rubble of smashed ice now. But Morg was still there, her wings outstretched on the ledge, the only part of the cave still standing, and spreading out across the beach came a pack of wolves the color of ink.

"Winterwolves!" Mrs. Fickletint gasped.

Zeb raised a shaking finger to the sky as a dozen dark shapes flew through the sunset toward them. "And the nightswans are back!"

Then the sea before the rubble of ice burst open and an ogre eel rose up. Zeb's heart thumped. They were outnumbered and outsized and utterly surrounded by Morg's dark magic. He fumbled inside his rucksack for the omniscribble while Snaggle roared flames to keep Morg away.

Zeb glanced at the words on the scroll. It talked of the egg the very first phoenix had hatched from and of the feathers and tears this phoenix shed to create the Faraway and the Unmapped Kingdoms. Zeb scanned the story to where it stopped. To the blank space waiting for an ending. He put the omniscribble to the scroll, but no matter how many times he tried to write a new phoenix into life to save the Unmapped Kingdoms and the Faraway, he couldn't. The pen wouldn't write a single word.

He looked up. "I thought Dollop said the omniscribble could write on any surface!"

"Keep trying!" Oonie yelled as the winterwolves stalked closer and the nightswans swarmed above them.

It was then Zeb noticed the small print etched into the side of the pen: GUARANTEED TO WORK ON ALL SURFACES WITH NO INK—UNLESS TEMPERATURES ARE BELOW FREEZING, IN WHICH CASE IT WON'T WORK AT ALL. He let the quill slip between his fingers as despair crept in.

Snaggle roared again and again, but his flames were no match for Morg's dark magic now that it was closing in on all sides. With one swipe of her wings, she turned each blast of fire to ice, which shattered and fell to the ground. The winterwolves howled in anticipation.

"This is it," Zeb cried. "This is the end, isn't it?"

He clung to Oonie and Mrs. Fickletint, knowing that he'd never see Fox Petty-Squabble again, that her promise hadn't been strong enough to beat the dark magic lying in its way. Not even their Crackledawn dragon could crush it. Because Morg was brewing more magic between her palms now, and this was bigger and darker than anything she'd conjured before. The winterwolves broke into a gallop, the ogre eel hissed, the nightswans dived—and then Oonie stood up.

She cocked her head to one side, as if listening for something. Zeb strained his ears, but he could hear nothing beyond the sound of the Midnights closing in. Oonie could hear something, though, and she threw her voice out over the ice.

"One cold winter day," she shouted, "a boy, a girl, and a chameleon rode a Crackledawn dragon across Silvercrag to try to save the world!"

Mrs. Fickletint was weeping from Oonie's pocket, and even Snaggle was bracing himself for what Morg was about to unleash.

Oonie went on, despite the dark magic rushing in and Morg raising her arm high. "Their crew was small," she shouted, "but it never gave up hope. And so, when the end of the world reared up before them, they called upon those keeping the last of the Unmapped magic going!"

Morg laughed. "You think a story can save you now?"

Oonie ignored the harpy. "The crew called upon the Unmapped dragons! Red ones with star-studded wings, blue ones with river-long tails, silver ones with icicled teeth, and green ones with webbed talons and amber eyes! They called upon every single dragon in the Unmapped Kingdoms—*and they came!*"

She felt for Zeb's hand and hauled him up. "I can hear the dark magic coming for us, Zeb, just like you can. But I can hear the sunchatter back in Crackledawn suddenly, even though we're miles away now. And it's different to what I've heard before. This isn't just a few notes; it's a full-blown symphony. *All* the sunchatter left in Crackledawn is ringing out one last time, and it sounds like hope rising! I think the sunchatter is urging us to keep going!"

Zeb's heart was pounding. Morg's dark magic was just moments away from finishing them all, but he could see his captain clearly now. She was brilliant at finding sunchatter, but she was even better at finding hope. No one else could have heard hope singing all the way back in Crackledawn, but Oonie had heard it because she had been born for this very moment. The end of the world was drawing close, but Oonie was still fighting with the only thing they had left: a story.

Snaggle rose to stand with his crew too. Then he, Zeb, and Mrs. Fickletint closed their eyes tight, hoped hard, and imagined all the Unmapped dragons Oonie had called soaring through the sky to help them.

"Quite finished?" Morg sneered as she drew her arm back, ready to unleash her dark magic on the Unmapped Kingdoms once and for all.

An earsplitting cry pierced the dusk. Then another rang out, followed by another and another and another.

Snaggle jerked his head. Zeb and Mrs. Fickletint gasped.

But Oonie only smiled. "Harpies are strong, but stories are stronger."

The cries tore across the darkening sky, and the nightswans scattered first. Then the winterwolves stopped in their tracks and the ogre eel sunk a little lower. And when the crew opened their eyes, they saw hundreds of winged silhouettes beating through the twilight as the sky filled with dragons. Red ones with star-studded wings, blue ones with river-long tails, silver ones with icicled teeth, and green ones with webbed talons and amber eyes! They were all there, just as they had been in Oonie's story! And these dragons had come to fight.

They plowed into the winterwolves, they tore after the

nightswans, and as they set upon the ogre eel, Snaggle seized his chance and whisked the crew onto his back before launching into the sky. At that very moment, Morg rose up on glittering wings and hurled her ball of magic after them.

Zeb ducked, but neither he nor Mrs. Fickletint managed to warn Oonie in time, and the dark magic thundered into her. She clutched Zeb's arm, her face full of fear, and then she and Mrs. Fickletint slipped soundlessly from Snaggle's back and fell through the sky.

Chapter 27

OONIE!" Zeb roared. "MRS. FICKLETINT!"

Snaggle dived down toward the sea. But there was a battle raging below them—a furious clash of nightswans, dragons, and ogre eels. The little girl and her chameleon were nowhere to be seen.

"Where are they, Snaggle?" Zeb cried.

The Crackledawn dragon wanted to go on after Oonie and Mrs. Fickletint—he would have followed them to the ends of the earth—but he could see that Morg was tearing through the sky after them. And there was a glow at the horizon now; the moon was only minutes away. . . .

Snaggle scoured the battle one last time before pushing up into the sky. Then two Silvercrag dragons set upon Morg, dragging her back to the fight with their icicled teeth. Zeb knew this was his chance to somehow save the world, but he couldn't see through his tears. All he could think about were Oonie and Mrs. Fickletint.

Snaggle twisted his head round and nudged Zeb, as if trying to tell him that he *had* to go on. There was no other way.

"What's the point of a world without Oonie and Mrs. Fickletint?" Zeb sniffed. "And what's the point of having the Ember Scroll and the Stargold Wings if I can't even write an ending?"

Zeb scanned the battle below for a sign of his friends, but no matter how hard he looked, no matter how desperately he willed them to appear, he couldn't see them. The sadness rocked inside him. They *couldn't* be gone—not when they'd gotten this far. Zeb was meant to tell the story of a new phoenix rising to save the world *and* his crew, but he was high in the sky now—without a quill—and Morg was steadily breaking out of the Silvercrag dragons' hold.

But the thing about stories is that beginnings can grow out of endings. Oonie had conjured a sky full of dragons when the end of the world drew close. Zeb had learned to trust when he said goodbye to the pain of his past. And then there was the phoenix itself—a magical creature born out of the embers of the phoenix before it.

Morg lobbied the Silvercrag dragons with more and more curses until she forced her way free. Then she flew, full tilt, after Zeb, but the Crackledawn dragon was flying faster still.

Zeb glanced at the Ember Scroll, shining in the gathering dark and rolling and unfurling at the edges as it tried to reach for the Stargold Wings. It was waiting for an ending, and all this time Zeb had assumed that meant he had to write one onto the parchment. But stories didn't have to be written down. You could *tell* stories—Oonie had proved that—and you could live them. Snaggle flew on, and Zeb tried to block out the harpy careering toward him and the surging sadness he felt every time he thought of Oonie and Mrs. Fickletint. He knew now what he would do.

Steadying himself against the wind, Zeb lifted the Stargold Wings out of their pouch and held them on the Ember Scroll. The parchment curled protectively over the wings, and Zeb released his grip on them. When the scroll opened a second later, he saw the Stargold Wings had split down the middle and were glowing once more. The wings fixed themselves on either side of the parchment, and then Zeb lowered the Ember Scroll toward the Crackledawn dragon racing through the sky.

"Snaggle," he panted as the scroll rippled in the wind, "I need you to breathe fire one more time."

Snaggle's eyes widened as he realized what Zeb was asking. He had already broken a rule tonight, and this, burning the very thing they'd journeyed so far to find, didn't make sense at all.

"Trust me," Zeb urged. "Please. Trust me."

Snaggle swung his head toward the Ember Scroll. Then, after one quick glance at Zeb, he sent his flames into the parchment.

"WHAT ARE YOU DOING?!" Morg screamed as she reared up before the fire.

Zeb loosened his hold on the Ember Scroll, then he let it float off into the sky, pursued by the screeching harpy. He had given the story an ending, and he knew, from Oonie, that it was hope that turned endings into beginnings. So, as Snaggle beat his wings to hold them where they were up in the sky, Zeb hoped hard, pouring every drop of his faith into the Ember Scroll as it sailed into the dark. Still Morg raced on, closer and closer to the burning story. And then, just as the harpy reached out a grappling hand toward it, the Ember Scroll exploded.

Sparks scattered like stars, and the whole world shook so that even those back in the Faraway felt it. Where the burning parchment had been was the creature the Unmapped Kingdoms had longed for every single day since Morg rose up out of Everdark almost five thousand years ago.

A phoenix.

Zeb's jaw dropped. It was the most magnificent thing he had seen in all of Crackledawn. And as it rose into the night, its golden feathers trailing flames, its sweeping tail ribbons of fire, the sky itself came alive. Shooting stars fell, comets soared, and a full moon rose.

Morg turned then and made a frantic, cowardly attempt to flee. But there was not room for a harpy *and* a phoenix in the world. And as the phoenix hung in the air, its burning wings outstretched, a blinding light flashed across the kingdom. The harpy screeched, one final bloodcurdling scream filled with terror, because she knew that her time had come to an end. She had clawed her way out of a never-ending well. She had conjured a ship and sailed into Crackledawn. She broken through to Silvercrag and cursed an entire kingdom. But she was no match for a phoenix. Her wings shriveled, her feathers dropped off, her body crumbled, and she fell through the sky as a handful of glittering soot. The winterwolves dissolved, the nightswans faded, and the ogre eels vanished completely. And, just like that, the harpy's reign of terror ended.

Zeb watched as the phoenix whirled through the sky and the rest of the Unmapped dragons, who usually roamed the world alone, rose up together to join it. Then the night was filled with their roars and with the eagled cry of the phoenix, because—at long last—a new era had been born and the Faraway had been rescued.

Zeb should have been happy. He, Zebedee Bolt, had saved the world. But his mind was frozen with thoughts of Oonie and Mrs. Fickletint. Snaggle glided beneath the phoenix, and Zeb saw that his amber eyes were sad. The Crackledawn dragon had answered their call, found the Final Curtain, scaled the Impossible Peaks, *and* helped them beat Morg. But he had broken the only rule dragons kept.

And then Zeb spotted something tearing round the coastline. Something large and blue with a matted mane and a river-long tail that scattered dragonflies, hummingbirds, and tropical flowers in its wake. It was one of Jungledrop's dragons, and on its back there rode a purple chameleon and a girl who knew the taste of moonlight.

"Oonie?" Zeb breathed, hardly daring to believe it. Then louder because there could be no doubt now: "OONIE! MRS. FICKLETINT!"

The Jungledrop dragon soared through the sky toward them, shaking snow from its tangled mane, and then—to Mrs. Fickletint's horror—it tossed them from its back toward Snaggle before racing off to join the other dragons. Snaggle caught the girl and the chameleon between his spikes, and Zeb held them both close.

"I thought I'd never see you again," he sobbed. "The world felt so empty without you!"

Oonie hugged Zeb tight. "Nothing can break up our crew, Zeb. Not even Morg and all her dark magic."

Zeb and Oonie laughed, and even Mrs. Fickletint managed a shaky grin, despite the trauma that had unfolded after she and Oonie fell from Snaggle's back. "Tangled in another nightswan web," she tutted, "dragged off round the coast, nearly eaten whole by a winterwolf, then rescued by a Jungledrop dragon in desperate need of a hairbrush. Whatever next?! Still"—the chameleon hopped onto Zeb's leg, clambered up his coat, and kissed his nose—"we saved the world."

The phoenix drew close, and its flame-rippled majesty

stunned Zeb to the core. From the ancestors of this creature, the whole world had sprung. Kingdoms had blossomed and continents, oceans, and galaxies had been born. The phoenix hovered in the air before them. Then it dipped its beak, as if thanking them for all that they had done, before turning to look at Snaggle.

The dragon bowed his head in respect and in sorrow, for he knew all too well the crime he had committed. The phoenix spoke in a way that neither Zeb nor Oonie and Mrs. Fickletint could understand—a series of caws and clicks—but Snaggle understood. He listened, his wide eyes shining, as the phoenix delivered its verdict on Snaggle's fate. Then the phoenix wheeled away, back into the sky with the rest of the Unmapped dragons.

Zeb leaned forward over Snaggle's neck as he soared through the sky. "What did the phoenix say? Surely you're pardoned now?"

Oonie nodded. "Everyone will understand that you killed another dragon to save us—and the world?"

"It wasn't as if it was a very nice dragon anyway," Mrs. Fickletint added.

Snaggle swung his head round and nuzzled his crew.

And though they didn't know what had passed between the Crackledawn and the phoenix, and Snaggle didn't rush through the sky to be with the rest of his kind, they could see a hope of sorts burning in his eyes now. The phoenix cried out again, the dragons roared, and as the sky rang with victory, Silvercrag stirred back into life.

Skystallions poured over the Impossible Peaks. Frost giants lumbered round the coastline, their shoulders laden with Silvercrag's Unmappers. And eagle owls glided out of secret mountain tunnels. But it wasn't just those in Silvercrag whom the phoenix had summoned. As Snaggle swooped down toward the sea, Zeb saw boats appearing on the horizon to the west, each one lit with the soft glow of a Bother-Ahead Beacon.

"Crackledawn's Unmappers!" Mrs. Fickletint cried in disbelief. "They've managed to cross between kingdoms!"

The boats sailed on through the silver sea toward them, and Zeb grabbed Oonie's arm as a dhow with a dragonhead prow came into view. "It's—it's the *Kerfuffle*! With Trampletusk and Dollop on board!" He squinted as Snaggle raced closer. "And isn't that Mr. Fickletint beside them, along with your twenty-seven children?"

Mrs. Fickletint beamed and then she waved to them before turning hastily back to Snaggle: "Whatever you do, don't fly *too* close; I am *not* getting roped into childcare now. . . ." Snaggle glided over the newcomers, and Mrs. Fickletint gasped. "Bless my soul if that isn't Greyhobble, Timberdust, and Crumpet sailing forth on their boat *Dragonclaw*! Our Lofty Husks have arrived, and they're safe and well despite all that Morg threw at them!"

Zeb's eyes caught on flash upon flash of mirror-bright scales rising and falling beneath the waves. And then a very flustered head poked out of the water. "It's Perpetual Faff!"

"With all her merglimmers *and* her guzzlebag!" Mrs. Fickletint chuckled. "I dread to think how much faffing was involved to get them all to this point!"

"And what about Rumblestar's Unmappers?" Oonie asked. "Are they here yet too?"

Zeb grinned. "If they travel by hot-air balloon, then yes, they're here! There's a whole fleet of balloons filled with men, women, and children dressed in overalls and wearing flying goggles, and"—he peered a little closer—"there are lots of short hairy things waving crossbows in the balloons with them!"

"Snow trolls!" Oonie laughed. "I've always wanted to meet one!"

Mrs. Fickletint raised her brow as a hot-air balloon carrying two ogres and three wizened-looking witches sailed into view. "Even Rumblestar's storm ogres and drizzle hags appear to have been invited. I must have a word with the phoenix about this guest list. . . ."

"And which kingdom has hippogriffs?" Zeb cried. "Because there's a whole bunch of them storming across the sky from the east, and they're carrying all sorts of things: golden panthers, a ghost in a loincloth, and a really talkative parrot!"

"The swiftwings from Jungledrop!" Mrs. Fickletint blinked. "And, my word, that parrot has good genes; she saved her kingdom from Morg five hundred years ago, and here she is, still going strong!"

The sea, sky, and shore filled with Unmappers, Lofty Husks, and magical beasts, and every single one was cheering for the crew. Because they had beaten Morg, they had rescued the Faraway, and they had rid the Unmapped Kingdoms of dark magic forever. Zeb, Oonie, and Mrs. Fickletint grinned and laughed and hugged again.

Then a voice called out above all the rest. "Zebedee Bolt!"

Zeb looked down to see a boat glinting in the moonlight, and at its helm, a woman with fire-red hair and a promise that had not been broken. His breath caught.

"I told you I'd come back for you! That I'd cross worlds and kingdoms to find you!"

Zeb's heart surged. Fox Petty-Squabble had kept her promise! And this was a promise that had followed him into the Unmapped Kingdoms, stood firm when surrounded by Morg's Midnights, and broken into Silvercrag at the call of the phoenix.

Snaggle dived down toward the boat and landed, with a thump, on the prow. Fox clambered over the benches until she stood before the dragon.

Then she smiled. "It's good to see you, Zeb."

And while Mrs. Fickletint and Oonie whispered to each other about asking for the autograph of the legendary Fox Petty-Squabble, Zeb slipped off Snaggle's back into the boat. Silvercrag rang with the sound of cheers, but Zeb could only hear Fox's voice in that moment.

"I'll take care of you," she said. "There'll be no more sleeping in armchairs and running away. We'll find somewhere to live, the two of us together. And yours will be the room with the piano."

While the sky danced with fireworks and shooting stars, Zeb fell into Fox's arms. And it felt like coming home.

Chapter 28

The phoenix flew, in a sweeping arc, over the last of the Impossible Peaks, and as it did so, more magic poured from its flaming wings. Bonfires appeared on the beaches, and the air filled with the smell of spices as banqueting tables—piled high with cinnamon buns, warmed gingerbread, and mugs of hot chocolate laden with marshmallows—materialized out of thin air. Zeb watched in awe as the rubble that had once been a cave built up into a frosted fairground: an ice rink filled with shimmering tunnels; a Ferris wheel jutting over the sea; bumper cars made of snow; and pine trees decorated with stardust.

The Unmappers spilled out of boats and hot-air balloons and slid from the backs of swiftwings and frost giants to celebrate together, swapping stories about their kingdoms. And before long, there were skystallions galloping through the shallows, cloud giants breathing moonbows, and silver whales sculpting every possible magical beast from their blowholes.

Everyone wanted to talk to the crew of the *Kerfuffle* and ask them about their dangerous voyage. After Zeb, Oonie, and Mrs. Fickletint had filled Trampletusk, Dollop, and Perpetual Faff in on everything that had happened, Mrs. Fickletint peeled off to see her family, and Zeb and Oonie sat down at the banqueting table with a group of young and very excited Unmappers from Crackledawn. Oonie's former classmates wanted to know everything about the quest, and Zeb noticed a shy kind of eagerness in Oonie that was altogether different from the defensive girl who had hauled him onto the *Kerfuffle*.

Snaggle had stuck around at first—he seemed reluctant to leave, and again Zeb wondered what the phoenix had said to him up in the sky. But when Zeb grabbed Oonie for a spin in the snow bumper cars with a bunch of Unmappers from Silvercrag, Snaggle took himself off for a walk and a think along the frosted shore.

Oonie and Zeb tore around the fairground together, laughing and chattering with Unmappers their age. Then Zeb spotted a Flyaway Tree, and before Mrs. Fickletint had time to wipe the remains of marshmallow from the mouths of her twenty-seven children, he cut down a feather, and he and Oonie flew on it, just like a broomstick, in a full loop-the-loop over the ocean (before crash-landing into a snowdrift).

Zeb looked up to see Fox grinning at him from one of the tables. She was surrounded by old friends, including the talkative parrot, Heckle—who seemed to be repeating what Fox thought, not what she said—and a golden panther called Deepglint. And Zeb felt that the fact that Fox had magical friends, and she hadn't told him off for crashing into a snowdrift, was probably a very good sign. She was, it appeared, the complete opposite of Derek Dunce.

Zeb glanced at the table filled with Lofty Husks, rulers from all four kingdoms gathered together for the first time in their history: Crackledawn's elves wrapped in velvet robes spoke with Rumblestar's wizards (and one plump elf, in particular, seemed to be quizzing them regarding the whereabouts of an extremely valuable hot water bottle wrapped in an eversnug fur). Jungledrop's golden panthers talked to Silvercrag's eagle owls, whose feathers shone brighter than moonlight. And from the night sky, the phoenix and all the Unmapped dragons but one looked down.

A sudden hush descended over the banqueting tables as a very old elf stood up on his chair.

"That's Greyhobble," Mrs. Fickletint explained to Zeb. "Terribly old, terribly wise, and terribly bad at telling jokes."

But Greyhobble had not called for quiet to tell a joke. "For almost five thousand years, Morg has plagued the Unmapped Kingdoms," he said. "She has destroyed homes and Unmappers, Lofty Husks and magical creatures. But tonight—thanks to the finest crew Crackledawn has ever mustered—we have peace and a future filled with joy and magic to look forward to."

The crew beamed with pride. Even the Crackledawn dragon—tucked away at the end of the beach—lifted his snout high.

"Oonie, Mrs. Fickletint, Zeb, and Snaggle: You are proof that with courage, compassion, and hope, anything is possible. And years to come, your story will still be told. The story of how, against the odds, a small but mighty crew took on a harpy—and won."

The cliffs rang with cheers again as every Lofty Husk, Unmapper, and magical beast rose to their feet and whooped and clapped. Zeb laughed. He had set off from 56 Rightangle Row thinking that he had been running away from the world.

But all the time, he had been running toward friendship and hope.

The cheers grew, then thousands of lanterns appeared in the sky, and as they drifted up toward the moon, the phoenix sent one more cry into the night before soaring off toward the horizon and the portal that could lead it home to Everdark.

The celebrations went on into the night, but the crew stayed together by the shore because they knew that one of them still had a journey to make. And from the way Snaggle was flexing his muscles and shaking the icicles from his throat, it was becoming increasingly clear who would be providing the lift.

Oonie sat in her furs on the frosted pebbles. "You have to go home, don't you?"

Zeb plucked at his cuff but said nothing.

Mrs. Fickletint hopped down from Oonie's shoulder and padded over the pebbles onto Zeb's knee. "We're going to miss you. A great deal, in fact, because you are one in a million, and Oonie and I were *so* very lucky to haul you out of the sea that day."

Zeb felt a familiar lump rise in his throat. "I don't think I'll ever find a crew like you in the Faraway."

Mrs. Fickletint smiled. "Oh, you will, Zeb. Because that's the beauty of the world: It is filled with extraordinary people—and the more living you do, the more wonders you find." She spread her little arms as far as they would go around Zeb's waist. "Just promise me you'll wear an undershirt in the winter months; I've heard it can get quite chilly in New York. And don't forget to get an early night every now and again; it works a treat for your sanity *and* your skin."

Zeb held the little chameleon close, then he set her down on the ground. She hurried into the warmth of Oonie's coat pocket.

Zeb turned to Oonie. "I used to think that being strong was all about having big biceps, but with you as the captain of our crew, I learned about hope. You taught me that if hope grows, miracles happen. Monsters get beaten and worlds get saved."

Oonie's voice was choked. "I'll never forget you, Zeb. And though I might not see as other people do, I know your heart, and it's brighter than sunlight, stronger than diamonds, and bigger than both our worlds put together."

Zeb tried his best not to cry, then he gave up and let the tears fall. "I won't forget you, either, Oonie." He sniffed. "Every time the sun rises back in the Faraway, I'll think of you out on the *Kerfuffle* hauling in sunchatter with Mrs. Fickletint." He was quiet for a moment. "What do beginnings smell like?"

Oonie thought about this, and then she said: "Peppercorns. They're spice and bite and full of promise."

Zeb threw his arms around her and Mrs. Fickletint, then the Crackledawn dragon wrapped his wings around everyone and purred. And Oonie and Mrs. Fickletint clung on to the dragon then, whispering thanks into his ears, because they didn't know, any more than Zeb, where Snaggle would end up.

Fox walked over to the crew, and while the Unmapped dragons wheeled in the sky and the celebrations ran on all down the beach, she turned to Zeb.

"Are you ready," she asked, "for a new beginning?"

Zeb squared his shoulders and nodded as they climbed up onto Snaggle's back.

"Peppercorns," he said, sniffing the air. "Definitely peppercorns."

Oonie and Mrs. Fickletint laughed. Then Snaggle lowered himself into a crouch and, just as he was about to launch off into the sky, the chameleon climbed onto Oonie's head and unleashed a torrent of secrets into the dragon's ear to fuel him on to the Faraway.

"Sometimes I find looking after twenty-seven children so draining, I lock myself inside my wibblebough sapling with a cup of tea while they tear around Wildhorn completely unsupervised. Once I used a nimblewisk to conjure up a birthday cake, then I passed it off as a home-baked treat. A few months ago, when I was feeling particularly vengeful after a night of Mr. Fickletint's snoring, I told the children to jump on him at sunrise."

Snaggle snorted, Oonie and Zeb laughed together one last time, then Snaggle burst into the sky and sailed out over the sea. Even as the sound of the celebrations faded, Zeb could still see Oonie on the shore waving up at the sky as Mrs. Fickletint hopped up and down on her shoulder. Then Zeb turned round again, and instead of holding on to Snaggle's spikes, he wrapped his arms around Fox, and they flew on until the only sound that could be heard were the waves rolling and heaving down below.

Zeb and Fox hadn't told Snaggle where to go; he had proved he had a knack for finding things, and he flew on now without a flicker of hesitation. After a while, Zeb felt a familiar tingling sensation—like electricity rushing through his bones—and though the ocean below them looked just the same as it had a moment before, he knew they had passed through an enchantment and out of the Unmapped Kingdoms.

Some time later, land came into sight—a clutter of high-rise buildings jutting into the sea and glinting in the breaking dawn.

"New York!" Zeb gasped. "There's the Statue of Liberty! And Central Park!"

"And Brooklyn!" Fox smiled. She knew there would be plenty of paperwork and tricky conversations ahead, but she knew that she and the boy would be happy here. Together, they would build a brilliant future. She looked over her shoulder. "We've come home, Zeb. And it looks as if only a few hours have passed since we left!"

Zeb held Fox tight as Snaggle plunged down through the sky. There were people on the streets now, more and more of them spilling out into Times Square. But they were not looking up at the dragon that morning. They were glued to the billboards flashing breaking news: Sea levels had, rather extraordinarily, dropped overnight; temperatures had plunged back to what they should have been on a crisp October morning; bushfires further afield had fizzled out in seconds; and reports were flooding back from the Arctic with sightings of polar bears, narwhals, and beluga whales. The city rang with cheers, and nobody noticed the boy who had been responsible for all this riding a Crackledawn dragon over their heads.

Snaggle slipped down into a quiet, unvisited sort of street, and landed with a crunch before an abandoned theater. Zeb looked at the broken window he'd climbed through during his getaway and thought of all that had happened since. He had left this world wanting to destroy it, but he was returning now having done everything in his power to keep its people, animals, and wild places safe.

Zeb and Fox slid off Snaggle's back, then the Crackledawn dragon turned to them. He held his head down level with Zeb's, and Zeb looked into his amber eyes.

"Oh, Snaggle," Zeb said. "You're meant to be wild and secretive and always alone, but you came when I called you. You stuck around through all sorts of dangers. And you broke the one dragon rule to protect me and my crew."

Snaggle's eyes filled with tears, and Zeb's did the same.

"Whatever the phoenix and the other Unmapped dragons have decided about your future," Zeb said, "I think you're the most brilliant dragon there ever was."

He arched his arms around Snaggle's neck, and the dragon

nuzzled into him and purred. Snaggle was still wild, but a little part of him belonged to the boy now. The Crackledawn dragon pulled back and opened his mouth, and as he did so, the most astonishing thing happened.

Words came out.

"Well, well, well," Snaggle chuckled in a deep, soft voice. "Magic must work differently in the Faraway. I have carried sun scrolls here for as long as I can remember, but never once have I been seen, tried to speak, or indeed had anyone to speak to." He drew himself up. "I broke the dragon rule, and that rule was made at the beginning of time, so it cannot be undone and I must face the consequences."

Zeb's face fell.

"But"—and here Snaggle's eyes twinkled—"sometimes consequences are less disastrous than they sound. You see, the rest of the Unmapped dragons understood why I killed the bone dragon, and though they knew things couldn't go back to the way they were, they pleaded with the phoenix to create a new role for me."

Zeb and Fox frowned.

"Every night, hundreds of Crackledawn dragons arrive in the Faraway," Snaggle said, "and they leave sun scrolls in hidden places. The scrolls vanish at sunrise, giving you your sunlight for the day, but the problem is: Children from the Faraway can get up rather early—often when it's still dark—and they are far too inquisitive to leave secret things alone. They go poking and prodding and investigating. And for a while now, we Unmapped dragons have been worrying that sooner or later a Faraway child will discover a sun scroll and expose the Unmapped dragons. And we cannot have that, because dragons, as you well know, thrive on secrets."

Zeb could have listened to the dragon talking all day. His warm voice meandered like a slow-flowing river.

"What have they asked you to do?" Fox asked.

"Up until now I have mostly been delivering sun scrolls to Scotland—pretty country but ghastly weather, so I've been trying to brighten their days—but as of last night"—Snaggle winked—"I have been asked to patrol the Faraway when the sun scrolls arrive and distract children who might be snooping nearby. There won't be any roaring, of course, but I'll be rustling branches and growling nearby. I might even stretch to some misleading footsteps, if that's what it takes, or possibly a spot of whispering now that I know I can talk here. . . ."

Zeb couldn't believe what he was hearing. "So, you're *staying*? You're going to live in the Faraway?"

Snaggle burrowed his head into Zeb's shoulder. "Yes, dear boy. I'm staying. And though I'm wild, and terribly fierce when push comes to shove, you might just see me now and again." He drew back and looked at Fox. "Perhaps if the two of you were to go walking in Yosemite National Park or biking through Yellowstone, I might just happen to be there. . . . So long as you keep returning to your world's wild places, where I am less likely to be seen, then I will be waiting for you."

Fox grinned. "Oh, we'll keep returning; you can be sure of that."

"But how will you know where we are?" Zeb asked. "And won't you be sad not to go back to the Unmapped Kingdoms?"

Snaggle wrapped his tail around the boy. "You summoned me, Zeb. You forged a bond between us that can never be broken. *That's* how I will know where you are. I give you my word—a Crackledawn dragon's promise—that I will *always* show up for you." He cocked his head. "I may miss the Unmapped Kingdoms from time to time, but there is magic here, too, if you know where to look. And there are mountains, oceans, and jungles to explore. In fact, there are so many adventures ahead, I must remember to pace myself."

Snaggle folded his mighty wings around Zeb, who felt a rush of warmth spread out inside him. He had left the Faraway with nothing. But he had returned with a woman and a dragon who both knew the power of keeping promises. Zeb hugged Snaggle for a moment longer, then loosened his arms and stepped back.

Fox was there, her arm outstretched. Zeb slipped his hand into hers, then he took a deep breath in through his nose and smiled, because there was a distinct smell of peppercorns in the air. He threw one last look over his shoulder at the Crackledawn dragon, then, hand in hand with Fox Petty-Squabble, Zeb walked on into the sunrise.

Acknowledgments

Zebedee Bolt's list of people worth trusting in the Faraway:

1. Fox Petty-Squabble (obvs)
2. Snaggle (obvs)
3. The wonderful team at Simon & Schuster: Eve Wersocki-Morris, Louisa Danquah, Sarah Macmillan, Dan Fricker, Laura Hough, Rachel Denwood, Ali Dougal, Stephanie Purcell, Sarah McCabe, and the endlessly wise and kind Lucy Pearse
4. Inclusive Minds and Joanna Sholem, for her enthusiasm and insight
5. George Ermos for his brilliant cover artwork and map
6. Agent Hannah Sheppard for her ongoing loyalty
7. All the teachers, librarians, booksellers, parents, and carers who have introduced kids to the Unmapped Kingdoms
8. Authors Lauren St. John, Piers Torday, and Katherine Rundell whose wise counsel and friendship brought light and comfort during the pandemic. And gold-hearted writers Katie Webber, Kiran Millwood Hargrave, Ross Montgomery, Emma Carroll,

Cerrie Burnell, Robin Stevens, Michelle Harrison, Mel Taylor, Perdita Cargill, MG Leonard, Maz Evans, and Amy Wilson, whose encouragement and kindness are an anchor in these times

9. Abi's family for their unequaled love and support. Bring on the adventures in Scotland . . .

Embark on an exciting new magical adventure in the snowy kingdom of Erkenwald. Turn the page for a peek!

Eska

Eska sat, knees tucked under her chin and head bowed, on the pedestal inside the music box. Its glass dome curved around her, fixed tight to the silver base, and with her flimsy dress and bare feet, she might easily have passed for a mechanical ballerina. But Eska was no clockwork figure. She was a twelve-year-old girl with darting eyes and a pulse that trembled every time the Ice Queen drew near.

Eska closed her eyes and tried to wiggle her toes. They didn't move. She made to arch her back and then stretch her neck. Again, nothing moved. Even her hair—a tumble of red so full of knots it seemed to grow in circles—lay absolutely still down her back. But it was a ritual she attempted every morning in case, by some miracle, the Ice Queen's hold over her limbs had weakened. It never did, though. Not for a second. The music box had been Eska's prison for months and she could only blink wide blue eyes at the horrors that unfolded in Winterfang's vaulted hall.

She looked beyond the dome, through the ice arches in front of her, which faced out over Erkenwald. The first sunrise in six months spilled across the horizon. Frozen rivers shimmered, the snow on the tundra sparkled, and the sea was a dazzling jigsaw of ice and meltwater. It was mid-March then, Eska thought. That was when the light returned to the kingdom—she'd heard the Tusk guards talking.

Her chest tightened as she thought back to the day she'd awoken in the music box, her body locked under the Ice Queen's spell. The midnight sun had been burning and she had watched it for two whole months before the dark stole in. Eska swallowed. With the light returning now, she knew she had to have been the Ice Queen's prisoner for nine months, but even more frightening was the knowledge that she didn't have a single memory of her life before Winterfang. There must have been something else once—a home, a family, friends perhaps—since the spell the Ice Queen uttered every morning spoke of her as *the stolen child*. But stolen from where?

From whom? It was all a terrible blank. Because the Ice Queen didn't only steal people and voices: she stole memories, too, if it suited her.

At the sound of footsteps, Eska snapped out of her thoughts, and from the corner of her eye she watched a familiar scene unravel. The Ice Queen sat, very still, before an organ made of icicles in the middle of the hall, then she raised her hands to the keys. Eska waited. She knew what came next because it was the same every morning.

Chords drifted through the palace—up and down the snow-strewn staircases, into the towers surrounding the palace domes, across the bridge connecting the iceberg to the mainland, and then out over the miles of frozen tundra beyond. The chords were solemn, like the groaning of a faraway glacier, and as they swelled and throbbed, Eska winced. The Ice Queen was getting ready to feed on her stolen voices.

A melody rippled out from the silver trees lining the hall. Their roots sprawled over the ice floor, and from their bony branches, hundreds of glass baubles hung, each one filled with a golden glow. *This* was where the melody was coming from, because inside each ornament was a voice. And as the chords grew louder, the baubles shimmered and the voices of the Fur and Feather men and women singing a wordless anthem joined with the organ's steady pulse.

Eska watched as the golden glow from one of the baubles drifted toward the Ice Queen's mouth and slipped down her cold white throat. The organ grew louder as the Ice Queen swallowed, then she threw back her head and laughed.

"Another voice closer to immortality!"

She raked her nails across the keys. The chords clashed, the voices stopped, and the baubles dimmed. Then the Ice Queen snatched up her staff and strode toward the arches, her sequined gown swishing behind her.

Eska's insides churned as the woman knelt before the music box and slipped a key into the base. Then she uttered her spell and her voice came hard and pointed, as if full of unpleasant corners:

"Three turns to the left then half a turn right
with a key cut black as the deepest night.
The magic awakes, then limbs unfold
as the stolen child comes under my hold."

The Ice Queen turned the key and, as it wound three turns to the left then half a turn right, music began. It was different from the melody that came from the trees; this was a gentle, almost magical tinkling, like tiny bells chiming or dozens of stars falling to Earth.

And, at the sound, Eska felt her body stir. First her head lifted, then her hands pushed down and her legs extended until she was standing on the pedestal. She tried to hold the curse at bay, to take control of her body, but she was up on the balls of her feet now and her arms were outstretched. The Ice Queen breathed a crystal mist over the glass dome, making it disappear from sight, and, as the pedestal turned, round and round, Eska danced on trembling feet.

Unscrewing the orb from the top of her staff, the Ice Queen held it before Eska. "Your voice is cursed by the Sky Gods, child. But I can relieve you of it." She moved the orb nearer Eska's mouth. "Speak now—let your words slip into my orb—and you will no longer have to bear such a burden."

Eska's frail arms rose and fell and her body stooped and arched, but she said nothing. Minutes passed, the only sound in the room the fluttering of Eska's dress as she turned, then the music ground to a halt, the pedestal stilled, and Eska stopped mid-pirouette before folding herself up into a ball again.

The Ice Queen twisted the orb back on to her staff, then

she seized Eska's wrist. "I am not asking to hear your voice because I value your opinion. I am not asking to hear your voice because I care about your feelings. I am asking to hear your voice *because I own you.*" Her eyes darkened. "You bear the mark of the Sky Gods, Eska, the very Gods who used terrible magic to stir up hatred between the people of Erkenwald. But I will use your voice to tear the Sky Gods down and rid this kingdom of their evil forever."

Eska's mind whirled. The Ice Queen often spoke like this—about cursed marks and dreadful Gods—but, even though Eska could recall nothing from her past about either, some deep-rooted things couldn't be erased, like knowing right from wrong and sensing truth from lies. Something about the Ice Queen's words smelled of lies, as if she was spinning a story that just happened to suit her, and for this reason Eska kept her voice a secret inside her.

The Ice Queen loosened her grip. "You will remain locked inside this music box until I hear you speak." She paused. "And you will go without the dome tonight; perhaps a little cold is exactly what is needed to shock you into behaving."

Eska stayed silent, huddled on her pedestal, then there was a cough from somewhere nearby and the Ice Queen spun round.

A bald man dressed in sealskins and a walrus-tusk necklace stood before them. He was small and fat, with an oily smile, and as he dipped his head Eska glimpsed the edge of the tattoo of a large black eye stamped on to the back of his skull.

"Forgive my intrusion, Your Majesty."

The Ice Queen nodded. "Come, Slither. It seems I am still not getting through to the girl. My magic holds her body under its spell, but it cannot draw out her voice. She is mute—and perhaps she has always been that way—but somewhere inside her there must be a voice, even if she has never used it."

"I have some news that may interest you." Slither smirked. "The contraption I have been working on these last few months is almost finished."

The Ice Queen paced back and forth beside the music box, a smile forming on her blue lips. "You're quite sure it will work?"

Slither ran a hand over his bald head. "I am the most powerful shaman in Erkenwald. It will work."

"We cannot delay any longer. I must have Eska's voice in the next few days."

"There are still adjustments to make. I need at least a week before—"

The Ice Queen tilted her head and the sunlight flashed off her crown of snowflakes. "Work through the night, Slither. Get it done. To achieve immortality, I must steal every single voice in the kingdom before the midnight sun rises in two weeks' time." She paused. "Even your fiercest warriors have not been able to find the Fur and Feather children, but if I have Eska's voice, I can use it to summon the tribes to Winterfang. Then I will tear the Sky Gods down from the heavens and all will surrender to me."

Slither bowed and then scurried from the hall. The Ice Queen followed slowly, but, when she reached the shadows, she glanced over her shoulder at Eska.

"I *will* take your voice," she snarled. "I get everything I want. In the end."

Eska stayed with her head bent over her knees until the last of the Ice Queen's footsteps faded away. Then her eyes flicked open and fixed on the key. Distracted by Slither, the Ice Queen had left it in the lock. Eska remembered how the woman had turned it the wrong way by mistake one day and it had undone the spell over her body for a moment. If only she could reach it now . . .

But Eska's limbs were frozen; there was no chance of

escaping, and she could only gaze through the arches at the world beyond, wondering who she really was. A child cursed by the Sky Gods? Or somebody else entirely?

A cold wind swept through the hall and Eska blinked at the chill. The Ice Queen held her body in a music box and her memories in a locked chest somewhere deep within the palace—it was almost enough to make Eska give up hope of ever finding a way back into her past—almost but not quite.

Because Eska knew something the Ice Queen did not. She *could* speak.

She just didn't want to.

About the Author

ABI ELPHINSTONE grew up in Scotland, where she spent most of her childhood running wild across the moors, hiding in tree houses, and building dens in the woods. After being coaxed out of her tree houses, she studied English at Bristol University and then worked as an English teacher in Tanzania before returning to the United Kingdom to teach there. When she's not writing, Abi volunteers for the Coram Beanstalk charity, speaks in schools, and travels the world looking for her next story. Her latest adventures include living with the Kazakh eagle hunters in Mongolia and dogsledding across the Arctic.